ALSO BY DEBRA GALANT

*Rattled*

*Fear and Yoga in New Jersey*

# Cars
## from a Marriage

**DEBRA GALANT**

ST. MARTIN'S PRESS ✖ NEW YORK

This is a work of fiction. All of the characters, organizations, and events portrayed in this novel are either products of the author's imagination or are used fictitiously.

CARS FROM A MARRIAGE. Copyright 2010 by Debra Galant. All rights reserved. Printed in the United States of America. For information, address St. Martin's Press, 175 Fifth Avenue, New York, N.Y. 10010.

www.stmartins.com

*Book design by Jonathan Bennett*

Library of Congress Cataloging-in-Publication Data

Galant, Debra.
   Cars from a marriage / Debra Galant.—1st ed.
      p. cm.
   ISBN 978-0-312-36727-5
   1. Married people—Fiction.   2. Automobiles—Psychological aspects—
Fiction.   3. Marriage—Fiction.   4. Domestic fiction.   5. Psychological
fiction.   I. Title.
   PS3607.A385C37 2010
   813'.6—dc22

                                       2009045698

First Edition: May 2010

10  9  8  7  6  5  4  3  2  1

*For Margot and Noah,*
*my two bright shining headlights*

# Acknowledgments

Thanks first to Rhonda Scovill, chef extraordinaire, who sat patiently in the kitchen at the Virginia Center for the Creative Arts while I peppered her with questions about catering, and to Ginger Moran, whom I met during the same residency, who generously gave me a tour of my own characters' Charlottesville.

Thanks to my parents, Ray and Shirley Galant, for years of support, financial and otherwise, and to Margot, Noah, and Warren, the loves of my life.

To Liz George, who never complains when I leave Baristanet in her hands so I can go away to write.

To Dori Weintraub and Lisa Bankoff, who keep making it happen.

A loving shout-out to all the members of the Ex Libris club: Liza Dawson, Pam Satran, Sue Kasdon, Frank Gerard Godlewski, Nicky Mesiah, Fran Liscio, and Noel Nowicki.

And to Joyce Selter, who knows why.

# Cars

## from a Marriage

# One

## 1981—Ivy

I've always thought of cars as places to die. That's what high school driver's ed did to me. Sure, there was also the practical stuff: how close to follow, laws regarding school buses, what to do in a skid (the most terrifying, anti-intuitive lesson of all). But that's not what stuck. What stuck were the flickering black-and-white filmstrips narrated by dead drivers, forever regretting that one second they took their eyes off the road. Driver's ed ghost stories. They grabbed my throat like a garrote—sudden, violent, remorseless— convincing me that driving and death were not only interrelated but inevitable.

This was in the old days of Behind the Wheel, before lawyers were in charge, when the schools actually taught you to drive and put you in a car with your high school gym teacher. Mine, Mr. Kapsopoulos, or Mr. K for short, was an excitable Greek, taken to screaming at other drivers with a clenched fist: "Where'd you get your driver's license? Cereal box?" He taught us that the horn was more important than the brakes and, if we were on the highway, forbade us from slowing down when another car was merging from the right. He insisted it was the merging car's job to join the flow of traffic, but what, I wondered, if the driver in *that* car hadn't been taught by Mr. K? What if *he* was expecting a little help? All that mind reading, the judging of speeds and velocity, the opportunities for misunderstanding: to me, a fiery crash was as likely an outcome as any. I put off getting my license until I was twenty-three—much to the hilarity of my family and everybody in my hometown, Charlottesville. My dad was the local Buick dealer.

Ellis, on the other hand, grew up in New Jersey without even a twinge of car fear. Maybe they didn't subscribe to the Edgar Allan Poe school of driver's ed in New Jersey. Ellis marked the days leading up to his seventeenth birthday like some automotive Advent calendar. To the steering wheel born, I guess. In my imagination, his Behind the Wheel teacher spoke like Jeeves and held out a platter with caviar whenever he stopped at a light. To Ellis, the car was an extension of the bicycle, which was an extension of the trike, just another step in his trajectory from the womb to adulthood. If to me the car was Thanatos, to Ellis it was Eros. A conveyance handy for driving a date to the movies, feeling her up, maybe even getting luckier. If to me a car was to be driven slowly and cautiously, or preferably not at all, to Ellis a car was a toy—the shinier and faster, the better.

Did I ever think of this as a deal-breaker, in those first days we were dating? Perhaps if there was a Sedgewick-Inglebert Driving Compatibility Inventory, Ellis and I might have showed up to a high school cafeteria at eight-thirty one Saturday morning with our sharpened number two pencils, answered questions about yielding and the proper method of signaling parallel parking, and been told that our attitude toward cars was so clearly incompatible that we'd be better off never seeing each other again.

But there is no Sedgewick-Inglebert test. Besides, when I met Ellis, we were both living in New York City, where cars are optional. And of course, love is blind, especially at the beginning, especially in matters like following distances and turn signals.

I should probably explain that the New York City I had moved to, the New York of my psyche the year I met Ellis, was more a stage set than it was a real place. It was the Manhattan of Woody Allen movies, *Odd Couple* reruns, Marilyn Monroe standing on the air vent, and Marlo Thomas as "That Girl" smiling perkily from behind the counter in her Midtown candy shop. Before I moved to Manhattan, I'd been there only once, on a weekend excursion of the high school art club. We'd descended the magnificent spiral of the Guggenheim Museum, seen *The Effect of Gamma Rays on Man-in-the-Moon Marigolds,* and eaten what seemed like an extremely exotic meal at Benihana. That was it—the sum of my experience in Gotham. A decade later, I was as starry-eyed as a shortstop buttoning his pinstripe jersey in the Bronx for the first time. Boxy yellow taxis zoomed down Broadway as if for my personal amusement.

Like all adopted New Yorkers, I came for nothing less than complete transformation. For the past four years, I'd lived with Nick, a chef, in a cute little farmhouse nestled in the Blue Ridge, outside Charlottesville. I met Nick in my fourth year at UVa, when I'd decided to pick up a little money by waitressing in one of the new chic downtown restaurants. Those were the heady, early days of Charlottesville as a foodie place, and we all felt like we were part of something big and exciting. Nick had a noble Gallic nose and the chiseled angularity of someone who could cook with fresh butter and never gain weight. He knew his wines; he knew his cheeses; he knew how to pleasure a woman. I probably fell for his farmhouse hardest of all. It was only about twelve miles from the house where I'd grown up, where my parents still lived, yet it felt like it existed in an entirely separate universe, blessed by a stronger, brighter sun. I could see myself there forever, writing novels at the sturdy wooden kitchen table painted a playful 1950s shade of aqua.

But it was a fantasy—the whole thing with Nick—a fairy tale. I didn't fit in either in the high-class restaurant scene or with the celebrated authors who dropped into Nick's restaurant whenever their agents visited Charlottesville. I was too young to appreciate my youth and not smart enough to recognize my own intelligence. Everywhere I looked, I saw coeds who were more coltish, waitresses who were sexier, and brilliant older women professors who let their hair go white as if to telegraph their intellectual gravitas. I was just another former English major with a dozen unpublished short stories. And the butter that never showed up on Nick's hips was beginning to show on mine.

Looking back, it's hard to imagine the logic of my decision to move to New York. If I was a small fish in the pond that was Charlottesville, I'd be plankton in the mighty harbor of New York. But I was depressed by the same old parties with the same old snobs, with Nick's flirtations with new waitresses. And Nick could be cruel, too, especially when it came to my cooking. I once spent a whole day making chicken marsala. He took two bites and put down his fork, then got some of his own leftovers out of the refrigerator and ate them cold. He didn't say a thing. He didn't need to.

My part-time jobs—at Nick's restaurant, Williams Corner Bookstore, the *Virginia Quarterly Review* press—didn't add up to a career. The few pages that rolled through my manual Royal type-writer didn't add up to a novel. I had gotten to the point where I didn't know what I hated more: the pretensions of the central Virginia country elite, with their horsey weekends and their old-fashioned croquet parties where everyone wore white, or the rednecks at the 7-Eleven. I was at a dead end. Bailey, my sister, had managed to transplant herself to L.A. I would try New York.

So I sold my car for seven hundred dollars (it broke my father's heart to see me get so little for a car that had come off his lot) and, at Dad's insistence, converted the money into traveler's checks, carefully recording their serial numbers in my journal. My mother packed me deviled eggs to take on the Amtrak and reminded me to eat them in the first few hours, before they spoiled. When the train pulled out, I looked back and saw my parents grow smaller and smaller, until they were the size of wedding cake toppers. I felt a pinch of homesickness—and guilt, too, for leaving them without any daughters nearby. But they were healthy and had each other, and I was riding into my grand future.

It was late March. My first month or so, I stayed in the cramped den of a rent-controlled postwar apartment on the West Side, which belonged to a divorced voice teacher in her late fifties named Betty, the mother of my best friend from college, Tess. Betty would "adore" the company, Tess insisted.

But even though Betty occasionally made a pot of orange pekoe and invited me to sit in one of her stiff wingback chairs and talk about my day, I felt a sort of coolness, like she didn't want me getting too comfortable. Literally. Betty kept her apartment at sixty-five degrees, and I wasn't allowed in the living room during voice lessons. I had to wait for the short intervals between students to sprint to the dark galley kitchen, where I kept my own box of Lemon Zinger and a small supply of yogurt. Betty's twelve-year-old cat, Simon, had tuna breath and a problem with flatulence, and he slept in the same room I did. He arched his back whenever I walked in, reminding me I was the interloper—a gesture that brought to mind some of the crustier matriarchs of the Virginia aristocracy.

I adapted. I wore a sweatshirt over my pajamas and brought Simon a succession of cheap squeaky toy mice to try to win his affection. I splurged on treats for Betty, too, regularly stopping at Zabar's for chocolate croissants and nice-sized hunks of Gruyère. Although I'd shipped my old Royal typewriter to the apartment, the first time I typed a sentence, I realized that in such tight quarters, each keystroke sounded like a gunshot. A paragraph would have sounded like the St. Valentine's Day massacre. I didn't dare use it unless Betty was out.

But who cared? I was in New York. The first weekend, I rode all the way to Coney Island, wandered the narrow cobblestone alleys near Wall Street, and took the elevator to the top of the World Trade Center. You could pick up the Sunday *Times* on Saturday night and make a cheap dinner out of a gigantic slice of Original Ray's Pizza. I learned quickly that every Ray's was the "original" and disdained by real New Yorkers, but I still loved the thick, gooey, almost raw-in-the-middle slices.

My heart thrummed when I looked through all the entertainment listings in the *Village Voice*. If I didn't find a job before my seven hundred dollars ran out—although I was sure I would—I wanted to make sure I'd experienced everything it was possible to experience. At least everything that was free or cheap. And so my third week, seeing a "new-talent night" with a modest five-dollar cover at a downtown comedy club, I left Betty to watch *Knots Landing* and hopped the subway to see live comedy for the first time in my life.

The club was in the Village, a jumble of alleys that refused to participate in the city's rational north–south, east–west grid system. As a newcomer, I felt as if some higher power had just taken the map of Manhattan, pointed to Greenwich Village, and maliciously twisted it into a knot. I got off the subway in Washington Square, completely disoriented, and saw NYU kids, all of them relaxed, laughing, walking down through the park in little happy clutches. They weren't really much different from the kind of kids I'd seen at UVa my whole life, but I was jealous of the fact that they felt so at home, that their home was here, that they traveled in packs. Illogically, I took it personally, as if they were leaving me out on purpose. My cheeks burned; I couldn't bring myself to ask for directions. Instead, I walked in circles, determined to find the address on my own, feeling more turned around, out of place, and lonely with every step.

I found it, finally, underneath an Indian restaurant, down a narrow flight of concrete stairs. It looked exactly how I imagined a comedy club would look—exposed brick, long narrow tables at right angles to the stage, a microphone stand next to a tall wooden stool—but somehow shabbier. The chairs were plain, hard, and close together, and the room was even colder than Betty's. There was a bad smell, too: a mixture of spilled beer, ashtrays, and a men's room urinal not quite far enough down the hall.

I was led to a table by a girl about my age with spiky black hair, an eyebrow ring, and an expression of practiced scorn. There was a hardness to her that made me think she hadn't been to college but had been working at clubs and restaurants for years. Following her, I felt bland and conventional, like a sorority girl in an angora sweater. From the 1950s. I hadn't been a sorority girl. Growing up, I'd been the rebel, the freak, the one who was turned away from the country club for wearing denim. But if I was the least ladylike young lady in my family's circle of friends, here I was just a soft-faced girl, demure and slightly nervous.

She seated me right up front, next to the stage. Even I knew it was a bad idea to sit so close, but I was too intimidated to say anything. It was early, half an hour until the show, and I was the only one in the room. I started to wish I was back watching *Knots Landing*. What was I doing? Who went to see comedy by themselves? I pulled out a paperback I'd stuck in my bag—a biography of Zelda Fitzgerald—but couldn't concentrate. A harsh inner voice was too busy berating me: *You idiot. You rube. You stupid hick. Why didn't you ask for a different seat before you sat down?*

The girl came back a few minutes later and asked what I wanted. "Oh, nothing," I said, smiling. It came out like somebody who'd been trained, since childhood, never to trouble her host. That's what you were supposed to say when you went to somebody's house and they offered to get you something. "Oh, nothing, thank you." You didn't even accept a glass of water unless your host had offered three times. Then it was okay. It wasn't that I was trying to save the waitress any trouble. I was trying to save money. It just came out in that sappy, Southern, overly polite way—the way I'd been indoctrinated. Thank God I hadn't said *ma'am*.

The waitress sighed. She picked up a laminated card, which listed a variety of imported beers and expensive drinks, and pointed to the words TWO-DRINK MINIMUM.

"Oh," I said. My heart slipped a notch. The listing had just mentioned the five-dollar cover. It hadn't said anything about a two-drink minimum. If I'd known, I might not have come. Sure, it was a relatively small thing. But I hadn't found a job, and New York was sucking up money like an industrial vacuum. I felt duped and flustered, as if the entire purpose of the two-drink minimum was to humiliate me.

"Oh," I said. "I guess I'll have a Diet Coke."

The evening went downhill from there. The room gradually filled with couples and groups, all showily having fun. I felt like the kid in the cafeteria sitting alone. A few guys tried to hit on me, but they were losers, pathetic men with comb-overs and oily pickup lines. And then the show started. A single girl, by herself, sitting in the front? The comics pounced. Where was I from? (I might as well have been wearing a T-shirt that said OUT OF TOWN.) Where was my boyfriend? What? I didn't have a boyfriend? Why? Did I have herpes? What was I doing after the show? After a while, I had to pee, but the idea of being teased on my way to the bathroom kept me frozen in my seat.

Yet, even in my misery, there was one comedian who struck me as kind of cute. He looked like an overgrown baby chick, tall and skinny with wide-open eyes and fluffy hair in an Elvis Costello sort of do. He seemed nervous as he climbed on the stool, like he was afraid he might knock it over. I found that endearing. I liked his set—he was the only comic who didn't rely on profanity—and when he finished, I realized that I had, for a brief five minutes, forgotten how unhappy I was. But he was followed by a female comic who appeared to be on angel dust, stunning the audience into silence with an incoherent tirade about being fucked by her father when she was thirteen.

Finally, the show ended and the waitress slipped a check on my table. I felt like a hostage being released from a long ordeal. The whole evening had been a mistake. I should have waited until I'd made some friends. Maybe live comedy wasn't my thing. The club was skanky. I'd known it as soon as I walked in. I'd just been too embarrassed to turn around. And that bitchy waitress. What kind of employee treated customers that way? You walked into Honeycutt Motors, and you were greeted with a warm smile. Daddy would have fired that waitress in a minute.

I picked up the bill, then blinked twice, not sure I was seeing right. I'd been charged *four dollars apiece* for my Diet Cokes. Four dollars for a Diet Coke, and they hadn't even brought me a whole can! Never in my life had I been charged more than a dollar fifty for soda. True, I was coming to New York from Charlottesville, where things were considerably cheaper, but even so. Four dollars for a Diet Coke?

The waitress came back, her mouth twisted like she'd been sucking lemons, and waited for me to produce the money. She was making it clear, in case I still didn't get it, that I was just another tedious chore in her evening, like sliding chairs under the table and sweeping the floor after the last customer left. There wasn't an ounce of warmth, not the merest acknowledgment that we were both human beings on the same planet, let alone two girls the same age in the same city.

And that was when I snapped. The whole evening had punctured my Macy's balloon of a Manhattan daydream. I suddenly understood that I was outmatched by this city, that the Woody Allen–Marilyn Monroe–*Odd Couple*–*That Girl* fantasy I'd been floating on so buoyantly for the past couple weeks was just that—a fantasy. What an idiot I was, staking my future on something as real as an episode of *My Favorite Martian*. I was going to find fame and fortune in New York? I was going to sit in cafés and write the Great American Novel? Right. I couldn't even manage to order a Diet Coke without being humiliated.

But I still had an ounce of fight left. I picked up the bill, held it up to the waitress's face, and with a dramatic flourish, tore it in half. I wasn't just mad; I was seething: a French revolutionary avenging the excesses of Marie Antoinette. "Four dollars for a Diet Coke?" I said through clenched teeth. "I may be from out of town, but I'm not an idiot."

The girl flinched. For the first time that evening, she looked at me as if I wasn't a piece of furniture. She looked at me like I was a rabid dog, maybe a piece of furniture that had turned into a rabid dog. She tried backing up, but she was right against the raised stage and wearing ridiculous clunky platform boots. I saw her eyes dart around, looking for a manager. She reminded me of the kids in the gym at the end of the movie *Carrie*. I felt righteous, even powerful, as I stared her down. Finally, she moved a chair and stalked off. I heard her mutter "crazy bitch" under her breath.

Then, abruptly, the Great Comedy Club Revolt of 1981 was over. I crumpled to the table and began to sob. It was awful. An embarrassment. I was doing what a Southern lady never did: calling attention to myself. But I was no more capable of stopping than of holding back a monsoon. If I had to look at that waitress again, if she sneered at me once more or brought over a manager, I'd shrivel up and melt right into the earth.

Suddenly, I felt the slight pressure of a hand on my shoulder. I looked up to see the cute comedian.

He pulled out his wallet, put a twenty on the table, and with the slightest touch to my elbow, stood me up. "Let's blow this taco stand," he said, retrieving my purse from the floor. He led me out of the comedy club and onto the street. I walked next to him trustingly, like a child, not knowing why, not knowing where, the city lights distorted into hallucinatory coronas through my tears. When he stopped a few blocks later and opened up the passenger door of a dinged-up car, I got in.

As he crossed in front of the car to his side, it occurred to me that I'd just done what I'd been warned since childhood never to do: gotten into a car with a complete stranger. But it didn't matter.

He wasn't a stranger. Not really. I felt like I'd known him all my life. Or if he was a stranger, he was that stranger you meet in the forest in the middle of a fairy tale, the one who saves you. He got in the car, reached in his pocket, and pulled out a handkerchief. A handkerchief! It was so old-fashioned. A gentleman, no less. He wiped my cheek and then handed over the handkerchief. "You're a mess," he said. He had the warmest smile. "I'm Ellis. Where you going?" At that moment, I knew: I was home.

It wasn't just that Ellis had rescued me from my moment of disgrace. Part of the charm was that he swept me away in a *car*. Anywhere else, that would have been unremarkable, but in New York City? Who bothered owning a car in New York City, where there were subways, buses, and taxis in abundance, and where parking garages cost hundreds of dollars a month? I'd have hardly been more surprised had Ellis lifted me up onto a steed.

But a car was even better. The glass and metal provided a hard protective shell, which kept the dangers of the city out—the weird, the homeless, the deranged—and yet, wondrously, still available for my observation. It was like watching a movie. I ruined Ellis's handkerchief, turning it black with mascara. I would have to offer to buy him a new one. He drove comfortably, one hand on the wheel, unperturbed by maniacal taxi drivers, like someone enjoying sunset on a yacht. Once he found out I was new to town, he started pointing out sights. And when he found out I hadn't eaten dinner, he took me to the Empire Diner, a little chrome dining car with art deco lettering, where I had a hamburger, fat greasy onion rings, and the first malted milk shake of my life.

I fell in love with Ellis that night, and when he pulled up in front of Betty's apartment building, we sat for an hour and a half telling our life stories, not budging when a few cars, trying to get a jump on alternate-side-of-the-street parking, flashed their lights. I was reluctant to open the door and break the spell, afraid I'd never see him again, even though we'd already written down each other's phone numbers on napkins. I even thought of leaving something behind, Cinderella-style, just to make sure. The only thing that could release me was a kiss. I was actually embarrassed when Ellis finally leaned over to put his mouth on mine, thinking of the onion rings, but the kiss was long and exploring and filled with promises.

In retrospect, Ellis's '74 Mustang was a pathetic little sardine-can of a motor vehicle. But from that first night, when it conveyed me comfortably and conveniently home, until our trip to meet Ellis's mother in the Berkshires that Thanksgiving, I had not a single complaint. Nor would I tolerate anybody else's criticism. Within two weeks of meeting Ellis, I was sure that I'd won the lottery of life and was calling everyone I knew. I went on and on about the four-dollar Cokes, how he'd rescued me, what a gentleman he was, always opening the door—who did that anymore?—and how extraordinary it was to be ferried around New York City. My mantra had become "Love means never having to take the subway." It never failed to crack me up.

All Bailey wanted to know was, "What does he drive?" Embarrassingly, for the daughter of a car dealer, I hadn't even noticed. But Bailey lived in L.A., where such things mattered, and she persisted. Finally I remembered it was the same kind of car that Eric Hutchison drove in eleventh grade. "A Mustang?" Bailey snorted.

"Something like that."

"Eternal teenager." Bailey, at the time, was dating a plastic surgeon who drove a Jaguar. My father wasn't quite so dismissive, but I could tell he'd have been happier if I'd been dating a Buick man.

Because we started going out in the spring, I didn't know about the small problem with the Mustang's heating system (it didn't work) or that the windshield was apt to fog up in damp weather. Nor was I fazed by the large dent in the passenger door. I had come to see the dent the way Ellis did, as an anti-theft device. It turned out that he parked the car on the street.

From that first night, Ellis was both protector and personal docent, opening up New York City like a treasure chest, every weekend presenting a new trinket: the Unisphere from the 1964 World's Fair; a whole block of Indian restaurants in the East Village; the Dakota, where John Lennon had lived and died. And in the process, we also, slowly, unwrapped ourselves—our histories, our love lives, our childhoods, our dreams.

Ellis was Jewish, which made him exotic by Charlottesville standards. I was fascinated, though a little repelled, by his stories about his mother. Sheba, the shrink. How he had to walk around in socks and whisper in his own house because his mother was always in the den with clients. How the brothers learned to fight— even having punch-in-the-stomach, fall-on-the-floor wrestling matches—without making a noise, so as not to disturb a session.

How they were the only kids in the neighborhood who didn't get to watch TV, because Sheba was convinced it would interfere with their psychosocial development. Her strange coldness and reserve. For a woman who allegedly dealt in feelings, she was oddly clinical when Ellis got upset as a kid, never taking him into her arms but instead offering him a box of tissues. He rarely spoke about his father. There'd been a messy divorce. A hint of some betrayal, nothing explained.

Sheba seemed like the polar opposite of my mother, who was so chirpy, she might have flown right out of Disney's *Cinderella*. My mom went around the house singing and humming, hugging us so randomly that by the time I was in high school, I'd dart into my bedroom if I heard her on the stairs. Mom delighted in making our special breakfasts every weekend: silver-dollar pancakes for Bailey, French toast for me. It was the kind of childhood everybody wants—family dinners, loving parents, tons of presents under the tree—but it held hardly anything for an aspiring writer to work with. The cold and withholding Sheba, with the strange name and the mysterious divorce, was far more interesting.

Ellis, it turned out, was not really a stand-up comic. Not professionally, anyway. He was trying it out, going to open-mic sessions and new-talent nights. Though I always made sure to tell people I was dating a comedian, this being a very cool thing, I was spooked by comedy clubs after that first experience and made excuses not to see Ellis perform. As for the club where we'd met, I wouldn't even set foot on that *block*. On nights when Ellis had a gig there, I stayed home, worrying just a little that there might be a fresh transplant to the city for him to rescue.

For a real job, Ellis worked four days a week as a guide for the Gray Line, standing at the front of the bus with a microphone, delivering his shtick, and trying not to fall when the driver slammed the brakes. It figured that Ellis's job would involve wheels and a microphone. I didn't worry that what he did wasn't conventionally ambitious. I trusted in his brilliance.

By May, I'd found a job, covering stemware, kitchenware, and linens for a little trade magazine called *The Restaurant Roll,* and had moved out of Betty's den and into an apartment share twelve blocks uptown. Not exactly my fantasy career, but at least it made decent use of my restaurant experience and paid well. Ellis and I spent all our weekends together. By fall, I was starting to daydream about moving in. Things had gotten comfortable, and the sightseeing phase was over. We were happy on a Saturday night just to bring in some samosas and watch an old movie on TV. I knew we'd reached a certain threshold of intimacy when Ellis started listening to his phone machine messages in front of me. His former girlfriends weren't calling anymore.

And then came the invitation that threw the progress of our relationship into sudden sharp relief, a summons from Sheba to spend Thanksgiving in the Berkshires.

At first, I was deliriously happy. Ellis's mother wanted to meet me. An excellent sign. He must have been talking about me a lot. But my euphoria was soon replaced by a nervousness bordering on obsession. What if Sheba didn't like me? How potent were her psychological powers? I convinced myself that Sheba the Shrink could read minds, that she'd be able to read mine, that she would find my character flawed, my personality borderline.

Even if I'd been perfectly normal *before* the invitation to Thanksgiving, wasn't my obsessive fear of Sheba's rejection proof of some fatal flaw?

Then there was the long-distance pouting of my mother, who had jumped onto the Martha Stewart bandwagon early, and whose already legendary Thanksgivings had become geometrically more complex each year. She was so certain that I'd be joining the family that she'd already made me a reservation on Amtrak.

"Sorry, Mom. I'm going to Ellis's mother's house in the Berkshires."

"Oh," she said, sounding wounded. "That's wonderful." But she quickly recovered. "So you and Ellis will come for Christmas, right?"

Thus began the inevitable competition between the future mothers-in-law, which would make sibling rivalry seem like child's play.

My mood swung wildly: bliss, panic, and filial guilt finally overtaken by a sense of adventure, even excitement. Without evidence, with neither photographs nor corroboration from Ellis, I began to construct a mental picture of Sheba's Berkshires house. I built it in the style of Frank Lloyd Wright, with windows overlooking a copse of birches. I decorated the living room with black leather sling chairs and a white bearskin rug. Presiding over it all was a massive stone fireplace. There would be nothing fussy, crocheted, or embroidered. And there'd be books, thousands of books. Smart books, too. No orphaned *Reader's*

*Digest*s or paperback beach reads, but volumes of Proust, Dostoevsky, Sartre.

In short, it would be the opposite of my parents' endearing little colonial filled with so many of my mother's antiques that you couldn't find a flat surface to put your coffee down.

A few days before the trip, my mother reminded me to wear the ankle-length blue down coat, the one I'd bought at Belk's the year before. "It'll be cold," she said, as if this were special, privileged information. But the down coat looked like a sleeping bag. I'd just bought a cute little faux fur jacket at Strawberry, and this was the fashion statement I intended to present to Ellis, his brother, his mother, and their stepfather.

An hour into our trip, I realized the desperate state of Ellis's heater. I sat shivering in the passenger seat, hunched into a tight ball, my cute little faux fur jacket offering as much insulation from the elements as a toilet seat cover. My mother had been right. I should have worn the down.

The trip had started pleasantly enough. I handed Ellis a new boxed set of cassettes, *The News from Lake Wobegon,* which I'd bought for the journey, and he, in turn, passed me a joint. Neither of us had been able to get off early from work, so it was dark when we left, but once we finally got out of the city, the next fifty miles or so rolled by pleasantly enough as Keillor purred hypnotically about the Chatterbox Café and bachelor farmers. Somewhere in Connecticut, though, I began shivering too much to pay attention. This was the first time I'd felt anything but grateful about Ellis's car. Now I reverted to being the daughter of a car dealer, appalled my boyfriend had taken me off to the mountains in November in a car without working heat.

Then it began to snow. Serious snow—not some delicate laceworks, but giant clumps. Like God, that bully, was starting a one-way snowball fight. I held my breath, wondering whether Ellis's windshield wipers would be as ineffectual as his heater, then relaxed slightly as they batted furiously at the onslaught. Still, coming from Virginia, I was filled with alarm at the combination of snow and driving. It hadn't occurred to me to listen to a weather forecast. It must have been a few days since I'd talked to my mother, because if there'd been even a hint of snow predicted, she'd have begged me to reconsider.

I looked over at Ellis, who had turned off the tape player and was looking more alert. I willed myself to see him through a romantic scrim: Pa, from *Little House on the Prairie,* trudging home through a blizzard. Competent, strong, unflustered. As if reading my mind, he took his right hand off the steering wheel and patted my knee. "Don't worry." He smiled. "Up north, we learn to drive in snow." I replaced his hand on the wheel and swallowed my terror. This was what women were supposed to do, right? Keep their mouths shut and stand by their men. Stay out of the way. Suck our fear tightly inside our bellies. I tried to forget the pot we'd both smoked an hour earlier.

I remembered that men think about baseball statistics to keep from coming when they're making love, and in the same spirit, I decided to do a mental inventory of every article of clothing I'd ever owned. Favorite coats, going back to when I was a kid. All the shoes in my closet. How many jeans I owned and in what sizes. In my mind, I folded sweaters and stacked them neatly in an imaginary closet. I was cataloging my blouses when the car went into a skid.

We were flying, leaving the familiar world of friction and gravity, skittering toward oblivion. I slammed a phantom brake, and as if responding to my command, the car suddenly hooked left. Sharply. And then we began to spin. I squeezed my eyes shut and braced for the clash of metal on metal, for shattered glass, blood. In real time, it couldn't have lasted more than a second. But during that second, time opened into an infinity of fear. It was like staring down into your own grave.

And then, miraculously, I felt the car unwind itself from the centrifuge. I opened my eyes, and we were back where we were supposed to be, heading forward.

"Ellis!" I screamed.

"What?"

"You almost got us killed."

My heart was pounding. It was the first time I'd ever been afraid in the car with Ellis. True, his city driving did occasionally seem a tad aggressive. Once or twice I'd held my breath when he squeezed between a row of taxis and a stopped bus. But I'd never really felt like I was going to die.

My fear turned to anger. Ellis's job was to *protect* me, not get me killed. This was stupid. We shouldn't be driving. I didn't care how much supposed "experience" he had driving in the snow. We should stop.

And then I noticed a strange thing. Ellis was angry, too. He stared straight ahead, his jaw set, his top teeth biting into his bottom lip, as if his feelings were so dangerous, they needed to be prevented, physically, from flying out.

"*What?*" I said.

No answer.

It was unbelievable. Ellis was angry at *me*? "My God, Ellis," I said. "We've got to stop. I don't know what's going on in there"—I gestured at his head—"why you're so *mad*. But I'm . . . I'm terrified."

"One little skid? That's all it takes?"

"It wasn't just a *skid*. It was a . . . a . . ." I searched for the word. "A fishtail! A three-sixty!"

"God, you're such a drama queen."

*Drama queen?* Had he really said *drama queen*? Was this my prince, my rescuer, my tender playmate of the past eight months? I felt like I'd been punched.

"I'm not allowed to be scared?" I could hear my voice rising into the hysterical range. Not attractive.

"Sure, be scared. Be scared all you want." Here was something I'd never heard from Ellis before, at least not directed at me: sarcasm.

I searched my memory, reviewing the time we'd been together. Had we ever had a fight? Of course we'd had *disagreements*. We'd even had a couple of normal I-think-we-should-probably-see-other-people periods. We'd had differences about what movie to see, where to go to dinner, please stop snoring, why were you flirting with that girl at the party? But never a real fight.

I was just beginning to suspect there were hidden edges to our relationship. Rule number one: I would get limitless love as long as I gave limitless approval.

The snow kept falling, a rare November blizzard. And the wind was picking up. I didn't know what was worse: Ellis being angry at me, or the fact that the world had been reduced to a bleary windshield and our two headlights, with snow so big and wet, it looked like it had been invented just to mock us. No, that's not true. I did know which was worse. Death was worse. I'd lived without Ellis, and it might have been a pale, echoless version of the life I'd been living since April. But it was still life.

"Ellis. We've got to stop."

"Where?" he said, indicating the nothingness outside our car. "Where?"

"I don't know. A motel?"

"Do you *see* a motel?"

I leaned forward, peeking through the little semicircle created by the windshield wipers. There was nothing. The world had been reduced to a car, a snowstorm, an angry boyfriend, almost certain death.

"The next exit, then?"

He shrugged, as if he didn't want to encourage stupid questions. Contempt. Definitely contempt.

I crossed my arms. "We should have stopped before, when it started snowing."

Ellis looked away from the road to glare at me. "I know that in *Virginia,* people don't know how to drive in snow." He enunciated each word distinctly, and the word *Virginia* came out like an insult. Like Alabama or Mississippi, a place full of hicks and a history of slavery. "Here in the Northeast, we learn to drive in snow." I could see this working its way into a future comedy routine, and I didn't like it.

"Yeah, right. That was an excellent demonstration before."

We drove for a while in silence. I tucked my hands under my armpits, then used them to warm my nose. For a while, the simple struggle for heat absorbed me. Then fear crept back in. I started thinking about everybody I'd ever known who died in a car crash. The four seniors who were killed my sophomore year, and how we all came back to school that Monday and the principal broke down crying during assembly. The grief counselors. The flowers and teddy bears that accumulated in massive piles in front of the four lockers. Did I mention this was just a few months before I started driver's ed?

Then there was the Japanese family up the street that I babysat for occasionally. One night the mother went out to the store for milk and eggs and was killed by a drunk driver on the way home. I sat for the kids once after that happened, before the family moved away. Their rec room had turned into a mausoleum. The kids, always superpolite and reserved, even before the accident, were silent for hours. It was as if the air had been sucked out of the house, and grief had taken its place. When the husband got home and began digging in his wallet to pay me, I waved him off, fleeing for the door. I'd felt like I was suffocating.

I looked over to see Ellis, grim and concentrating, his hands clutching the wheel tightly.

"So," I said, "tell me again about your mother."

I was offering an olive branch. I didn't care about his mother, not at that moment, anyway, but ever since the car had spun around, there hadn't been one pleasant word between us. I had to restart conversation, without complaining about my discomfort or the danger.

Ellis exhaled audibly, as if considering whether he wanted to talk to me. "What do you want to know?"

"I don't know. Anything."

"Okay," he said, turning to me with just the faintest trace of a smile. "She hates Thanksgiving."

I burst out laughing. "Sheba hates Thanksgiving?" We were risking life and limb to drive to her house, in the snow, to join her for a holiday she hated? "This is a joke, right?"

"No." He looked wounded. "She really hates Thanksgiving."

"Okay, I'll play. *Why* does she hate Thanksgiving?"

"Never mind."

"No, seriously. You can't start something like this and not finish."

He stared straight ahead. "You think it's a joke."

"I think it's funny that we're driving through a *blizzard* to get to your mother's house for Thanksgiving, a holiday which I now learn she hates. Especially when we could have gone down to see *my* mother, who loves Thanksgiving. But I really want to know. Why"—I struggled for a neutral tone—"does your mother hate Thanksgiving?"

Ellis absently started thrumming his fingers on the steering wheel. "Well, first of all, she can't make turkey. Every time she tries, it turns out all burned and dried out, or else bloody in the middle."

I shook my head. Even I had made a turkey. Anybody could make a turkey. That was the easy part, my mother always said. There was no peeling, grating, chopping, or measuring. You just put the bird in the oven and basted it every few hours. I laughed so hard now, my shoulders were shaking. Tears rolled down my face.

"But that's not all."

"What else?"

"It's the time of year my dad moved out. Our first holiday as a broken family."

"I'm sorry. I shouldn't have joked."

"It's okay."

We drove a few minutes in silence. I wanted to know more, to find out whether there'd been years of fighting, or an affair. But I held back.

And then I saw it, a shadow on the side of the road up ahead. Not trees, something vaguely rectangular. Could it be—?

"There! Ellis, look! Stop!"

But he didn't stop. The car continued, its headlights briefly touching what was indeed a roadside motel, what they called a *motor hotel* in the old days, before the era of the interstate highway. It was only a blur in the snow, but you could just make out the shape. It was the kind of place people stayed before there were Holiday Inns. Where traveling salesmen and lovers sometimes still stayed. Where my mother would *never* stay. I could picture the sagging mattress, the thin bedspread, the moldy rug, the stained toilet. I didn't care. I couldn't even tell if the motel was open. It could have been boarded up years ago. But it was a chance!

"Ellis!"

He didn't even slow down.

I couldn't believe it. This was the guy who'd rescued me from the comedy club, whom I'd started to believe I would live with forever? What an asshole! Suddenly I saw Ellis for what he was: a heartless jerk on a power trip, driving through a snowstorm just to prove that he was in charge. He'd made up his mind, and nothing I said or did could change it.

I felt like my head was going to explode, like one of those old Warner Bros. cartoon characters. I grabbed the door handle.

"Let me out!"

"Ivy."

"I'm serious, Ellis. Let me the fuck out of this car."

I cracked the door open, and a blast of cold air came in, along with a sheet of fresh snow. The snow blanketed my lap, my legs, and most of the floor.

Ellis reached across me, the car swerving, and closed the door. "Are you trying to get us killed?"

God knew, I wasn't trying to get us killed. I just wanted out. Out of this stupid car, this stupid trip, this stupid relationship. Ellis obviously wasn't the person I'd thought he was. He was a fucking prick. He didn't want a girlfriend—or, God forbid, a wife—he wanted a plastic blowup doll to sit obediently in the car seat next to him.

I bent over and sobbed. The world had never known such disappointment, such misery. I was crying for my poor miserable body, for my frozen fingers, my wounded pride, my flawed exit.

But mostly I was mourning for the couple who had started out bright and expectant in New York City just a few hours earlier.

Then I felt the car decelerate. Ellis was pulling over to the side of the road. I didn't stop howling until we were at a complete standstill.

Ellis was stroking my hair. "Okay," he said.

"Okay what?"

"We'll go back. To the motel."

I didn't see how. It was too slick and narrow to pull a U-turn. There was no exit in sight, probably for miles. But Ellis threw the car in reverse. He rested his arm on the back of my seat and looked in the direction of the rear window. Which, of course, was completely covered with snow.

"Wait." He jumped out and wiped the back window with the sleeve of his coat.

It didn't stay clear very long, but Ellis managed. I stopped sniffling and sat straight up as the car made its way backwards. I was still afraid that we'd be hit from behind. If we died because of this maneuver, it would be my fault.

Finally, we reached the motel. It was dark. Not a light on anywhere, not a car in the parking lot. Now we could see what the place was called, the Cloverleaf Motel, but clearly its NO VACANCY hadn't been turned on for years.

"Now what?" I said.

Ellis got out. He walked across the parking lot and started trying doors. He moved methodically, beginning at the far left. Finally, two rooms from the end, a door budged.

I didn't have to be coaxed. I bolted out of the car and stood next to Ellis.

We hesitated, not knowing what to expect—rats, skeletons, Jimmy Hoffa, a feral cat—and then advanced slowly. The room was black, and as cold as the car. But it had what it was supposed to have: a bed. The windows weren't broken. Snow wasn't coming in. Best of all, it wasn't moving.

"Okay," Ellis said. "You stay here. I'll get a flashlight."

I waited, not liking the darkness, but not sure I'd like what the flashlight revealed either.

Ellis came back and led me to the bed. "Wait," I said, brushing the snow to the floor. He tucked me in, put his coat over me, covered me in the blanket, then looked in a dresser drawer and found another one. "I'll be back," he said. I heard the sound of breaking glass, and then Ellis returned with two more blankets.

He got in bed next to me, rolled on top of me, and with the weight and heat of his body, I began to thaw. I didn't think I would be able to fall asleep, but I must have, because I woke up the next day to discover that the world was again filled with light. The blinding light that comes the morning after a snow.

It was Thanksgiving.

Ellis was looking at me tenderly, his left index finger tracing my lips.

"Ellis, I'm sorry."

"Shhhh."

"But—"

"Let's get going."

He took some of the blankets, draping them on me for the car ride to Sheba's. It was still ridiculously freezing in the Mustang. But as it turned out, we were only about forty-five minutes away.

We got to the house, which was nothing like I had imagined, not Frank Lloyd Wright at all, but an ordinary white former farmhouse, very small. They had heard the car pull up, and all came to the door—Sheba; Sheba's husband, Harold; Ellis's brother, Paul; Paul's wife, Julie; their little daughter, Kirsten. There was a rush of introductions, kisses, laughter. "We were worried," Julie said. "We kept calling the highway patrol, to see if there were any accidents."

Sheba backed up slowly, deliberately, to take my full measure— and they all made way for her. She was a tall woman with raven hair, save one white streak that swept back from her forehead, Cruella De Vil–style. She inspected me head to toe, and I knew I looked like a wreck, Cinderella after the clock struck twelve. Was I supposed to curtsy? There was a collective intake of breath as everybody waited. Even Kirsten.

Ellis finally broke the silence. "Mom," he said, putting his arm around me, "meet my fiancée, Ivy."

## *Two*

## 1983—ELLIS

1982 BUICK LESABRE,

AUTOMATIC, SIX-CYLINDER, LIGHT GREEN


We had just eaten the worst Chinese meal ever and were now sitting in bumper-to-bumper traffic, trying to get back to the city. The MSG made my blood feel as sluggish as the traffic, and Ivy had gas, and nothing on the road was moving. Another wasted Sunday.

Ivy kept trying to defend the place, which we'd found in a little suburban strip mall, wedged between a Hit or Miss and a GNC, after a long day of house-hunting. It was important to her campaign to move us to the suburbs that I find the Chinese food in New Jersey at least palatable.

"Really, Ivy, canned pineapple in the moo shu pork?"

"I thought it was interesting."

"Interesting. Hmmph. And those 'spicy mixed vegetables'? Those were *vegetables*? Maybe according to Ronald Reagan."

"Just because they come out of can doesn't mean they're not vegetables."

"Ivy, do you hear what you're saying? Out of a *can*? And chopsticks. When I asked for chopsticks, he looked at me like I was speaking a foreign language."

31

"But they did have them."

"You have to agree, that place sucked."

"Well," she finally admitted, "the cockroach in the fried rice did kind of skeeve me out."

"See! Case closed! We can't move to New Jersey."

The New York City skyline, gray and remote, was just visible on the horizon.

At first I couldn't figure out how Ivy got it in her head that we should move to New Jersey. Then I put two and two together. My mother. Sheba wanted grandchildren. Ipso facto, the suburbs. You might have thought that Sheba had been some kind of *Leave It to Beaver* mom, setting out cookies and milk after school and volunteering for the PTA. (Fat chance.) Certainly this couldn't be the same mother who had moved us to the city right after she and my dad split up, tearing me away from all my friends in the middle of my senior year in high school?

Well. My mom was one thing. I'd been getting head fakes and Statue of Liberty plays from her all my life. But Ivy, my wide-eyed Southern girl, who'd moved to New York just two years earlier because it was the most exciting place on earth? *My* Ivy, who never tired of the gaudy brilliance of Times Square, who loved the grit of the city streets, the narrow canyons formed by the skyscrapers, the graffiti on the subway, the wind off the Hudson, Sabrett hot dogs, knockoff handbags, Chinatown, the Greenwich Village Halloween Parade, female impersonators? *She* wanted the suburbs?

It made no sense. Ivy had just been promoted from stemware

and linens to the "Chef of the Week" beat and now got invitations to the best restaurants in the city several times a week. What was she going to do? Get up before dessert and run to the Port Authority to catch the 10:15? It wasn't like she was going to, God forbid, get into a car and drive home. Not once in the time we'd been together had she ever gotten behind the wheel, even after I broke my wrist playing softball in Central Park. Of course, then I'd still had the Mustang, which was a stick. But even after her father insisted on giving us the hulking Buick LeSabre, which of course came with automatic transmission ("So Ivy can drive it, too"), she never did. Even when we visited Virginia. The girl simply didn't drive, at least not in my experience. Did she think she'd drag me to New Jersey to become her chauffeur?

Yet here we were, driving out to New Jersey every Sunday, looking in Montclair, Maplewood, Ridgewood, Westfield, all the towns that *New York* magazine said wouldn't make you vomit if you moved there. Shaking hands with real estate agents in primary-colored blazers, riding around in their bloated Cadillacs, walking through houses with cramped bedrooms, pink powder rooms and avocado-green kitchens that just needed "a little remodeling"—the bane of our particular price range. We'd drive right past all the houses that might just woo a city boy—sprawling Victorians with wraparound porches, noble Georgians with white columns—and wind up, inevitably, in front of a small boxy house with an Astroturf-covered front porch and a BEWARE OF DOG sign on a chain-link fence. *That* was what we found in our price range.

During these tours, Ivy and the bushy-tailed Realtor du jour would always be five steps ahead of me, talking conspiratorially about how this or that room would make a perfect nursery. Ivy would beam at the word *nursery* and I'd think, *Hmmm, does she realize that this baby thing actually requires sex?* (This particular activity having become increasingly rare.) They had mighty imaginations, my wife and these Realtors. You could build a closet *there*—"Simple!"—or a half bath *there*. They'd stand in a room with some Laura Ashley wallpaper (that's what they told me the stuff with the little flowers was) and cutesy country baskets and imagine it all replaced by something French Provincial, whatever that was. I'd look at the homey embroidered pillows and think, *Who the hell are my neighbors going to be in a place like this? Ma and Pa Walton?*

I took my revenge by insisting on seeing each basement. The third Realtor we'd met, one of the rare men in the real estate henhouse, had always included the basement as part of the tour, teaching me to check for asbestos, leaks in the foundation, rot, mold, standing water. He'd also mentioned that just about any- where in Jersey we'd have to test for radon. This was the stuff I lived for, the possibility that we'd discover invisible toxins and Ivy would go running back to our prewar one-bedroom on West End Avenue and kiss the black-and-white tile on the bathroom floor. Sometimes my fantasies would go Stephen King. Maybe I'd find some Satanic scribblings or a decomposing body and *that* would send Ivy screaming back to her senses. At least it would pep things up a little.

No such luck. "Wait," I'd say, just as the Realtor was about to stash the key back in the lockbox. "I'm going downstairs." Ivy would sigh heavily, like a mother who's just smelled a dirty diaper after bundling a squirmy toddler into three layers of snowsuit. We were short on time, she'd remind me. Who cared about the basement? But I'd go down, look at the crappy laundry room, the boilerman's toilet, the asbestos-covered pipes, the damp floor, and bound back upstairs like a cat bearing a dead mouse, ready to deliver the bad news. Or sometimes, if there was no bad news to report—just a tidy workbench and a side-by-side washer-dryer— I'd stay down there for a few minutes and light a joint. It didn't matter what I found or didn't find. By the time I got upstairs, they were already looking at the next listing and tapping their feet, hot to trot.

And then there were the rides home. We'd face the inevitable back-to-the-city Sunday traffic, people returning from weekends in New Hope or the Poconos. I'd experiment with various approaches: the Lincoln, the Holland, the GW, getting bad traffic advice from the liars on WCBS and WINS, while Ivy went on about some *darling* little colonial on Hawthorne Place. And I'd be thinking: *This isn't the deal I signed up for. This is a goddamn bait and switch.*

Not that I didn't love Ivy. I *did* love Ivy. Who didn't love Ivy? She was Asti Spumante, bubbly and sweet, a mile-a-minute talker who could liven up a morgue. Yes, she was neurotic, but in that fabulously cute Diane Keaton way, all long eyelashes and apologies and ten-dollar vocabulary words. Of course I loved Ivy. Of course I was happy I'd married her.

I just felt that slowly but surely, my soul was leaking out, like the air in a bicycle that had been sitting unused all winter.

It had been months since I'd done any stand-up. Comedy clubs made Ivy uncomfortable. She didn't like the bathrooms, she said, but I knew it went back to the goddamn four-dollar Diet Cokes. And I was a working stiff now, a suit. I was doing entertainment PR at the lowest possible level, pitching stories about celebrity impersonators in Vegas and Atlantic City. Not bad, as far as grown-up jobs went, even if it was a little sleazy, but I did have to wear a tie, carry a briefcase, and set an alarm clock.

Now it looked like I was also going to be sentenced to a life of terrible Chinese food and endless discussions about throw pillows. My fortune cookie, that great wisecracker, had it nailed: "As long as you don't ask for much, you'll be happy." It worked equally well if you read it the way I'd learned to read fortunes in college, adding *between the sheets* at the end.

There was a game Ivy and I played, sometimes in the car, imagining ourselves as parents, turning around to reprimand some squawking preschoolers in the backseat. It was just another iteration of the Game of Grown-up we'd played for the past two years: Buying a Diamond Engagement Ring, Registering at Bloomingdale's, Applying for a Mortgage and Going Before a Coop Board. Only those games had been real. We'd actually gone to Forty-seventh Street to pick out a ring, picked out china patterns, found and moved into an apartment together. In this game, though, we were playacting at Real Grown-uphood: that irreversible process of diving into the genetic pool.

Ivy turned around. "Now, Cornelius"—part of the game was assigning ridiculous names to our nonexistent offspring—"no more kicking the back of Daddy's seat. If you don't settle down, you won't get one of those great big fudge sundaes Grandma Sheba likes to make."

. Ha ha. Ivy was already enjoying little pokes at Sheba, who never in her life had made a fudge sundae, for herself or anyone, and who prided herself on maintaining the same weight since her wedding day. The first wedding day.

"And, Horatio," I countered, looking into the rearview mirror and pretending to address a child in the backseat. "If you keep hitting Cornelius, Grandma Katherine won't take you out in the rowboat. And we know how you love the rowboat."

Ivy snorted. It was a well-known fact that her mother never learned how to swim, paid someone to take the swimming test for her in college, and detested boats in any form.

"And no television or candy," Ivy admonished.

"And you have to sleep in the closet," I added.

We both laughed. Why were we intent on torturing our non-children?

At least it made the time pass. The interstate was a parking lot; we hadn't moved three miles in the last half an hour. I paused in my discipline of Horatio and Cornelius to turn on the radio. And here it was: jackknifed oil tanker at the entrance to the tunnel. Spilled oil, slick roadways, traffic backed up for miles. Great. Now they told us.

I pounded the wheel. "Shit."

"What?" Ivy said, yawning. She hadn't heard anything, probably hadn't even noticed that we weren't moving.

"It's going to be July Fourth before we're home, that's what."

She went back to her knitting, placidly moving pale blue angora from one needle to the other. Another scarf. If she were any more relaxed, she'd be sleeping.

I, on the other hand, was livid. If I had to look at that CHOOSE LIFE bumper sticker on the stupid van in front of us for one more *second,* I might just have to ram it in the ass. It was March— March Madness—there were basketball games to be watched. I'd already given up half my day. It was going to be dark before we got home.

I squinted at the green signs hanging a few hundred yards down the road in hopes of recognizing something. If only there was an exit I knew. Where were we, exactly? Newark? Harrison? Irvington? Elizabeth? Nothing looked familiar.

Fuck, it didn't matter. I was getting off. My dad always said that you could get from one end of New Jersey to the other end on back roads. Nothing could be worse than sitting in this. I saw an opening in the right lane, darted in, then popped through to the shoulder. A few hundred feet and I was sailing down a ramp to, well, somewhere. I was so happy to be moving again, I floored it for sheer joy, slamming the brakes when I got to the traffic light at the bottom of the exit.

"Shit," Ivy said, looking up. "I dropped a whole row!"

*Forbear,* I told myself. *Forbear. There's no point picking a fight right now.* I willed myself to explain everything as softly and patiently as a kindergarten teacher. "Traffic's backed up for miles. I'm going to take local roads."

"Where are we?" she said, looking at the beer cans and discarded tires that leaned up against the underpass.

I was pretty sure we were in Newark. If not Newark, Irvington. Maybe Harrison. It wouldn't make any difference to Ivy anyway, would it? Did she have any associations with the name
Newark? Did she know about the riots? The slums? The crack
dealers? Surely, she must. Although, being from Virginia, maybe
she didn't. There was a lot of stuff she didn't know. Son of Sam
was just a vague headline to her; the names John Lindsay and
Nelson Rockefeller barely rang a bell. Maybe she didn't know that
Newark meant drug dealers and street gangs.

Well, it wouldn't take her long to figure it out. In just a block,
we'd passed burned-out, boarded-up buildings. Black kids in
baggy pants swaggered through a postapocalyptic landscape, gaz-
ing at us through narrowed eyes.

Ivy put down her knitting needles. "Is this . . . safe?"

I felt sorry for her. I knew what she was thinking. She was
scared, but she didn't want to sound like a racist. In Virginia, she'd
known racists. She'd sacrificed popularity in high school by refusing to laugh at nigger jokes. She even hated much milder forms of
prejudice, like when her father talked about tipping "the boy"—a
fifty-eight-year-old black man who ran the service department—
or her mother gathered hand-me-downs for "the girl." Ivy lived in
an idealistic bubble, where skin color didn't matter and wasn't supposed to be mentioned. It was one of the most endearing things
about her.

But *these* black people were scaring her. These weren't the nice
"Yes, sir," "How you doin', ma'am?" black folks who fixed cars or
cleaned white folks' homes back in Albemarle County. These
were city brothers. They looked like they might kill for sport.

From where I sat, there were advantages to her discomfort. It was useful to my cause to show her that New Jersey wasn't all picket fences and good schools. Newark bordered South Orange, which was right next to Maplewood, only five miles from Montclair. Probably not enough to derail Ivy's suburban aspirations, but a man could hope.

"But," she said, snapping the automatic door locks shut, "you do know where you're going, right?"

I shrugged.

Ivy went three shades paler. She even put down her knitting. Her eyebrows were pinched and her mouth had gone small and tight. It was hard to witness so much fear in the woman I loved, even if I did enjoy giving her a reality lesson.

"Look in the glove compartment," I said. "See if we have a Jersey map."

This was really just a diversionary tactic. Ivy couldn't read a map to save her life. She liked to talk about how she'd used her subway map so much when she got to New York that she'd worn it out, but I had a hard time believing it. Certainly, she'd been no help with a map since she'd been riding in *my* passenger seat. She didn't even seem to be able to fold one. She might recognize a state, even a city, on a map, but never fast enough for you to decide on an exit. And ask her to find an alternate route? You might as well ask her to rebuild a carburetor.

Dutifully, she rummaged through the stack. "New York," she said, leaning into the glove box while I passed a church marred by graffiti. "Long Island ... Vermont ... Wait! I think Anne gave us one." She turned around to retrieve a Realtor's package from the backseat. She found the map and opened it awkwardly. "Now, what am I looking for?"

Good old Ivy. She might be scared half to death, but when you gave her an assignment, she was perky as all get-out. A real Girl Scout.

Ivy leaned down and inspected the map, trying earnestly to connect our location in the physical world to the large piece of paper spread across her lap. I came to a stoplight and peered at it myself. And then I noticed. We were being watched. It hadn't occurred to me until just then: if this landscape was alien to us, we must have looked equally alien to the people in it. Ivy might as well have been holding a sign: TWO WHITE KIDS! LOST! COME AND GET 'EM!

Suddenly, there was a tap on my window. Ivy reacted as if it had been a firecracker.

I looked up, expecting to see a squeegee man, like we had in New York, wanting to wash our windshield for a buck. But there was no squeegee, just a heavily bundled-up black man of indeterminate age who'd bent down to my level and was trying to get my attention. I rolled the window down an inch, and he leaned in, reeking of unwashed clothes and applejack, pointing a dirty black stub of a finger toward the map on Ivy's lap.

"Lost?" he mumbled through rotting teeth.

"No!" Ivy said. She dropped the map on the floor, stomped her feet on it, and bounced back up with a manic smile. "Not lost at all! Just looking for an old family friend. A policeman." She muttered at me through clenched teeth: "Go!"

"But the light's still red."

"*Go.*"

I left so fast, I thought the guy might fall down. "What's your problem?" I said, looking around to see if any cops had caught us running a red light. "He was just offering to help."

Ivy crossed her arms. "Maybe. Or maybe he was going to *kill us.*"

Okay, I'd jumped, too, when the guy tapped the window. But we both had our roles, and mine was to stare down danger with Bond-like nonchalance. I was the man. I drove. I navigated. I brought home the health insurance. Someday I'd be shoveling snow and assembling toy train sets. I calmly faced down potential muggers and homeless people. *All part of the job, ma'am.*

"Really, Ivy. Let's not overreact."

She squeezed her eyes tight. She looked like she was concentrating. Controlling her anger? Composing the perfect zinger? Trying to remember some time a former boyfriend, or maybe her father, had gotten her out of a dangerous spot? Finally, she opened her eyes.

"Ellis?"

"Yes?"

"I have to go to the bathroom."

Ahhh. I should have figured that out myself.

Ivy needing a bathroom was one of our recurring themes, and it could make even an ordinary road trip into a manic scavenger hunt. Her intestines were like an island dictator, ready to erupt at the slightest provocation. She knew every bathroom in every hotel and bookstore in the city. An important meeting the next day would have her doubled up the whole night before. So a guy tapping on her window in darkest Newark? Of course she had to go to the bathroom.

But where? Ivy may have seen herself as a rebel against the prissiness of Southern womanhood—she had made me promise that if she died first, I wouldn't let anybody bury her in pantyhose—but when it came to standards of hygiene and sanitation, there wasn't a whole lot of distance between her and her mother. You could argue that her greatest accomplishment over the past two years was training me to differentiate between suitable and unsuitable pit stops at sixty-five miles per hour. Old gas stations with outdoor toilets, the kind that you had to ask for a key to unlock? Out of the question. They were unheated, dirty, and usually out of toilet paper. And God knew what you could find in there. Discarded drug needles or dead babies. She'd read about these things. Gettys were the only exception. They were known for taking pride in the state of their bathrooms. Better a McDonald's. Best of all, a full-service hotel.

There was nothing in this pitiless slum that even came close. We could only hope for a McDonald's.

"Um. Can you wait a little bit?"

"I don't think so."

I reached over and squeezed her hand. "Okay. We'll find something."

The sky was darkening rapidly. We drove. More gutted buildings. An off-brand fried-chicken restaurant. I glanced at Ivy. She shook her head. Most of the city was closed—it was, after all, a Sunday—check-cashing establishments and liquor stores locked tight behind corrugated metal window covers.

And then, suddenly, like a mirage, we both saw it. The round blue sign with a white *H* in the middle.

"A hospital!" Ivy shouted, her voice so overfilled with joy, you might have thought she was suffering from a broken leg rather than an overactive bowel. I followed the sign, and sure enough, about ten blocks later, there it was: a shining edifice of modern sanitation.

I headed toward the parking deck, but Ivy couldn't wait. "There." She pointed to the emergency room. "And look, there's a parking place."

Ivy was out the door even before I'd managed to wedge the LeSabre between a Chevy and a roofing truck. I scooped the crumpled map off the floor and tried to smooth it out, figuring I would take it inside and look at it under fluorescent lights.

Anybody but Ivy would have found the idea of barging into an inner-city ER to use the ladies' room preposterous. But I knew she'd have no problem. ER waiting rooms had to have bathrooms, and Ivy would have the place scoped out within seconds.

The waiting room was so brightly lit that each of its miserable inhabitants appeared like characters on a stage. *Waiting for Dr. Godot?* In one corner, a woman in her teens or twenties sat with a sick toddler who looked as pale and lifeless as a fish out of water, flat across her lap. Four other little kids scampered around her. One found a place on her mother's knee to lay her head and started dreamily sucking her thumb. Two stared up at the TV, which had some movie on in Spanish. Another kept jumping off a chair, climbing back, jumping off again. The mother didn't even seem to notice. Across from them sat two desiccated octogenarians, the husband doubled over in pain—gastric or coronary, I couldn't tell. A drunk was walking around the perimeter of the room, talking loudly to himself, occasionally kicking a trash can.

I found an empty chair and sat down. It would be easy to find the hospital on the map and from there, to trace a route home.

Ivy emerged from a hallway, looking much more relaxed, wiping wet hands on her jeans. She saw me and smiled. It was a perfect Ivy smile, the rainbow after a storm, bestowing peace and second chances. Had anybody really been mad? Was she mad that I'd rolled down the window at that stoplight? Was I mad that I'd spent another Sunday house-hunting in the suburbs? The smile reached out to me like a beam of light. Then she looked around the room, taking in the suffering, and her smile vanished.

It occurred to me that we alone, of everyone else here, could just walk right out of there.

Ivy was crossing toward me when the front doors of the ER swung open and an ambulance crew rushed in, wheeling a gurney at full speed. Blood spattered on the hospital's white linoleum floor. I heard somebody shout, "Sixteen-year-old, shot twice in the chest, large gauge!" They rushed straight past the triage nurse, through stainless steel double doors.

"Wow," Ivy said, taking the seat next to me. "That was something."

"I was afraid they were going to run you over."

She looked down at my map. "So, did you figure it out?"

"Yep. Did you, by any chance, see a coffee machine?"

Before she could answer, the front door to the emergency room swung open again. A group of kids rushed in, wearing baggy pants and tight knit caps, followed by two policemen. _"Mother-fuckers!"_ I heard someone yell. The kids went straight for the stainless steel doors the gurney had disappeared through—"DeShawn! Brother, can you hear me?"—but the cops blocked them.

It was getting messy. Any minute now, someone was going to pull a knife. Or a gun. Already, some people in the waiting room were on the floor, hiding under chairs. Only the octogenarian couple seemed unfazed. Probably, they were hard of hearing. Or maybe they'd clocked enough time on the planet not to care.

I grabbed Ivy and pulled her out the front door.

I'd never liked the LeSabre. I knew it was a generous gift—brand new, no dents, a working heater—but I'd always resented the fact that I was forced to take it, that my father-in-law had picked it out. Still, there was one good thing about the LeSabre: automatic locks. I pulled my key fob out of my pocket and pointed it at the car. The locks popped up obediently.

Ivy was just opening her door when suddenly I heard another _"Motherfucker!"_ and turned around to see two of the kids who'd rushed in calling for DeShawn. One held a gun. He waved it wildly. "Keys!" he demanded.

I tossed them and watched the LeSabre squeal off. A cop followed, running. There were gunshots. It had all happened so fast, I hadn't had time to think: Was Ivy in the car?

I started chasing it when a cop knocked me to the ground. "Stay down!" he barked.

Then all hell erupted. Screams. More gunshots. Sirens. It was like a movie but not a movie. I'd seen this a million times, always on a screen. Never for real. But this time it was real. Surround sound, three-dimensional, in full living color. And then all of a sudden, as fast as it had started, it was over. The sirens were fading, hell moving into someone else's neighborhood. Slowly, I lifted my head and looked around. There she was, about ten feet away, lying flat on her stomach. "Ivy!" I yelled. *My God,* I thought. *She's dead.* Then she turned her head and looked at me. I'd never been so relieved in my entire life.

I crawled over.

"I crapped my pants," she whispered.

"It's okay."

It was well into the night before we got out of there. One of the nurses brought Ivy a clean orderly's uniform to change into and let her take a shower in the intern's lounge. We had to repeat the story to the cops at least five times. The interviews took place in the ER. Each new cop, taking our names and address, would cock his head, look slightly perplexed. What were we doing there, in Newark, outside the emergency room? Ivy, turning red, lowering her eyelashes, left me to answer. "My wife had to go to the bathroom. You see, there was this backup, the oil tanker . . ." They all jotted it down. Since we were right there, they insisted, we ought to be evaluated. That took another two hours, with the X-rays. Aside from a few abrasions, we were fine. The damage, I knew, was psychological. "You're damn lucky," one of the cops had declared. They'd gathered spent gun shells just inches away from where Ivy dropped to the ground.

We took a cab back to New York, fell into bed, and held each other for hours.

For days we clung to each other like that. Fiercely. In the middle of the night, sometimes Ivy would wake up and grab me even tighter. We each told the story at work and to our parents, waiting for the sympathetic gasp. After the third or fourth telling, I realized that this would be part of our shared lore. Eventually, we would add comic flourishes. I could imagine a time, years from now, when we'd tell it at dinner parties, taking turns.

For now, though, it threw everything into sharp perspective. That one split second, seeing Ivy on the ground, thinking she was dead. Well, if I wasn't absolutely sure before, I knew now: I loved Ivy more than anything. Suddenly I didn't care if we stayed in the city or moved to the suburbs. Of course, I preferred the city. But if that's what made her happy—a house, trees, a backyard—okay, then. I could make that sacrifice. If I hadn't been so angry about house-hunting, so impatient to go back to watching basketball, I might not have gotten off at Newark. . . .

I gulped when I thought about that. We hadn't *had* to go through this ordeal. Ivy had been knitting tranquilly—we'd lost that, too, her scarf and her knitting needles, when the car squealed off—and I'd been the asshole who couldn't stand one more minute sitting in traffic. If I'd stayed on the highway, nothing would have happened.

A few days later, a policeman called me at work. The LeSabre had been found slammed against the wall of a highway underpass, and was impounded in a police lot in Newark. They'd already swept what was left of it for prints, so we could pick it up if we wanted. Although, the cop said, we probably wouldn't want to bother. It looked like a smashed accordion; the back window was broken; there were bullet holes everywhere. Did we have comprehensive? Yes? Well, then, they'd send us photos and a report to file with our insurance company. Our insurance would pay the city to tow the car to a dump.

It struck me as nervy for the city of Newark to charge my insurance company to tow away a car they'd shot at themselves.

But when I got off the phone, I looked down at the notes I'd scratched while the policeman talked to me, and the words jumped out. There, in my own handwriting, "total loss." My heart leaped. I felt my mouth curl up in a smile. It was, I knew, completely inappropriate. The LeSabre was a total loss! Smashed, gone, history! I was happy. I mean, to think of the human tragedy that smashed car represented. The kids who stole it dead or in jail. Their friend DeShawn, surely dead. All those dead-end lives. And poor Ivy, still half in shock. But—I leaned back in my chair and closed my eyes, still smiling—the big old hulking LeSabre was gone. What would I get to replace it? A Datson 280ZX was a sweet piece of machinery. Maybe a Camaro. An MG?

On my way home, I stopped at a newsstand and picked up a car magazine and a copy of the *Daily News,* which had the best car ads. I was ready to make a project of it—just the way Ivy was making a project of the house. It was, when I thought about it, my just reward. I *had,* after all, had a gun held on me. There was, I noticed, a little spring in my step. But as I got closer to the apartment, I slowed down. I had to remember to tamp down my enthusiasm. Ivy's father had, after all, given us the car as an engagement present. It wouldn't be seemly to come in whistling over its demise. I decided to stop at the little Korean grocery on the corner and pick up roses. I hadn't brought Ivy flowers in a long time.

I unlocked the door and smelled something fabulous. It was a brisket, I could tell. Ivy, an excellent cook, had learned from my sister-in-law how to make a Jewish brisket. There were other wonderful smells. I recognized buttermilk biscuits, carrots simmering in brown sugar and curry powder. I heard Ivy humming in the kitchen. She came out, smiling, wiping her hands on her apron. It was, I realized, the first time I'd seen her smiling since Newark.

"What's going on?" I asked. "It smells wonderful in here."

She stood on tiptoe to kiss me, then pressed her nose into the roses. "These smell wonderful, too." She took the flowers and twirled around.

"So," I repeated, "what's going on?"

"We're celebrating." Beaming, Ivy reached in her apron pocket. With a flourish, she pulled out a key on a brand-new fob. "Daddy sent us up a new car. It was delivered this afternoon. He said to keep the insurance money for a house down payment! Isn't that great?"

She handed me the key, to which she'd somehow attached a red ribbon. I looked down and saw, of course, the famous Buick tri-shield logo. I closed my hand over it and forced a smile. "Great!" I said. "That's so generous." There went the 280ZX. Unless, of course, I sold it . . . the new Buick. . . .

"Dad thinks we'll get a lot of money for the car. It was practically new."

"That's great, honey."

"They felt so terrible about what happened, so worried."

My smile felt as stiff as a shirt cardboard, but Ivy didn't seem to notice. I kept nodding enthusiastically. "Another LeSabre?"

"A Skylark."

"Wow," I said. "I'm going to change, okay?"

I walked into the bedroom and hid the car magazine in the bottom drawer of my dresser. Ivy didn't need to see this, didn't need to know what I'd been thinking. I couldn't ruin her surprise. *This is the first time she's smiled since Sunday.* And Jack, good old Jack Honeycutt, coming through with a *second* car in two years. And yet . . . why was Jack picking out my cars? I felt a prick of resentment, disloyalty.

I closed the drawer, hung up my suit, and changed into an old pair of jeans. It was time to go out and join Ivy, but I looked down again at the bottom drawer. I smiled. It was like hiding *Playboy*. Porn. Automotive porn. I opened the drawer once more and pulled out the magazine, flipping through until I saw a picture of the 280ZX. I ran my index finger over the little picture.

"Ellis!" Ivy called. "Dinner's ready."

I replaced the magazine and took a deep breath. It had been such a short-lived fantasy. I was sad to have to let it go. But Ivy was alive—remember?—and there was a brisket waiting in the kitchen. My wife was practically dancing on air. I closed the drawer and called back, "Coming!"

# Three

## 1989—IVY

1987 BUICK CENTURY WAGON,

AUTOMATIC, FOUR-CYLINDER, WHITE, WOOD TRIM

How did I manage to re-create my family dynamics despite fleeing three hundred miles from the Honeycutt homestead in Virginia and marrying a Jewish comedian? Well, not so much a comedian anymore, but still a very funny guy and a mover and shaker in the entertainment business, on a first-name basis with Michael (Ovitz) and Harrison (Ford). Who would ever have thought, when I went to New York to find my fame and fortune, I'd wind up just like my mom—a stay-at-home mother to two little girls, with a side business in the domestic arts? Mom sold antiques. Here I was, dabbling in catering, baking brownies for PTA bake sales, the mother of Charlotte, five, and Lily, not quite two, and wondering what had become of my not-so-brilliant career.

And that wasn't where the similarity ended. Charlotte was just like me: the serious one, an early reader, already wearing glasses, who loved going to the library and making her own bookmarks out of construction paper, bless her little heart. And Lily, still in diapers, was already a pistol. Lily had the wispy flaxen hair of an angel, but her shiny brown eyes were all devil. She charmed everybody. You could tell she was going to be a boy magnet just like her

53

Aunt Bailey. Lily was born to be adored, to wave at crowds from a convertible.

Just as Ellis had predicted, I'd quit my job at the *Roll*. I couldn't handle the chef beat anymore, not from New Jersey. The free dinners weren't nearly so fun when you had to run off to the Port Authority. For a while, I cut back to part-time, writing the old stemware beat from my third-floor office. But when Charlotte came along, it didn't seem worth it to hire a babysitter just to keep writing about goblets, and Ellis was doing well enough that we didn't really need the second income. I got it in my head to try some creative writing again and picked up some old short stories from my Charlottesville days, tinkering over them while Charlotte was napping. I even joined a writers' group and sent a few things off. Nothing sold. They probably weren't any good. And then one of the moms who ran the PTA bake sales asked if I'd bake some cookies for a party she was giving, and Just Desserts was born.

Ellis, meanwhile, had moved up the food chain in entertainment PR and wasn't representing Michael Jackson impersonators anymore or driving down to Atlantic City. He was a *macher*—I had picked up a little Yiddish—a big shot, the in-house fixer for HWG Group in New York, which represented everybody from Liza Minnelli to Eddie Murphy. His job was to take a celebrity crisis and spin it into gold. Better yet, platinum. He dealt with rock stars sneaking out of rehab, directors caught with kiddie porn, celebrity marriages splitting. The job had nice perks, like staying at the Beverly Hills Hotel. Rumor was, next year he would go to the Oscars.

And our marriage? It was okay. Sweet, I think. Ellis had adjusted, finally, to living in the suburbs, to the train commute, to being a dad. Maybe it seemed a little dull compared with the glossy lives of his celebrity clients, but we were blessed with friends and both loved to entertain. We'd wound up in a sturdy hundred-year-old house, not huge, but filled with fireplaces and window seats, all kinds of welcoming little nooks and crannies. On weekends it was often crowded with three or four other families, kids watching a Disney movie on the VCR, parents standing around drinking wine while we cooked.

And so everything was in balance. Sort of. I was still a reluctant driver, afraid to drive on the Parkway or the Turnpike, but okay puttering around town in the wood-paneled wagon Dad had sent up when he found out I was pregnant with Lily. Ellis sold the Skylark and got a bright red Triumph TR6, which he shined up like an apple every Saturday, and which drew state troopers like moths to a flame. We argued about his speeding tickets, which wouldn't have been so bad at two hundred dollars a pop if they hadn't all counted as points against our car insurance. And I was often nervous sitting in the passenger seat—I called it the "death seat"—when we went on a highway. But I didn't have much of a choice. The only thing scarier than sitting in the death seat would have been driving myself.

The call for the job had come unexpectedly, during one of Lily's naps at the end of a very long week. Monday night, Ellis had come down with what we'd both assumed was food poisoning after a lunch of steak tartare at 21, but the next day, Charlotte got sick, too, and then the baby. A bug. I'd been cleaning brown stains out of little pink sweatpants since Tuesday. But at least Charlotte had woken up on Friday temperature-free and asking for toast, so I'd sent her to school. Just one day until the weekend, and Ellis finally would be around to help.

When Lily went down for her morning nap, I plopped on the couch and turned on *All My Children,* a guilty pleasure left over from when I was sick as a kid and my mom let me lie on the couch with ginger ale and watch the soaps. I could have used a shower, but all I wanted to do was rest. I'm sure I looked like something out of a refugee camp. I hadn't put on makeup or brushed my hair in days. But I didn't care. I was exhausted. I'd just situated the pillows right where I wanted them when the phone rang. *Please,* I prayed. *Don't let it be the school nurse.* The last thing I needed was to have to wake Lily and drag her out to get Charlotte from school.

But it wasn't the nurse. The voice on the other end of the phone sounded like cashmere. Cashmere-covered steel. You could imagine her next call being the White House. This was obvious after just two words—"Mrs. Honeycutt"—a command rather than a question. As if I were in her employ already.

"*Ms.* Honeycutt, actually," I said. "My husband's—"

"Miss Honeycutt," she said, cutting me off. "I'm Sarah Barnes. Let me get right to the point."

Let me stop here to say that I hate the words *let me get right to the point.* Rarely do they portend anything good. I was starting to think Sarah Barnes might be a high-class bill collector or a secretary in Jeff Katzenberg's office with some bad news for

Ellis. Or—I felt my heart spasm—one of my mother's rich friends, with the sad duty of telling me my parents were dead. My heart seized while I waited.

"I understand you do desserts," she said.

I exhaled. Nobody was dead. Our house wasn't about to be repossessed. The secretary of Health, Education, and Welfare wasn't calling to put me in jail for sending Charlotte to school less than twenty-four hours since her last fever. The woman with the imperious voice wasn't calling to punish or humiliate me. She was calling with a catering job.

I sat up, willing myself to sound professional, or at least awake. "I do desserts. Just Desserts, actually. That's the name of my—"

"Can you work on short notice?"

"How short?"

"Tomorrow."

"Tomorrow," I repeated.

I brought the phone into the kitchen and looked at the mess. My kitchen belonged in a fraternity house. The sink was piled with dishes. Foul-smelling dish towels littered the floor. I almost tripped over a pail of dirty water from the last spit-up I'd cleaned. Underneath the table was a trail of crayons and cut-up construction paper from yesterday, when Charlotte had started feeling better.

And that was just the kitchen. There were still mountains of laundry; we hadn't gone grocery shopping since last Saturday; I didn't know how sick Lily would be when she woke up, whether Charlotte was better, or if I was going to come down with the bug myself.

On the other hand, tomorrow was Saturday. Ellis would be home to help.

"Tell me," I said, noncommittal.

"I'm having a tea for seventy-five, and my caterer pulled out at the last minute. Damn her to hell."

"Seventy-five?" I croaked.

"What are your specialties?"

I blurted out the names of my most impressive-sounding cookies and tarts, most of them from Martha Stewart. Meringue kisses. Kiwi tartlets. Romanian walnut crescents.

"Fine, and can you throw in some little sandwiches, too, with the crusts cut off? Watercress? Cucumber? Butter? I heard about you from a friend of a friend, and, well, to be honest, I've already called five caterers already and you're the last on my list."

How flattering.

"Believe me, I'll make it worth your while. And you'll have the start of a client list that will last you for years."

She quoted a price four times higher than the one in my head. Rush-job pricing.

"You can do scones, right?"

"Sure," I said. I'd made scones, once. "Where? And what time?"

"Ridgewood Women's Club. Tea is at three. The building will be open at noon for you to set up."

"Okay." I gulped. "I'll be there." She hung up so fast, I forgot to get her phone number.

I took advantage of Lily's nap to clean the kitchen and figure out a plan of attack. After loading the dishwasher, I scrubbed the counters with bleach. God knew, there were germs all over the place. I didn't want to be the caterer known for poisoning the fine ladies of Ridgewood.

Even if I hadn't been completely exhausted, overwhelmed with running a sick house, the numbers would have seemed staggering. Up until this point, I'd supplied desserts to a few home jewelry parties and a dinner party or two—nothing so formal as a sit-down tea at a women's club. Even given the anorexic tendencies of rich women, I wasn't sure how many cookies I needed to bake— and Sarah Barnes had left a distressing amount of detail to my discretion. I estimated: three cookies, one scone, and four quarter sandwiches for each person. That would be 225 cookies, 75 scones, and 300 sandwiches. I wiped my forehead. I should have said no, I berated myself. I should have told her that I wasn't *that* kind of caterer. I was just an amateur, a mom who liked to mess around in the kitchen. I couldn't possibly rise to the challenge.

Then I realized I couldn't back out. I didn't have her number. Besides, I was the last one on her list.

I talked sternly to myself. "Organization, Ivy!" I said. "Courage!" I could manage, really. This wasn't beyond me. I might have eighteen trays of cookies to bake, and ten trays of scones, but you could fit more than one cookie sheet in the oven at a time. While the cookies were baking, I could de-crust the bread and peel and slice the cucumbers.

Yes, it would all work out. Lily would feel better when she got up from her nap. I could put her in front of *Baby Songs* while I finalized my shopping list. Charlotte would come home from school her old self and go straight to her bedroom to read. I'd order pizza for dinner, and as soon as Ellis got home, I'd run to the store and buy everything I needed. I'd get all my batters made before I went to bed, and get up before dawn on Saturday. Ellis would have to keep the girls occupied all morning— preferably out of the house. Then about eleven-thirty, he'd come home, load the car, and drive me to Ridgewood.

I went to the kitchen and pulled out my worn copy of Martha Stewart *Entertaining* and got to work. Kiwi tartlet. The recipe called for milk, egg yolks, flour, cornstarch, butter, heavy cream, apricot preserves, cognac (could I skip the cognac?), and, of course, kiwis. It yielded twelve three-inch tartlets. Wait. Three-inch tartlets? Nobody needed a three-inch tartlet. I'd cut them back to two inches. Then, the recipe would yield eighteen, right? I could triple it. Quadruple it. Oh man, my head was already starting to spin. Why had I mentioned kiwi tartlets anyway? Were kiwis even in season?

I was about to look up the seasonal properties of the kiwi when I heard a loud cry coming from the baby's room. I ran upstairs to find Lily standing in her crib, screaming, her face beet red. She'd torn off her clothes, including her diaper, and there was a little trail of brown dripping down her right leg. She was also madly scratching her stomach. The light in the room was dim and the shades were down. I didn't want to see what I thought I saw: little red bumps all over her body.

I diapered and dressed Lily as fast as I could, wiping the poop off her leg and ignoring, for the moment, the mess in the crib. I went into the bathroom and found some Benadryl. Then I plugged

Lily with a pacifier, turned on a video, sat down on the sofa, and bounced her on my knee while I called Ellis.

His secretary, Doreen, answered.

"I have to talk to Ellis," I said.

Usually Doreen put me right through, but this time she hesitated. "Let me see if he can take your call." I heard her put the phone down and ask Ellis if he had time to talk to me.

This pissed me off. Why couldn't I talk to my husband? I bounced Lily harder; her pacifier came out and she started bawling. I picked the pacifier off the floor, wiped it on my sweatshirt, and put it back in.

Finally, Ellis came on. "Honey," he said, "I have an emergency."

"Oh yeah. I have an emergency, too. I got a last-minute catering job tomorrow for seventy-five people, everything in the house is complete and total chaos, and Lily just woke up with chicken pox. I need you to come home early."

"Ivy," Ellis said, "Leo Disario was found dead."

"What?"

"Found in a hotel room in Las Vegas by a maid. Probably a drug overdose. Maybe suicide. I have to go out and identify the body. Among other things."

I was stunned. Leo Disario was one of Ellis's favorite clients. He was a foul-mouthed comedian who headlined in clubs in New York and L.A., and was about to break out into a major concert career. He also had angry ex-wives on both coasts, and Al Sharpton thought he was a racist, which was why Ellis knew him so well. I wouldn't say Leo had a heart of gold, but he wasn't as bad offstage as he was on. He always insisted on picking up the check when Ellis took him to dinner, and if I was there, he apologized after at least half his profanities.

"Leo Disario is dead?"

"That's what I'm saying."

"I can't believe it."

"I know. And, honey, I know you're having a rough day, but I have a plane to catch in an hour."

*"What?"*

"Ivy, I told you. I have to go out and identify his body."

*"But you can't!"* I screeched. Lily spit out her pacifier again and screamed loud enough to wake the dead.

"Listen," Ellis said, assuming the even tone of an experienced hostage negotiator. "This is what I do. Celebrity emergencies. It doesn't get any worse than this."

"Yes, it does! Do you hear this?" I held the phone in front of Lily for a second. I was crying now, too. "You know, going there isn't going to change anything. You can't bring him back."

"I'm sorry, Ivy," Ellis said. "There's a car waiting for me. If you need me, I'll be at the Grand." He hung up even though I was still arguing.

"But who," I cried to the dial tone, "is going to drive me to Ridgewood tomorrow?"

It was a measure of my neurosis about driving that the crisis immediately became about driving to Ridgewood. Before I'd called Ellis, all I could think about was the challenge of all that baking.

That was now dwarfed by a more serious ordeal: driving twenty miles, by myself, on the Garden State Parkway.

Did I mention that I was afraid of driving? I think maybe I did. Ellis was right. We never should have moved to Jersey. If we still lived in Manhattan, I'd never have gotten a call from the Ridgewood Women's Club to cater their stupid tea party. I wouldn't be some lame suburban dessert caterer in the first place. I'd still be a restaurant writer. And I wouldn't be expected to drive, period. My fear of getting on a highway wouldn't be some kind of monstrous character flaw. It would be a small eccentricity I could clutch proudly, like a toy poodle, while standing on a street corner in high heels, hailing a taxi.

Except for one short soul-jarring journey on Route 46, which I made the mistake of trying shortly after we moved to the suburbs, I'd managed to avoid them all: I-280, I-78, the Garden State, the Turnpike—unless, of course, somebody else was driving. This took considerable planning. A birthday party invitation for Chuck E. Cheese (which would have involved the Parkway, Route 22, and then a New Jersey jug handle) could involve days of strategizing if the party didn't fall on a weekend, when Ellis was around. I'd have to grill Charlotte on who all the birthday girl's other little friends were and pore over my class list until I could find a mom I wasn't embarrassed to ask for a ride. If they suggested a carpool, a reasonable-enough concept, I'd have to think fast, come up with some really good reason I couldn't manage even one leg of the trip. Or decide whether the mother was simpatico enough to reveal my dark secret: I was afraid to drive on a highway.

Why, oh why, had I agree to take this job? Yes, the money was good. Yes, Sarah Barnes had promised me I'd wind up with a fabulous new client list. But if all the clients were going to be up in Bergen County, what was the point? I stared at the phone and considered punching *69, which would dial her back. I had enough excuses, didn't I? A toddler with chicken pox, a husband away on an unexpected business trip. But I knew I wasn't going to back out, even if I could reach her, and it wasn't just the money. Canceling a job was flaky, and canceling a job over a phobia was double flaky.

I cursed Ellis, and poor Leo Disario, a thousand times. That was between writing out my grocery list and calling the pediatrician, who said there was really nothing I could do, except use calamine lotion and Benadryl and keep Lily away from other kids. This meant I couldn't pawn little Typhoid Lily off on any of the usual suspects—my best friend, Rita, for example, whose son, Cody, was the same age. Or the woman two blocks away, in the big old Victorian with the wraparound porch, who would watch kids for six dollars an hour, no appointment necessary. Her one rule: no contagious diseases.

No, I was stuck, stuck with the whole thing. Eventually the Benadryl kicked in and Lily was drooling sedately and staring blankly at videos. I'd rolled out a practice sheet of raisin scones. The raisins burned even though the scone wasn't cooked all the way through. Trial and error. Next time, I'd skip the raisins. And then it was time to pick up Charlotte and go to the grocery store.

Let's just skip that part. Lily caterwauling while standing up in the grocery cart, Charlotte trailing along lethargically, the sympa-

thetic and not-so-sympathetic looks of middle-aged women waiting behind me. I'd covered the eruptions on Lily's face with
calamine, then blended it all over with makeup and hoped the
light in the baking aisle would be low enough that no one would
notice. Most didn't. But there were those occasional sideways looks
from people who identified us, accurately, as the afternoon's super-
market freak show. By the end of the shopping trip, Lily had torn
at all the pustules on her face and smeared calamine and makeup
all over her clothes and her hair. The cucumbers were soft, the
kiwis underripe, and there was no watercress whatsoever.

When we got home, I ordered pizza, then bribed Charlotte five
dollars to "babysit" her little sister, which meant jollying her up in
the playpen in the living room. I set to work on the batter. After
I'd used up every mixing bowl and plastic container in the house, I
called up Rita and burst into tears, begging her to come over
with more bowls, Tupperware, and whatever baking sheets she
had around. She was almost ready to join me for an all-night
baking party—Ted would watch the kids—when I mentioned
Lily's chicken pox. She hesitated. Then apologized. She had to
draw the line. It was three weeks until Christmas—the incubation
period of chicken pox, give or take a week—and she couldn't risk
it. She would, however, have Ted drive over and leave some mixing
bowls and cookie sheets on the front porch.

"But if you've had it, you can't get it and give it to Cody," I
whined.

"I'm really sorry," she said. "I just can't chance it."

My best friend.

*　*　*

At 1:45 A.M., when the girls were asleep, I opened the fridge for more eggs and discovered I was out. Obviously, I'd miscalculated, which didn't bode well for the rest of my math. "Oh, fuck!" I yelled, kicking the refrigerator. "Fuck, fuck, fuck, fuck." I thought about leaving them asleep and running out to Krauser's. What was going to happen in fifteen minutes? Then I remembered: Babies could fall headfirst out of cribs; there could be electrical fires; someone could break into the house. *I* could get shot at Krauser's and the kids would wake up without Daddy *or* Mommy at home. No, I couldn't put eggs ahead of my children's welfare. Damn it.

I thought about going upstairs, waking Charlotte, and wrapping a coat over her footy pajamas. I thought about lifting Lily from the crib, bundling her up, rocking her gently so she wouldn't wake up, then buckling her into her car seat. Taking the two girls to the store wasn't out of the question. It was just . . .

Exhausting. I slumped into a chair and decided to call Ellis. I looked up the area code for Las Vegas and asked information for the MGM Grand. It was ten-forty-five, local time. I figured he'd be in already, and any morgue visit would have to wait until morning. Maybe he'd be in his room. I could cry. I could rage. He would comfort me. But he wasn't in. I let the phone ring seven times before giving up.

Suddenly I noticed that my back hurt, something that often sneaked up on me when I was feeling stress. It was a sign I needed to slow down. The eggs would have to wait. I didn't even need to set an alarm—the girls woke up at 6 A.M. like clockwork—but I set it anyway. I'd pull it all together in the morning.

But do you really think I was going to fall asleep? With Ellis gone? The possibility of bad guys breaking in? Lily having chicken pox? All the work I had left? And especially, the *drive to Ridgewood*? Hardly. I had a lot more worrying to do. Sure, I'd managed to distract myself with flour and butter and keeping the girls occupied and getting them to sleep, but the minute my head hit the pillow, my heart started racing. All I could think of was the merge, the fiery merge. I go through the tollbooth and glide down the entry ramp, getting ready to join the flow of traffic at exactly the same time as the driver in the right lane arrives at that spot. Speed up or slow down, I can't decide. And he can't, either. The last thing I see before we all die is Charlotte's face, staring at me with surprise and confusion.

Then there's Ellis at our funerals, utterly heartbroken and filled with guilt. If only he'd put off that business trip . . .

I'd already turned the clock away from me so I wouldn't be spooked by how late it was, but curiosity got the best of me and I turned it around. 3:18. Damn Ellis! Why was his job always the most important thing? Why couldn't somebody else at HWG take this trip? How could he abandon me with sick children? I turned on the light and found the paper that I'd written the hotel number on. I called again. Still no answer.

When the alarm clock sounded at 6 A.M., I woke up electrified. The cookies! The highway! It was all there waiting for me. I turned over and discovered Charlotte in bed next to me. That was how I was sure I'd actually fallen asleep, because I didn't remember her coming in. But now I saw her face was covered with the same bulging pus sacs that Lily had, bloody from her scratching them in her sleep. I tiptoed to the bathroom, got the calamine lotion out, and gently spread it on her face. Miraculously, she stayed asleep, and Lily did, too, allowing me to go downstairs and get started.

There I met the first calamity of the day. Sitting on the table was my big stainless mixing bowl. I didn't remember leaving it out. Surely, I'd emptied all my batters in plastic containers and stacked them in the refrigerator. Surely, I hadn't left something I was working on sitting out all night. But there it was, the filling for the kiwi tarts. I must have gone upstairs a minute to check on Lily, or maybe it was when I called Ellis. The bowl wasn't going to fit—that's right—and I was planning to look for some more plastic containers. I'd run out. But something must have distracted me. And there it was, filled with egg yolks and heavy cream, sitting all night at room temperature and brewing salmonella.

I could have wept. That was at least four dozen kiwi tarts, maybe five dozen. I wasn't sure of the math. And I had to throw it out. It killed me. But I didn't have enough catering clients, to go around poisoning the ones I had. I didn't cry. I didn't have time. I had to be brisk, efficient. Not cheerful—I wouldn't go that far— but I didn't have time for tears. I picked up the bowl, marched into the powder room, and dumped the mess down the toilet.

Snap decision. Instead of homemade custard, I'd fill the buggers with lemon curd from the A&P. At $5.95 a jar, that should be good enough for anyone.

I washed my hands, turned on the oven, set to work. I pulled out my big marble pastry boards, floured them, and rolled out dough, then started the baking assembly line. While cookies were baking,

I de-crusted the heavy Pepperidge Farm white bread I'd bought at the store and started peeling my cucumbers. In my mind, I juggled a list of things I would have to get once the girls woke up. Eggs and lemon curd. That was to start. Every once in a while, my heart would give a little leap when I thought about the drive to Ridgewood. But then a timer would go off, and I'd jump and pull more cookies out of the oven.

The girls had slept late. So much for my automatic alarm clocks. But I was lucky to have a few good hours to myself. Finally, I heard the baby gate upstairs squeak open and Charlotte thump heavily down the stairs. A minute later, she showed up in the kitchen, holding her baby sister like a prize pig. I shook my head and smiled in spite of myself. They looked so damn cute. True, taking Lily out of the crib was unauthorized, but they were both so *proud* of themselves. I stopped for a minute and congratulated myself on just how lucky I was to have two such happy little girls, who by all rights could have woken up miserable.

Then Lily pointed to the kitchen window, and I learned the real source of their morning glee: "Look, Mommy. Snow."

How had I failed to notice that?

If Lily had said, *Look, Mommy. Sea monsters,* I don't think I would have been more shocked. It was dark when I'd woken up, and I'd been concentrating so hard, I hadn't even noticed the sun come up. Well, no wonder. There wasn't much sun when it snowed, was there? I looked out and saw giant tumbleweeds of snow, falling as gently as parachutes, more beautiful than just about anything that could ruin your day and maybe even kill you. "Oh, shit!" I said, running to the front door to see what the snow was doing to the roads. "Oh, shit!" cried my little echoes, running barefoot behind me. So far, there was just a few inches. But when I stepped out on the porch in my slippers to look up at the impenetrable gray sky, I could see that there was more coming. Even the atmosphere was conspiring against me.

Then I heard the door slam behind me, and Lily giggling.

I was locked out. "Charlotte!" I yelled. "It's not funny." Only Charlotte was big enough to unlatch the door; Lily couldn't even reach the doorknob. I listened, shivering, for the sound of the lock retracting, but it still stayed maddeningly shut. After a few seconds, I started pounding. "Charlotte Louise Halpern, if you don't open the door right this second, you're not going to have ice cream for a whole year!" After books, Charlotte lived for ice cream. Lily answered: "Charlotte bathroom." I waited, hugging myself for warmth. A minute later, I knocked on the door again. Nothing. Not even a giggle.

I suddenly realized how absurd I must have looked if anybody was watching—a grown woman, in bathrobe and slippers, pounding on her own front door during a snowstorm. But nobody was watching. In fact, I realized suddenly, nobody *inside* the house was paying attention, either. It occurred to me that closing the door must have been Lily's little joke, and that she'd tottered away, moving on to other toddler things, not mentioning to Charlotte that she had locked me out. And it wasn't just my freezing ass I had to worry about. Who knew what kind of trouble Lily could get into without a grown-up in the house? I thought about the baby gate open upstairs and imagined Lily climbing up, then tumbling back down head over heels and lying unconscious at the bottom of the landing.

I tried one more time, pounding even harder, but the door was solid. The noise barely registered. *"Charlotte!"* The snow had wrapped the entire neighborhood in a dense silence. I felt like the only person in the whole world.

Nothing.

I would have to walk over to the Rileys to get a spare key. I knew it was early for a Saturday, but what choice did I have? I couldn't stand outside half-dressed until it was decent to wake up the neighbors. I pounded on the Rileys' door, wondering if anybody in that house would hear me. Pat Riley, the tough bird next door, who never smiled except at the neighborhood Christmas party, where she stood vigil over the eggnog, looked down at my wet slippers. She invited me in as she silently rummaged through a mug in her kitchen for our spare key. I saw coffee dripping from an automatic coffeemaker and longed for a cup, but didn't dare waste another second. Nor did she offer.

Suddenly it occurred to me: the answer to my troubles! Fifteen-year-old Colleen Riley, Pat's youngest daughter and the only one still living at home, a fifteen-year-old field hockey player with red hair and knobby knees. She hadn't babysat for us since before Lily was born, but I could make it worth her while. The going rate for teenagers was five dollars an hour. I'd give her ten dollars. "Pat," I said, my heart pounding like I was asking for a date. "Has Colleen had the chicken pox?"

Pat Riley hadn't raised six kids without learning all the angles. She knew what I was getting at as soon as she heard

Colleen's name. "Sure," she said. "But if you're looking for her to sit, you're out of luck. She's at a sleepover and I don't expect any of them to wake up before noon. And then, with the weather"— she shrugged—"who knows when she'll be home?"

I tried to imagine what it would be like to have Charlotte out with friends and not know when she would be returning. I couldn't.

"Where's Ellis?" Pat asked, handing me the key.

"Vegas."

I ran back through the snow, unlocked the door with relief, and threw off my sopping slippers. I stood on the heat vent for a second and a half to thaw out my frozen feet before noticing the drone of the oven timer and the smell of something burning. I ran into the kitchen, turned off the oven, grabbed an oven mitt, and pulled out three trays of coal-like lumps that were intended to be Romanian walnut crescents. Then the smoke detector started wailing. But that wasn't the bad part.

The bad part was that Lily had climbed up on the kitchen table and made mincemeat of my morning's work. Charlotte stood next to her, her face covered with crumbs.

Where meringue kisses and unfilled tart shells had been lined up neatly on cooling racks, there were now only half-eaten cookies. My first batch of decent scones was smashed like ruins. Charlotte stopped as soon as she saw me, but Lily was still greedily stuffing cookies in her mouth, looking like some crazed contestant on a Nickelodeon game show. Eight hours of planning, shopping, mixing, and baking—smeared on their pus-filled faces, spread through their matted hair, oozing through their sticky little fingers.

*"Ellis!"* I screamed.

"Daddy's not here," Charlotte said.

"Yes," echoed Lily. "Daddy's not here."

"Don't you remember, Mommy?" Charlotte added, a little condescendingly for someone who'd just been licking her left wrist. "Daddy's on a business trip."

Yes, she was right. Daddy wasn't here, the son of a bitch. And Mommy had reached her limit.

I lifted Lily out of her crib and deposited her, more roughly than necessary, into the playpen. Then I came back into the kitchen and stood over Charlotte. "How could you?" I screamed. I took a cookie and threw it across the room. It was easy to forget that Charlotte was five. She always seemed so mature, almost like a third little adult.

She stared at me, her lip puckered, ready to cry. "It was Lily's idea. . . ."

The smoke detector was still emitting its hysterical squeal. "Lily?" I shouted. "You listen to a baby?"

I slammed the cookie sheets and cooling racks to the floor. The crash made Charlotte jump and set off a new round of screams, from Lily in the next room. It was over. It was all over. The women of Ridgewood would have to eat Pepperidge Farm.

"Now are you happy?" I slumped in a chair and noticed that the bottoms of my pajamas were still soaking. In the chaos of the cookies and the smoke detector, I'd forgotten that part. That Charlotte had locked me outside. Or Lily had. My toes were still little Popsicles. I suddenly remembered pounding on the front door, then slogging in slippers through the wet snow, and how I'd *worried* about them getting hurt somehow. And here they'd been, stuffing their little faces.

Charlotte made the mistake of picking just that moment to grab a scrap of shortbread that had been sitting, temptingly, next to her right hand. The audacity! A synapse inside me tripped, sudden and violent as a bolt of lightning. I lunged, grabbing a hunk of Charlotte's hair, and gave it a vengeful tug.

She ran upstairs, and for a while, it was a contest to see which of the three of us could cry the loudest. The smoke detector was still screaming. The whole fucking house had turned into the "Ride of the Valkyries." I put my head in my hands and sobbed until I was raw inside. What had I done? What kind of monster was I?

What had happened? All I'd done was to try my best. I'd worked hard, been organized. I'd made lists, set my alarm for 6 A.M. I *hadn't* deserted my children in the middle of the night to get eggs. I hadn't tempted fate. What went wrong? It wasn't supposed to work out this way.

I walked into the living room and picked up the phone. It was only 5 A.M., Vegas time, but why should Ellis sleep peacefully in a warm city? I had to batter him, too. The phone rang three times, and for one terrible moment, I wondered if he'd gone to his room at all last night—and if not, where was he?—but on the fourth ring, he answered. I pummeled him with rage and blame; he said calm, helpful things in return. I told him how I'd pulled Charlotte's hair. "She'll get over it," he said, absolving me. "Those smoke detectors can make you crazy."

Eventually, the batteries in the damn thing died, its shrill ending in a long sour blast that sounded like a dying cow. I took it as a sign that it was time to clean the kitchen and check on the children.

Lily had cried herself to sleep in the playpen. My heart heavy, I trudged upstairs to Charlotte's room. She was sitting at her desk, writing me a letter on lined paper, apologizing for ruining the cookies. I took the pencil out of her hand and reached over to draw her close. She flinched a little, my punishment. But I held her tight, daring even to smooth her hair—her precious hair—and repeated, like an incantation, "I'm sorry. I'm so sorry. Mommies make mistakes." I felt her expel a huge breath, her small body quivering, like a minor exorcism.

I decided to believe Ellis. Charlotte would get over it. I looked out her bedroom window, watching as the snow accumulated on the roofs, wrapping the whole world in a white blanket. The tea in Ridgewood would be canceled, too. I was sure of it.

"Come on," I said. "Let's get your snowsuit on." I shouldn't have—the chicken pox—but I needed, we both needed, an act of grace. I'd bundle her up in warm layers and let her stay outside for only a few minutes. Lily, too.

*Four*

1991—ELLIS

1987 BUICK CENTURY WAGON,
AUTOMATIC, FOUR-CYLINDER, WHITE, WOOD TRIM

Marry a shiksa, you get Christmas. It's a package deal. I understood that's what I'd signed up for at the beginning, but you never know how you're really going to feel about it until you've gone out to a Cut Your Own Tree farm, performed your own ceremonial Little Georgie Washington on a Scotch pine, tied it to your luggage rack, and barreled down I-78 with it flapping on top of your car.

Trust me, there was nothing in my upbringing, training, temperament, or skill set that made me a natural candidate for such duty. And I was sure my ancestors going all the way back to Abraham were spinning in their graves. But this was what Ivy wanted and, she assured me, what Charlotte and Lily wanted—*really* wanted—too. Ivy was wrong, though. Lily wanted it, but not Charlotte, who'd just started going to Hebrew school in September. Charlotte was always the sensitive one, and she needed to make things all fit together in her head. The Christmas tree trip was flipping her out, because it pitted her mother against her Hebrew school teacher, who'd been saying that it was wrong to celebrate Christmas if you were a Jew, wrong to have a Christmas tree in your house. I tried to explain this to Ivy, but it was mid-December, and the Christmas Express was clattering full speed down the tracks. And Ivy was wallowing in a nice-sized piece of Christmas self-pity, because this was the first time in her life that she wasn't going to celebrate Christmas in the house at Canterbury Road. Her parents had decided to fly out to L.A. and spend the holiday with Bailey.

True, I could have backed out of this whole Christmas deal if I'd had my eyes open right from the beginning. We'd been engaged only a month the first time I experienced a Honeycutt Family Christmas. Fair was fair, after all. We'd spent Thanksgiving with my mom. And if I'd heard all the way up to Pittsfield that Thanksgiving was Ivy's mother's absolute favorite holiday, well, I should have realized that was just a little Ivy hyperbole. Thanksgiving was great, but it was more like an *appetizer* leading up to the big meal. And it wasn't just Ivy's mom who was crazy about Christmas. Her dad was gaga over it, too.

Jack Honeycutt was one of those guys who hung a Christmas wreath on the grille of his car. In fact, all the cars on the edge of his car lot, all the ones facing the road, sported little wreaths. The two weeks before Christmas, he wore a little elf hat and tried to get all the guys in the showroom to wear them, too. From Thanksgiving on, his radio was always playing Christmas music, and if he had any excuse at all, he'd dress up in a Santa Claus suit. Naturally, he *owned* his own Santa suit, the way most men own a tux. I guess it was a pretty good investment in the long run, and safe, too. Who outgrows a Santa outfit? If the Rotary Club didn't ask him to dress up as Santa, he'd be Santa for a year-end-sale commercial for Honeycutt Motors. Sometimes both. The record, I'd heard, was Jack playing Santa four times in one season.

But don't think that just because Jack Honeycutt was Santa incarnate that Ivy's mother was any slouch when it came to Christmas. Katherine Honeycutt was part of that breed of women who hardly exist anymore, at least not where we live, women who make a thorough production of Christmas and yet never once complain about it. You could see where Ivy got her talent in the cookie department. Katherine didn't bake Christmas cookies by the dozen; she baked them by the gross, putting them in antique cookie tins decorated with pictures of poinsettia and distributing them to all her friends and customers and Jack's customers and employees, along with the other shopkeepers on her end of Main Street, all of whom had more than enough Christmas cookies of their own.

When it came to decorations, Katherine didn't even try to exercise restraint. The woman couldn't help it. After all, she ran an antiques shop. She'd come across a vintage nativity scene with the three wise men or a china serving platter decorated with holly or an eighteenth-century cross-stitched Christmas stocking and just not have the strength to resist. The Honeycutt living room and dining room were never studies in minimalism, but come December, there wasn't a spare inch in either one. You could scarcely find a place to put down a drink. There were Christmas tea towels in the kitchen, Christmas hand towels in the bathroom, and even, one year, some Santa Claus toilet paper that it actually seemed kind of a shame to have to wipe yourself with.

Katherine's prized possession was a collection of delicate glass ornaments that had passed through five generations of Honeycutts and Gambles, each of which could be traced to the exact descendant—and event—that had brought it into the family. The birth of Emily Ann Gamble in 1896, the marriage of John Fowler Honeycutt in 1918—*and here's the Dresden glass hot air balloon ornament, bought by Grandma Emily in honor of Ivy's birth, see that?* The Honeycutts had a special tradition of unwrapping and then hanging these precious orbs while listening to a Perry Como Christmas album and drinking eggnog. That first Christmas with Ivy, I broke not one, but two, of the precious Honeycutt ornaments in the first hour. They masked their horror bravely. Jack laughingly blamed it on the rum.

And that was just the beginning of the buildup. There was visiting the whole week leading up to Christmas, which reached its apotheosis on the day of Christmas Eve, when the doorbell rang all day, and cookies were exchanged with lilting complaints about weight gain, and everybody wore sweaters with reindeer or snowflakes.

Then there was a great sit-down dinner, limited to kinfolk, which was still a pretty big crowd, followed by a candlelight service in a small wooden colonial chapel and, back home, a ceremonial offering of cookies and milk for Santa Claus in front of the fireplace (whether young children were present or not). Ivy and I shared one chaste kiss under the mistletoe before going up to our separate bedrooms, which in my case meant Bailey's old room, because Bailey didn't come home that year. Bailey's winking prom queen pictures gave me a hard-on, which I relieved, shamefully, under her pink chenille bedspread once I was certain everyone had fallen asleep.

So I knew. I could have backed out of the whole thing then, in 1981. It would have been awkward, true, to end a one-month-old engagement, but it was possible. We hadn't tied the knot. But I was crazy about the girl, and her childlike love of Christmas was just one more thing to be crazy about, and secretly, of course, I was crazy about Christmas, too. After all, it was the one thing I'd been deprived of growing up.

My parents, mindful of the Holocaust and the necessity of identifying with one's co-religionists, *even if they were wrong,* paid dues to a synagogue and sent me to Hebrew school. Being shrinks, though, their real gods were Freud and Jung and Adler. They looked at things like dietary laws and the High Holidays as outmoded and superstitious vestiges of a repressive civilization. When the question came up of whether to let us have a "Chanukah bush," they were, typically, divided. My dad was all for indulging us, arguing that the American Christmas was a secular holiday anyway, and that trees and stockings and nutcrackers were harmless. But my mother, who always won, saw Christianity more darkly. She was a First Amendment fundamentalist who thought that making Jewish kids sing "Silent Night" in school was coercive, and she couldn't very well write letters to the school board while having a Christmas tree in her very own house, whether you called it a Chanukah bush or not.

Her one concession to the season was the *Charlie Brown Christmas* special, which she let us watch in the rec room with TV trays and Stouffer's TV dinners, a rare concession that was also granted for the annual airing of *The Wizard of Oz*. Sometimes I'd look over at her during those Charlie Brown specials and see her mouth turn up slightly and wonder how Charlie Brown and Lucy and Linus could coax that relaxed, faraway smile out of her when we could not. Then the Vince Guaraldi music would come on, and the credits would scroll up, and that's all we would get of Christmas except the meager crumbs dropped by our classmates and the general culture.

So going to the Honeycutts that first year was like being in Candyland. I could finally suck at the tit of the Great American Yuletide until I was drowsy-drunk and lie there like a soused pig on Bailey's pink chenille bedspread and then get back up and slurp some more, and nobody was going to do anything but look over at me and smile.

But now it was ten years later. I wasn't a boyfriend; I was a husband, a father—and a dues-paying member of a synagogue. Maybe some of Sheba's principled stoicism had leached into me. I was tired of joining in reindeer games.

Ivy had a way of not listening. It was a Sunday morning, and we were in the kitchen—me finishing a cup of coffee and her looking at recipes for teacakes to bring on the ride out to the Christmas tree farm. If it had been October, and we were going apple picking, I would have reminded Ivy the orchards all sold doughnuts and cider, and that bringing teacakes was really coals to Newcastle, and she would have laughed and decided to make them anyway, just to put her own stamp on it. And I would have thought, *Fine. That's unnecessary, but really very sweet.*

But this morning, I wasn't feeling at all generous, and Ivy making teacakes as part of a jolly old trip to cut down a Christmas tree felt, well, a little manipulative. I could understand her wanting a real Christmas tree, I really could, but this whole *Little House on the Prairie* thing seemed excessive, and the fact that she'd sprung it on us—on me—without *asking,* made me furious. She'd just announced it, a done deal, as if I had no say at all in how we spent our Sundays.

I tried to bring it up while she was tidying the kitchen, but she kept turning on the faucet and clanking things around in the sink, as if purposely trying to drown me out. "It's confusing for the kids," I argued. "We agreed that it's good for them to have a religion, and we joined a synagogue. And now—"

"Which do you like better? The lemon or apple cinnamon?" Ivy asked, as if we'd been talking teacakes all along. "Or should I go completely traditional and just do butter and sugar?" She had a cookbook spread out on the table, and her mouth was twisted the way it always was when she was trying to make a culinary decision.

Ivy's lemon teacakes were almost worth abandoning your principles, but I didn't say anything.

"Lemon?" she asked, as if reading my mind. She walked to the jelly cupboard and looked into the breadbox. "And PB-and-J or ham biscuits? I mean, if the ham stays out in the car too long, could it make us sick or something?"

"Ivy!" I walked over and grabbed her shoulders, turning her around to face me. "You're not listening." She wasn't expecting it, and seemed to have no idea why I was so angry. She looked wounded, like a girl whose pigtails have just been dunked in the inkwell.

I was still holding her shoulders. "I've been trying to talk to you."

She shrugged away and walked over to pour herself a cup of coffee. She added milk and sugar, stirred it, found a napkin, folded it, pulled out a chair, sat down, crossed her legs, straightened her back—all with slow and silent dignity. Finally, she took a sip of coffee. Only then did she look up. "Okay," she said. "I'm waiting."

"I've been saying that I don't think this little jaunt to the country to cut down a Christmas tree is a good idea."

"You're telling me I can't have a Christmas tree."

"I didn't say that."

I should explain. I've never denied Ivy her Christmas trees. We'd always had one, starting with that little three-footer I helped her buy and bring back to her apartment that very first December. But Christmas trees were always problematic, given our annual drive down to Virginia. One of the things that comes as a surprise if you don't grow up with them is that the damn things are a fire hazard. They have to be watered. I remember that first year in Montclair, with the tree all pretty and decorated, twinkling away in the corner of the living room, and Ivy, very pregnant, suddenly turning to me with a wistful look and saying, "What are we going to do about it while we're away?'

"Do about what?"

"The tree." And then she explained the thing about the fire hazard. I could imagine my mother rolling her eyes—*those wacky Christians!*—but kept it to myself.

Ivy thought about hiring a teenager to come in and water the damn thing every day while we were away, like taking care of cats, but it seemed kind of ridiculous. And so, the day before we left, she took down all the ornaments and asked me to pull the tree out to the street. It became her sad little ritual, taking down the Christmas tree before we left for Virginia. And then one year, while picking up socks at Kmart, she saw an artificial tree—silver with touches of textured fake snow—and it hit her like an Elvis sighting. This tree would solve all her problems! You didn't have to water it! It didn't take itself too seriously! The tree was so kitsch that it was religiously neutral. Even if Sheba should happen to stop by—something that wouldn't happen without an engraved invitation, but just supposing—the tree wouldn't offend. (That was the theory, anyway.) When Ivy spotted flashing jalapeño pepper lights in the next aisle, it was like the exclamation point at the end of the miracle! And here was the best part: She knew she'd get her real evergreen fix at her parents', so she really didn't have to give up anything.

But this year, we weren't going to her parents', and if she wanted the Great American Christmas, she was going to have to give it to herself. This year the wink-wink, nudge-nudge irony of the aluminum Christmas tree just wasn't going to cut it. She wanted a real tree—the real smell of Scotch pine—in her own house.

"So you're saying I can't have a Christmas tree at all," Ivy repeated.

"No," I said. But I wasn't sure. Maybe that was what I was saying. Maybe it wasn't just the Christmas tree farm I was objecting to, but the whole idea of transferring the Honeycutt Family Christmas to the Halpern house. Maybe I had the moral high ground and maybe I didn't. Maybe I was just trying to pick a fight.

"I just don't think it's fair the way you sprang it on me," I said.

That part, at least, was true. Ivy had just announced it unilaterally at dinner on Thursday night.

Thursday had been one of those rare weeknights when I got home from work early enough to have dinner with the family. I never knew what I'd be walking into when I got home, especially in winter when it started getting dark before five. It was the time Ivy referred to as "the arsenic hour," a period of hyperactive children and frayed maternal nerves, and I was never surprised to come home and find Ivy conked out in bed. But this night, Ivy seemed uncharacteristically unfrazzled. She'd prepared spaghetti and meatballs and was grating Parmesan when I walked in.

"Perfect timing," she said, smiling. That was also a relief. She was so often angry that I was late. "Go tell the girls it's dinner." It was the trifecta of domesticity: Ivy in a good mood, dinner ready, and the girls happily watching *Rugrats*. I should have realized something was up.

I went into the living room, clicked off the television, and bent down to hoist Lily off the sofa and swing her into the air. It was something I'd been doing since Charlotte was a toddler, but now Charlotte was too big and it was Lily's turn. Ivy warned me I'd pull out my back one day—Lily was already thirty-five pounds— but "Up in the air, flying like an airplane!" was a small joy of fatherhood. Tonight, though, Lily was having none of it. "Stop!" she said, thrashing her legs and landing a nice sharp kick to my chest. "It's almost *over*."

That started souring my mood, the idea that Lily preferred Tommy and Angelica, the characters on *Rugrats,* to her own dad. When I was a boy, I sometimes waited down the block to see my dad's Chevy turn the corner onto our street at dinnertime. I'd chase his car to our house and, even before he got out, start telling him about my day. Granted, things were more regular then. My dad turned that corner between 5:50 and 5:55 every night. But was it too much to ask that children actually be happy to see the person who worked all day to put food on the table?

And it was another reminder of how spoiled Lily was getting. This sometimes happened to the golden child. Having too much charm could make a person insufferable.

"Too bad," I said.

Charlotte had been observing silently—she probably wanted to see the end of *Rugrats* herself—though as soon as she saw I was serious, she got up to wash her hands. But Lily pouted and stamped her feet, trudging into the kitchen still complaining about her show.

"Now, hush," Ivy said, and I should have realized, with the word *hush,* that something was up. *Hush* was a Southern word, a Katherine-ism. "I have something to tell you girls." She cut up a baguette and took a tub of margarine from the refrigerator, drawing out the suspense. "This weekend, we're going to drive out to the country to cut down our own Christmas tree!"

Lily immediately sprang up from her seat and started doing a happy dance. You'd have hardly guessed this was the little monster who'd kicked me a few minutes earlier. *"Yay,"* she said. "Christmas tree! Christmas tree! We're going to cut down a Christmas tree!"

Ivy shot me a sly smile—as if to say, *See,* this *is how you handle children*—and then reminded Lily to sit down and behave like a young lady. Then she explained how *her* father, PopPop Jack, used to take them out to cut down Christmas trees when she was a little girl and how this weekend—Saturday or Sunday, she wasn't sure—"our daddy" would use an *actual saw* and everybody would get hot cocoa. We might even see Santa Claus.

This was all news to me. "Oh, really. I don't remember having a saw."

"Don't worry." Ivy winked. "They provide them."

"Can I bring Hannah?" Lily asked. Hannah Bloom was Lily's best friend and constant companion. "Pretty please? Pretty please with sugar on top?" The little demon of five minutes ago now had her hands folded politely together and was looking at Ivy with saucer-sized eyes. She appealed only to Ivy, not to me.

"I don't know," Ivy said. "It's kind of a family thing. And also . . ." She hesitated. "Hannah's Jewish."

Another little voice piped up. "But aren't we Jewish, too?" It was Charlotte, who'd slunk down in her chair and was watching everything very closely.

Well, Charlotte had asked it, the $64,000 question. I don't know what Ivy was thinking, but I was picturing Charlotte in her little plaid jumper and white turtleneck a few months earlier at synagogue, when she'd been given a tiny little Torah and had paraded it around the aisles. It was called consecration, a welcoming of the temple's newest religious students, and it was part of the festival of Simchat Torah, with klezmer music and dancing and, afterwards, candy apples. It was foreign to me, since my family never went to synagogue except on the days my brother and I were bar mitzvahed, but it was definitely charming. And the sight of Charlotte solemnly carrying that little Torah had melted even my heathen heart.

"Well," Ivy said. "We are Jewish. Sort of. That is, Daddy is Jewish. And I guess you two are going to be Jewish, too." Charlotte was gnawing at a fingernail and now even Lily looked worried, as if this technicality raised by her older sister was going to spoil everything. "But *I'm* not. So I guess you could say that we're getting this Christmas tree for Mommy, and I'm inviting you to come along and celebrate."

Ivy smiled. She'd finessed it. She was *inviting* us—we poor benighted Jews—to come along and celebrate her quaint little custom called Christmas. How about that?

"So can Hannah come, too?" Lily asked again.

"Sure," said Ivy.

"*Yay!*"

Charlotte and I exchanged glances and went back to our spaghetti. But Lily and Ivy were revving themselves up about the Christmas tree expedition. I wasn't sure I'd be able to get this horse back in the barn. But I was planning to talk to Ivy later.

Hannah's mother, Shara, tried to press a twenty on us in case there was anything Hannah might want to buy in the course of our expedition, but we shook our heads and told her not to worry. Hannah didn't need money. And we'd be back before dark. Hannah snuggled into the backseat next to Lily, showing off a new Beanie Baby her grandmother had just sent. Through the rearview mirror, I noticed Charlotte peering over to take a look, but the smaller girls had huddled together conspiratorially and were keeping the Beanie from Charlotte's view.

"I don't know how we'll be able to keep Hannah down on the farm after this," Shara said with a laugh. "I keep telling Todd we ought to go out and cut down a menorah, but he isn't having any of it." The cheerful way she said it, you knew she either had complete confidence in her daughter's Jewish identity or was just happy to dump her for a few hours.

I envied her. It had been brutal between Ivy and me in the kitchen that morning. I'd accused Ivy of "cramming Christmas down our throats," and she'd accused me of "extraordinary coldness." We both replayed old family dramas, me repeating my mother's dry intellectual arguments against Christmas almost word for word, and Ivy reliving an almost biblical level of sibling rivalry. "My parents always loved Bailey best," she said. "They're just rewarding her for moving three thousand miles away!" In the end, tears won out. I wound up holding Ivy and saying, "Of course you can have a tree, honey."

Charlotte must have been eavesdropping because she stepped into the kitchen just as we were making up. "Are we going to get a Christmas tree?" she asked. She sounded tentative, unsure where her allegiance should be. It made me think of King Solomon's advice to split the baby in half. I had to remember that when Ivy and I fought, it was like asking our children to choose between us. Well, at least Charlotte, who was so sensitive.

"Yes, sweetheart. We're going to go get Mommy a Christmas tree."

Ivy washed her face and went back to making teacakes. Before long, she was whistling Christmas songs. And my resentments? They were little black dung beetles crawling back into a rotting log, where they'd grow fatter and uglier and wait for next time.

"So do you have the directions?" Ivy asked as we pulled out of the Blooms' driveway.

"I thought *you* had the directions."

A small cloud passed over her face. "I thought—"

"Just kidding. It's pretty simple. Out 78 and a little past Flemington."

It was a glorious day, bright and in the mid-forties, cold enough to be authentically winter, warm enough to spend time outdoors. Ivy seemed sunny, too, and open-hearted. She could be nervous traveling on a highway, even with me driving, maybe *especially* with me driving—leaning over to check the speedometer, looking out for hidden cops—but she'd brought along some embroidery and was contentedly pushing her needle in and out through the hoop. She turned on the radio, and we listened to the Sunday rebroadcast of *A Prairie Home Companion*. Garrison talked about the character-building properties of Minnesota winters. There were Christmas carols for Ivy and jokes for me.

She reached over and took my hand. "Thanks."

"You're welcome."

We merged from the Parkway onto 78, and when we got past the turnoff to 24, Ivy passed out teacakes. I kept thinking how pleasant this was, and wondering why I'd made such an ass of myself earlier. Why was I so pinched and selfish that I couldn't grant Ivy her goddamned Christmas tree and her drive in the country? It wasn't so different from going apple picking or buying pumpkins, was it? We were just going out to cut down a tree. We weren't getting a crèche, or going to a baptism. There would be no holy rollers or snake handlers. It was just an outing in the country. We'd bring back a tree—it was just a *tree*—that would make the house smell nice and fresh. Such a small thing, really, to make Ivy happy.

Then I noticed some muffled sniffles coming from the backseat.

It was Charlotte. I looked in the rearview mirror and saw her looking down, fighting back tears, the book she'd brought flat on her lap, unopened. She was clearly fighting a battle for self-control, but when she caught my eyes in the mirror, she lost it. She started sucking big gulps of air, the prelude to outright crying. Poor Charlotte—my poor, dear, serious firstborn. It wasn't that she cried all the time, or that you couldn't eventually jolly her up. She just seemed a little too good for the world, a little too pure, and when she cried, it was because we—everybody—had somehow let her down.

Lily shrank from her sister like she was some crazy homeless person and moved closer to Hannah.

Ivy turned around. "What's wrong, honey bunch?"

Charlotte's chest was heaving so hard she couldn't talk. The words, the cause: stuck inside her.

It was my turn. Charlotte and I had a special bond. Ivy preferred Lily, the sunny one—even though by all reports, it was Charlotte whom she'd resembled as a child. Maybe that was why I loved Charlotte so much. She was like Ivy, back when Ivy was bookish and awkward and unfinished. I put my arm around the back of the seat and turned around. "What's the matter, sweetheart?"

"Keep your eyes on the road," Ivy snapped. "I'll take care of this."

I gave her a sarcastic little salute. "Aye, aye, Captain."

Charlotte cried harder. I heard Lily and Hannah giggling.

Ivy glared at me for half a second, then returned to the business of jollying up Charlotte. She actually unbuckled her seat belt so she could turn all the way around. First she threw a little warning glance at Lily and Hannah. Then she reached back and tenderly touched Charlotte's cheek. "What's wrong, baby?" she asked again.

"The Christmas tree. We're not supposed to."

"Oh, honey." I turned around to look at Charlotte. "It's okay. Really. We're not getting the Christmas tree for *ourselves*. We're getting it for *Mommy*."

I guess I must have slipped a little bit toward the right when I'd turned around, because a big SUV flying by right then honked at us. It was nothing, just a warning. I wasn't in his lane, not remotely. But a horn from another car was automatic grounds for hysteria.

Ivy whipped around and poked me in the arm, hard. "I said, watch the road."

I hate being poked, ever. But most of all when I'm driving. I felt a growing rage and stabbed Ivy back with my index finger. "Oh yes, Massa," I said. "I'm very sorry, Massa."

"Fuck you," said Ivy.

There it was, always under the surface. You'd never have known this girl was raised in Virginia, where ladies, supposedly, were brought up to talk like ladies. I certainly never heard Katherine use a swearword harder than *fudge*. Maybe it was a measure of how thin the veneer was that kept our whole life together, that shiny surface Ivy worked so hard to maintain. Or because she experienced threats everywhere—in the next lane, in her mother's judgment, in the snubs from women in the PTA. Most of the time, Ivy was like a shiny balloon: buoyant, happy, a welcome fixture in anybody's parade. But the slightest prick, and she popped.

I was used to it. I never liked it, but it didn't shock me. Even the girls had a fair acquaintance with Ivy shouting strings of obscenities, though it still made them flinch. But this time was worse. Hannah was in the car with us. Hannah was a witness. Like all families, we had our dirty little secrets, our silent conspiracies. But Hannah had heard everything. And that made what Ivy said shocking.

Suddenly, the only sound in the car was Garrison Keillor doing a Raw Bits commercial. Ivy snapped it off.

Now the car was completely silent. Charlotte had even stopped crying. None of the girls dared say anything. I actually felt a tiny bit sorry for Ivy. I knew she wanted to apologize, but she'd be hoping that, somehow, maybe Hannah would think she'd misheard her. If she apologized, Hannah would know she'd heard right.

"I hate you," Ivy whispered.

"Right back at you," I said with a false smile.

I heard a little whimper from the backseat.

*Well,* I thought, *the Blooms must fight once in a while. Maybe Shara lets loose like a sailor now and then.* But I wasn't all that concerned about Hannah. Kids could say all kinds of things, and you could always shrug it off. Who would believe a four-year-old? The real problem was that I really did hate Ivy just now. And it wasn't the Christmas tree, or the Christmas tree farm, or even the word *fuck.* It was the way she ordered me around like a slow-witted functionary.

"Charlotte," I said, reaching for something to replace the silence. "Let's talk about the Christmas tree. Tell me what's bothering you."

Ivy let out an annoyed sigh.

"It's okay," said Charlotte.

"No, sweetie. You were crying."

Charlotte shook her head and closed her eyes tightly. In the mirror, I saw her hands form tight little fists. She was trying hard not to rock the boat.

"Can't leave well enough alone, can you?" Ivy said under her breath.

"It's okay!" Charlotte shouted. "I don't care. Forget it. Just don't get divorced!"

Divorced? Where had she gotten an idea like that?

Charlotte dissolved into tears, followed by Lily and even Hannah.

"See what you've done," Ivy said.

The chorus of tears intensified.

What *I'd* done? I stared at Ivy in disbelief.

"You're doing it again!" Ivy yelled. "You're looking at me, and not the road. Goddamn it, Ellis, *are you trying to get us killed?*"

"Right," I said. "That's exactly it. I'm trying to get us killed." I glanced in the mirror and saw my opening. I was in the far left-hand lane, but managed to cross three lanes at once and slam to a stop on the shoulder. Horns blared, and the cries in the backseat grew louder, but we were safe. Perfectly safe. I turned the key, opened my door, and gestured gallantly at the steering wheel. "Okay, *you* drive."

I got out and stood up, stretching my legs and leaning back on the car like I had all the time in the world. I knew the girls were terrified, but I didn't care. I was too busy hating Ivy.

I saw people stare from their windows as their cars swooshed by, reminding me that I was disturbing the natural order of things. Even at sixty-five miles per hour, I could see worry on their faces. Should they stop? Should they help? Should they be a Good Samaritan? But luckily this was New Jersey. People could spare a little pity, but no time. And why should they? I wasn't bent over the hood or jacking up the car. I was just standing there.

On the other hand, what if a cop saw us and pulled over? Looked in and saw Ivy and the girls crying? I would look like a real asshole. *But, Officer, she was being a bitch. . . .* No, it wouldn't fly. I had to collect my pound of flesh and get this thing going.

I opened the car door. "Come on, big shot," I said to Ivy. "This is your party."

And this was where she folded, just as I'd known she would.

She looked up at me, pleading now, instead of telling me what to do. "Ellis. Please."

I liked the sound of the word *please*. The simple acknowledgment that she was asking for a favor. Because *she* wasn't going to move over and take the wheel, any more than Charlotte was, or Lily. Ivy was like a movie director whose actors had stalked off the set. Until she got me back on board, she wasn't going anywhere.

"Well?" I said.

She just looked at her lap, shaking her head.

I'd won. I got in, slammed the door, and started the car.

We drove in complete silence all the way to the Christmas tree farm. Even after we'd gotten there, it felt like we were just going through the motions, like Disney animatrons. The girls walked around with their shoulders slumped; even Santa Claus couldn't jolly them. I heard the laughter of other families all around us, like the tinkle of sleigh bells. What did they know that we didn't? I wondered.

# Five

## 1993—Ivy

1992 BUICK ROADMASTER ESTATE WAGON,

AUTOMATIC, V-8, SILVER

You might have found it funny had it been some anonymous guy in a plaid shirt and a billed cap, in an out-of-focus photo in some out-of-town newspaper, and you'd shake your head and look at the picture and think, *Poor schmuck, what a way to go: killed by a deer hitting his truck on the way home from a hunting weekend.* Ironic, huh? Like the prey getting some cosmic revenge on the predator. Only in this case, the coroner said, they both died instantly. No winner.

But it was my dad, so it wasn't funny. It was horrible.

First of all, he was just sixty-two, and he'd been to his doctor the month before and been declared fit as a fiddle. His blood pressure had been 120 over 80, his cholesterol just 170, and the only gut he had was the pillow he stuck in his Santa suit. The Honeycutt men had good tickers, my dad always said. My great-grandfather had lived to eighty-eight, and *his* father had made it past ninety. They didn't get cancer, either. They all died of old age, in their sleep, the death of the lucky and the virtuous.

It was my mother I'd worried about. Years ago, I had started hardening myself against the possibility of a late-night phone call.

She'd been diagnosed with breast cancer at fifty-three, had a double mastectomy, come back to fight it and win. But I'd seen her in the hospital bed a few hours after her surgery, a limp marionette tethered to a thousand tubes, flattened by pain and drained of color. And then the chemo. Mom never let anyone see her bare head, even my father. She took off her wig in her bathroom at night, put it on a stand, and replaced it with a silk scarf.

But, Dad—no, that was a shock. And it wasn't just that his health had always been good. It was the force of his personality. Dad was a salesman to the core, and while that might not impress a lot of snobs, a salesman—a real salesman—is a genius at the art of getting along with people. He can walk into a room, any room, and in minute, turn everyone there into his best friend. He's got a laugh that's strong and genuine, and even if he doesn't know you from Adam, he can put his hand on your shoulder with just the right pressure to convey warmth and concern, if that is what you need. He remembers your name and your husband's name and your kids' names and your dogs' names—and it's not just some sleazy trick. He's not doing it to snow you. He's doing it because he likes people, and people like him.

Well, in Dad's case, people *loved* him. The first EMT on the scene had bought a car from him in the mid-'80s; he wept when he saw who was behind the steering wheel. The news flew through Albemarle County, to fellow members of the Rotary Club, to generations of people he'd lent flatbeds to for parade floats, to diner waitresses and auto mechanics and, of course, the church. Baked dishes started arriving at the house on Canterbury Road. Three-cheese tuna casserole and Crozet sweet potato casserole and turkey hash and Swiss chicken, every combination of canned soup and protein possible, along with banana bread and brownies and apple pie. Enough food to stock a hurricane shelter, and my mom would need it, every last crumb. Because after the funeral, half the population of Charlottesville would be stopping by the house to offer their condolences and remind her that if she needed anything, anything at all, all she had to do was call.

I had spent the day with Charlotte's class on a field trip to Waterloo Village, herding children into the blacksmith shop, gristmill, and Leni-Lenape Indian village and ultimately into the main attraction, the Waterloo Village gift shop, where they could finally buy their Revolutionary War hats and colonial history coloring books. Waterloo was New Jersey's answer to Colonial Williamsburg, and coming from Virginia, birthplace of the presidents, I was underwhelmed. But it was a crisp November day, and Charlotte was young enough to be glad to have me along. She looked like she'd snagged J. D. Salinger as her seat mate.

We'd picked up Lily after the trip, and I was planning to put them in front of the television, go through the mail, see if there were any phone messages, then get to work on dinner. I was going to make crepes, savory for the main meal and sweet for the dessert, and was looking forward to going through *The Joy of Cooking* to get some ideas.

But after I dropped my purse and walked over to the answering machine, I knew something was up. It was flashing seven messages, about what I'd expect from a long weekend away, or even a whole week, not just six hours.

The first two were from my mother. "Ivy? Are you there?" she said, her voice sounding strained. "Please call home as soon as you can." The next few were from Aunt Helen and Aunt Rhonda, also asking me to call. I knew that something dire had to have happened, because I *never* heard from my aunts. I didn't even know they had my phone number. The last message was from Bailey, who broke with convention and just blurted it out on the answering machine. "Oh, Ivy," she sobbed. "Did you hear about Dad? Oh God, I can't believe it. Call me." The only question then was whether he was dead, or whether he'd had a stroke or a heart attack and was lying there unresponsive in the ICU at University Hospital.

"Oh, no," I said. I crumpled to the floor, next to the telephone table in the hallway, feeling like I'd been punched. I didn't dial immediately. I wanted to feel the solidity of my house first: the hardwood floor, the solid hum of the furnace, the TV in the living room. *This is still here,* I reminded myself. *No matter what happened.*

Bailey answered right away, as if she'd been waiting.

"Dad? Is he . . . ?"

"Oh, Ivy," she said. "Dad's gone."

I remember feeling like I'd been punched a second time, but that it was important to listen hard. As if, by the sheer power of my attention, I could turn everything right. It was just impossible that Dad was dead. My mind rushed to the only other option, the only other possibility behind the words *Dad's gone.* That Dad had, for inexplicable reasons, left Mom. Moved away. But even as I formed the thought, I knew it wasn't true. Dad running off with a tarty little waitress from the Tip Top diner? Leaving Mom? Giving up the dealership? It was like trying to transfer water from one hand to the other. The idea of it just slipped through my fingers, leaving me with the plainer meaning. The obvious one: Dad was dead.

"How?"

"His truck, hit by a deer."

I slapped my head. "Oh, God."

I'd thought of a heart attack and I'd thought of a stroke. How had I missed the possibility of a car accident, when I was always so sure that would be what got us all in the end?

But Dad? And a deer? He was the last person you thought would die in an automobile. Like Ellis, he wasn't the least bit afraid of driving. But he was more careful than Ellis, more respectful of the road, and of other drivers and safety in general. I remembered him coming home from a dealers' trip to Detroit, telling us about all the new safety features Buick had rolled out that year. He was thrilled when they figured out how to make retractable seat belts, because he said now people would use them. And even though, like most car men, he complained at first about government regulations that made air bags mandatory, ultimately he became their biggest fan.

"What happened to the air bag?" I asked Bailey.

"Oh, Ivy, I don't know," she wailed. "How can you think of something like that at a time like this?"

How could I not?

It was odd. I was always the emotional one, and Bailey was always matter-of-fact. When I was pregnant with Charlotte, I'd cried at long-distance telephone commercials. But now Bailey was the one crying. I heard my voice wobble, but somehow I was surprisingly steady—down there on the floor—able to manage straight questions. Maybe it was because I hadn't yet talked to Mom. Maybe that would break me. But for now, I just wanted to know everything, every single fact. If I just turned over every unlikely detail in my head, maybe I could refute it. Getting hit by a deer, for example. Wasn't Dad always the one warning *us* about that? Didn't he always say to go slow so we'd have more reaction time if a deer leaped out at us? Wasn't he always reminding us that deer usually traveled in twos and threes—that if we saw one, there'd probably be another? He was a hunter, for heaven's sake. What was God doing turning the tables on him?

But I didn't argue with Bailey. I'd heard Charlotte's footsteps—heavier than Lily's—and knew she was standing there, waiting. I couldn't bear to look at her yet. I knew my pain would travel into her with the speed of light, as soon as our eyes met. Even now, I knew her face would be grave, that she'd probably already picked up the scent of death. After all, why wasn't I in the kitchen, listening to the radio, cooking? Why was I sitting on the floor? And she'd be worrying that it was *her* father who died, not mine.

"Bailey," I said as evenly as I could, hoping to forestall another crying jag. "Do you have the arrangements?"

The funeral would be in a week. She was flying in tomorrow.

"Thanks. I'll call you later."

I hung up and motioned Charlotte to come sit on my lap, knowing that when I told her, it would really be official.

* * *

Ellis was my rock. I couldn't have gotten through it without him. For the first few hours, I was surprisingly calm. But when I got into bed that first night and closed my eyes, I couldn't stop seeing my father. And the most haunting thing? He was always smiling, as if he failed to understand the gravity of the situation. There he was, dressed up in his Santa suit—and there he was, running after me on my bicycle, teaching me how to ride. There he was in the living room, with a mock-stern face, teasing Bailey's prom date—then breaking into a grin and telling them to have a great time.

I could feel my pillow getting wet and thought, *Oh, boy—finally, I must be crying.*

Ellis held me. He wrapped his arms and legs around me, swaddling me like a cocoon. At least I felt warm, even as my thoughts grew increasingly gruesome. I thought of Dad's last seconds on earth, spotting that deer, going for the brakes. I thought of them pumping him with formaldehyde at the funeral home. I pictured the macabre ritual of the wake, with Dad laid out like a Thanksgiving turkey, a lifeless centerpiece. Eventually, Ellis's hold on me loosened, and he fell asleep. But he woke up several times and opened his eyes to check on me.

He had come home from work early that night and canceled a trip he had scheduled for L.A. later in the week. He sat there during dinner and quietly explained things to Lily, who was only six, and answered all Charlotte's questions. He called my mother and offered to help with the arrangements. And the next day, he packed the girls' suitcases and put everything in the car and drove us down there.

He was amazingly patient, anticipating my needs before I could think of them myself. He asked if we needed to stop at a store for me to buy anything for the funeral. Did I need a black dress? Or stockings? He covered every detail: He brought tissues, packed my favorite pillow, and most remarkably of all, drove the speed limit, even when it was just fifty-five miles per hour. As cars and trucks sped by on our left, and sometimes even on our right, I admired his restraint. He must have felt like a horse, pulling at the bit, and simultaneously like the rider, slowing himself down. But it did the trick. Finally, I was able to press the seat back and be lulled into the sleep that had eluded me in bed.

When someone you love dies, you expect the world to mourn along with you. Not just the people, but everything. The clouds should gather tears and hover over a gray landscape. Flags in front of schools and courthouses should be lowered to half-staff. And the supercilious shock jocks who coarsen the public airwaves should hold their tongues. At least for a few days, out of respect.

So when the sky holds forth bright blue, flags flutter atop their poles, and idiots on the radio keep blathering, it's hard not to feel that the universe is mocking you. During the last two and a half hours of our trip to Charlottesville, after we got past the force field of suburban Washington, the sky was so irrepressibly cheerful, it was hard to believe we were heading to a house of mourning. How could the world just go on as if nothing had happened?

The feeling continued as we landed in my parents' familiar driveway—it would be hard to start thinking of it as Mom's driveway—on Canterbury Road. There was a cinder of coal where my pink heart had beaten, but the house looked exactly the same. There was no evidence, except a boxed cake left on the front porch, that death had visited. The red brick walls didn't betray any tragedy, nor did the black shutters, the trim lawn, the hardy boxwoods. Everything looked just the same, as if he might come out at any moment and walk over to help Ellis with the suitcases. I don't know what I expected. That the house would literally slump in grief? Perhaps our own little personal rain cloud would hover respectfully over my father's roof? Or at least one of those huge purple-and-black ribbons they sometimes hang on firehouses?

Even my mother didn't show the signs of devastation I'd expected. She looked more like the director of a community theater production on opening night—checking the lighting, giving notes to the actors, inspecting the sets, the props, the ticket booth. Which, in a way, I suppose she was. I'd never thought of it that way, but a funeral—particularly for a man like my father, a substantial local businessman and community pillar—was a piece of community theater. There must have been dozens of details my mother had to coordinate: notices to the newspaper, arrangements with the funeral home, flowers, food. She greeted us with a great hug and a big smile, as if we'd all just driven in for a debutante ball. I guess it was just relief that we'd arrived safely and pleasure at seeing the girls. Still, it struck me as a little off.

But the biggest surprise was Bailey. When had I seen her last? Was it last Christmas? I couldn't remember. Bailey was lounging on the sofa in the living room, her ear to a phone, her blue-jeaned

left leg tossed lazily over the back of the sofa, the same position—
I realized suddenly—in which she'd spent most of her high
school years. She looked smashing. Her hair was blonder, her
boobs perkier, her face more radiant, as if time had been going
the opposite direction for her than it did for all the rest of us. It
didn't even look like she was trying. She was just wearing jeans
and a button-down men's-style shirt, but her jeans fit like she was
a teenager, and the button-down shirt, which strained a little at
the button over her chest, suggested a teasing kind of offhand
boyishness, as if Bailey wasn't even aware of the straining button.
Bailey looked even better than she had in high school, and that
was saying something. And then I remembered: Frank, the cos-
metic surgeon husband. I remembered that she lived in L.A.,
where the official religion was body worship and her husband was
a high priest. I thought all these judgmental and semi-treasonous
thoughts, wondering what had happened to the little sister who'd
been sobbing on the phone just the other day. Wondering how she
could look so damn *good* at a time like this.

Myself, I'd let my appearance slide in the last few years. I'd
put on some weight, and wore loose jeans and shapeless sweaters
to cover it up. I hadn't really noticed these things, not until I saw
Bailey. I looked like most of the other moms waiting at the bus
stop after school. And I hadn't bothered with any makeup since
I'd heard about Dad. There wouldn't be any point in putting on
mascara only to have it run down my cheeks. But seeing Bailey, I
realized that was also just a rationalization. Even before Dad had
died, I'd let my looks slip. But Bailey? She looked ready for the
paparazzi.

And then she hung up the phone, sprang up, and enclosed me in a vise grip of a hug. "Oh, Ivy. You look great!" she lied. She crouched down to hug the girls, but I could tell it was Lily who beguiled her. It must have been like telescoping back into the past and having a chance to greet herself as a child. And then she stood up and beamed her spectacular smile at Ellis. I mean, like one of those blinding spotlights they shine down on prisoners who try to make a run for it. I saw her sneak a full look at him, a complete up-and-down; then she put her hand out to shake his, as if she were meeting him for the first time. There was something coy about that gesture, practiced, almost predatory. She was, I registered, flirting with my husband. Ellis's cheeks suddenly flushed bright pink.

"Where's Frank?" I said.

"Oh, he couldn't clear his schedule," she said. "His office is a real mill." I imagined lumpy women with small breasts and large stomachs being loaded like logs onto a conveyer belt and being whittled down into Barbies.

I reached over and squeezed Ellis's hand.

"He really wanted to come," Bailey added, as if Frank were missing a dinner party rather than a funeral. "He and Ellis could have hung out." The absurdity of the declaration froze in the air. Ellis and Frank would hang out? And what? Play cards? She flashed another dazzling smile at Ellis. It was, I realized, her all-purpose Get Out of Jail Free card.

Was it the hypervigilant state I was in, ever since coming home and finding seven blinking messages on the answering machine, or just some vestigial sibling rivalry? But there it was.

Bailey, the charming younger sister, growing more charming and younger by the minute and, as always, stealing my friends. But Ellis couldn't be falling for this, could he? I mean, Ellis was too smart.

But it didn't last more than a second, this feeling, because just then my mother focused our attention on the practical: "Ellis, you two will be in Ivy's room, as usual. And the girls will be in the den." And the next thing, we were unloading the car and moving suitcases.

I think the Jewish people might have it right, getting the burial done by the next day. A few years earlier, we'd gotten a call about Ellis's aunt Sylvia on a Tuesday, and on Wednesday, we were standing there in the King Solomon Cemetery, watching his relatives toss shovelfuls of earth into an open hole.

By contrast, our Baptist tradition felt not just leisurely but shiftless. Like with Christmas, the visiting just stretched on and on. I guess there's some benefit to the doorbell always ringing and people coming by with casseroles and cakes. It was almost a full-time job for my mom to keep the coffee going. That certainly had to be better than sitting alone and contemplating her eternal loss, but there were five whole days before Dad's funeral, and that meant a lot of coffee, a lot of just sitting around. Or in Bailey's case, lying around. Which stumped me, it really did. It didn't seem to bother my mom to see Bailey sprawled on the sofa, watching TV or talking on the phone, like she was on vacation, and I was amazed that Bailey could feel so absolutely at home as well. Yes, it had been her sofa, her house growing up. It just seemed overly relaxed for a place you hadn't lived in for years, and particularly in a house of mourning. But that's charm, I guess, the ability to be completely yourself, and have everybody else buy into it.

And Bailey was a source of nonstop entertainment for Lily, always useful when you've got a six-year-old with too much time on her hands. They were two peas in pod, with identical gold hair, sprawling on the sofa together all day, every day, sharing the TV remote. Lily started out wanting to watch her shows, the whole kiddie morning lineup, and had some early success in selling the charms of *Sesame Street* to Aunt Bailey. But before long, Bailey had converted Lily into a Jerry Springer fan and introduced her to soaps and other forbidden joys. If anyone objected—if my mother walked out with a pot of coffee and said, "My Lord, Bailey, what in the world are you doing to corrupt my sweet little granddaughter?"—Bailey and Lily would break into conspiratorial laughter. Because Bailey was teaching Lily that, too—that attitude, that self-assurance of the too-readily adored. See how we deflect criticism, Lily? We laugh it off.

I decided to be the dutiful daughter rather than the hovering mom, and let Lily succumb to Bailey's charms. It would have been impossible anyway, like separating magnets. I tended to Mom, helping her answer the door, make coffee. I heard all her stories, some of them repeatedly. The call that Daddy was dead. How she'd felt a little pinch of worry when he drove off on the hunting trip. The story of how they'd met. And intriguing little asides, stories that started "Now, you can't tell this to anyone"— about various friends of hers who'd stopped talking to each other and therefore couldn't be accepted for condolence calls together. Some of the friendships had ended over petty things—a silver teapot returned tarnished—and others were truly astonishing, like the fact that Janet Clements had had an affair with Chester Wheeler and so could never be allowed to collide with his wife, Hope. All of them so old now, it was hard to imagine any of them screwing, let alone ruining each other's lives. And yet somehow, old Hope and Chester had stuck together, and so had Janet and Richard Clements.

Charlotte, my little reader, was devouring stories, too. As with all true readers, the sudden vista of uncommitted time represented an unexpected dividend. She'd packed three or four books and snuggled under a stack of antique quilts on the couch in the den, where she was allowed to read without interruption for hours. When she ran out of her own books the third or fourth night, I found her standing on tiptoes, checking out the books on my parents' shelves, which ran the gamut from *Peyton Place* to *Kovels' Know Your Antiques 1972*. I was relieved when she discovered *Gone with the Wind* and wondered how fast she would scarf that down. At the rate time was passing, Melanie's death-bed scene would get here before Dad's funeral, so I promised Charlotte a visit to Williams Corner Bookstore when we got a chance.

And Ellis? He behaved like a perfect gentleman, courteous and helpful, carrying or lifting anything that needed to be carried or lifted, driving anywhere that needed to be driven. But you could tell the days of waiting were making him antsy. He'd sneak off into the kitchen whenever he could to call New York or

L.A. It was a tricky time for a comic named Finn Brubaker—
Ellis now specialized in comedians—whose career had moved
several years earlier from nightclubs into guest appearances on
sitcoms and, finally, the movies, where he'd scored several roles
as the love interest's goofy sidekick. Until it had come out, on
the pages of a Hollywood gossip rag, that Finn had started life
as Fiona. That was the trip to L.A. Ellis had planned before my
father's run-in with the deer, a powwow to decide whether
Finn/Fiona would embrace his/her transsexuality and incorpo-
rate it into his/her comic persona, or whether to ignore or even
fight it.

Sometimes we'd be in the dining room, Mom and I, and we'd
hear a little snort from the kitchen, a truncated honk of masculine
laughter, when Ellis was on the phone. You could hear L.A. or
New York in that snort, the sophistication of a big-time operator.
And then we'd both think the same thing, Mom and I. We'd
realize there was a man in the house and that the man was not
Dad. It would surprise us, somehow, because the house had shifted
so irrevocably to the female with the arrival of two sets of daughters. And then we'd realize—or least I would—that it was different from Daddy's laugh. A little colder, unkinder, more cynical. It
made me wonder whether Ellis had always been like that and I
just had never seen it, or whether something harder had grown in
him over the years.

But then he'd come out a little while later, when his call was
done, having put on a new pot of coffee, and be the perfect husband and son-in-law again. He'd take whatever crumb-filled
dishes remained on the table back to the kitchen and refill our

cups, and then sit down with us, doing his bit to fill the long stretch of time our tradition had given us before Dad could be put to rest.

The day before the funeral, Bailey got up from the couch suddenly and announced that it was time to get the hell out of the house. She'd looked through the paper and found a kiddie matinee. Charlotte and Lily were too young for all this extended mourning, Bailey declared. They deserved some fun. Besides, we'd have all day tomorrow to cry our eyes out. I looked over at Mom, who nodded. "Bailey is right. The girls could use the fun," she said, grabbing her purse, but Bailey held up her hand. "My treat."

"Are you coming?" I asked Mom.

"No," she said. "I have some last-minute things. But you girls go."

"Ellis?"

"I'll pass, too. I've got some work. And maybe I'll go for a run."

Both Mom and Ellis looked relieved to be rid of us. And to be honest, I wouldn't have minded staying back myself. I was used to having a big house to myself every day while the girls were at school, and all this forced togetherness was grating on me. It would have been nice just to have the TV off, to let Bailey and Lily go out on a little adventure by themselves. Charlotte, deep into *Gone with the Wind,* wasn't bothering anyone. She'd be just as happy staying put, too.

"Okay!" Bailey said. "Girls' day out!"

"But—" Charlotte tried to protest.

"Oh, fiddle-dee-dee," Bailey said. "Did Miss Scarlett lie around

all day and read books? I don't think so. If she had, there wouldn't
have been any story." Charlotte grinned sheepishly, then dog-eared
the page she'd been holding. But I could tell she thought she was
trading down, that she'd crossed a threshold, with this book, from
children's stories to the endlessly complicated world of grown-ups,
and there was really no going back.

"So, sis," Bailey said, "you driving these days?"

The question caught me up short. Of course I was driving.
What did she think? That I lived in the suburbs like some kind
of hermit, trapped inside my house? That I dragged my girls to
school in a toy wagon and called a taxi every time I needed milk?
True, I didn't drive on the Garden State Parkway or the New
Jersey Turnpike. Or, God forbid, into the city. But I did *drive*.

"Of course," I said.

"Don't get your knickers in a twist. I was just remembering all
those years you didn't have your license. And thinking, I haven't
driven for almost a week, and I'd just love to go for a spin on the
old roads. Up to Crozet, maybe even Skyline Drive."

"I thought we were going to the movies?"

Bailey winked. "Right."

"Why don't you let Bailey drive?" Ellis said. "She's from L.A.
She's probably suffering withdrawal."

"Yeah, let Aunt Bailey drive!" echoed Lily, tugging Bailey's
hand. "Can I sit in the front?"

"No," I said categorically. "*I* sit in the front."

Bailey laughed and Ellis tossed her his keys.

I felt ganged up on. My fear of driving was a sore spot. It
wasn't exactly a secret—even the girls saw that I always sat in the

passenger seat when Ellis was around—but it was a vulnerability, something that made me feel less than adult. By taking the wheel and paying for the movies, Bailey would be in charge. I'd just be one of the girls along for the ride.

I stood there like a stupid lump. Why were they conspiring against me? Why were they bringing up the one thing that embarrassed me? I wanted to scream, but it was the day before my father's funeral, and I was here to support my mother, not to melt down.

I put on my coat and joined the procession of X chromosomes into the driveway.

Ellis walked us all out to the car, helped Lily with her seat belt, and then leaned in to give Bailey a tour of the dashboard. "There's heat and defrost. Lights are here, though I guess you'll be back before dark, and here's how the radio—"

"For God's sake, Ellis, it's not a spaceship!" I said. "And *I* can adjust the heat."

"We'll be fine." Bailey smiled her winning smile. "It's just a car." Then she rolled up the window, wiggled her fingers in Ellis's direction, and backed out. A little fast, I thought. Not the careful way Daddy had taught us. Certainly not getting out first and checking for children on tricycles. Not even really checking the mirrors. She backed out like someone who thought she was immortal, or maybe just someone whose golden good looks had always served as a sort of protective shield, absolving her of the need to worry about anything. For the millionth time in my life,

I wondered why she was the one designed like a sleek convertible, with a spoiler and pointy tailfins, born to zip down the road happy and fast, while I was the clunky sedan, burdened with practical and boring safety features. Why had all the neuroses landed on my shoulders?

And yet, miraculously, we were out on Canterbury Road and nobody had been killed.

The first thing Bailey did as she headed to town was turn on the radio and slide the tuner all the way to the right, settling on a rock station. She found her beat and started tapping the steering wheel. If you'd been looking for a metaphor to represent the difference between Bailey and me, the car radio was all you needed. Easy, breezy Bailey, the eternal teenager, bopping to her music, living in the moment. And me, all the way to the left at the public radio end of the dial, and always so, so serious. I was ticked that she'd changed the station without asking—it felt like someone coming in and moving my sofa—but I also felt stupid being so territorial. Were we going to go back to being little kids again, fighting over what to watch on TV? I held my tongue.

Bailey was oblivious. I had always thought it must have been good social skills that made Bailey so popular; well, good social skills and cheerleader looks. But now I was beginning to wonder. Maybe it was extreme selfishness that made people adore you. Because that was all she'd demonstrated during the past four days as she sprawled on the sofa, never lifting a finger to help. Maybe extreme self-absorption sent a signal to the world that you were *worth* being absorbed in. Maybe everyone just went along.

It was like deciding to be the birthday girl 365 days a year. You just put on your party hat and collected presents wherever you went. So here it was, the day before Daddy's funeral, and we were all going on an adventure! I was still a little confused about the *theme* of this little adventure. Was it a kiddie movie, as she'd promised the girls? Or a drive out to the country? I looked out the window for clues, disturbed to see how much Charlottesville had changed, all the new strip malls and national chain stores. But Bailey never seemed to lose her bearings. Ten minutes later, we were in front of the theater.

Lily was first to hop out, and I thought I'd have a heart attack, I was so sure she was going to race through the parking lot without looking. It would be Bailey's fault, too, getting her all riled up. But Bailey was quicker out of the car than I, and scooped Lily up, holding her upside down, exposing her flat belly and eliciting a gale of giggles. Danger averted.

"Thanks," I whispered to Bailey as we walked up to the ticket window.

"For what?" She seemed genuinely baffled. Perhaps she hadn't sensed any danger. She'd just gotten out of the car and scooped up her favorite niece. Maybe there hadn't been any danger. Maybe Lily was only racing to get to Bailey's door.

"Two children, please," Bailey said when we walked up to the ticket booth. I started to get out my wallet, but she gestured to put it away. Clearly this was her day to be magnanimous. I thought she was going to add *and two adults,* but she didn't. Instead, she put her arms over the girls' shoulders and marched them toward the usher. "You're in charge, sweetie pie," she said, slipping a ten into Charlotte's hand. "Now go buy the biggest bag of popcorn they sell. We'll be here the minute the movie's over."

Lily looked up, confused. "You're not coming, Aunt Bailey?"

I could see in Lily's face all the betrayal and disappointments yet to come: catty girlfriends, shitty boyfriends, mean bosses. I felt bad for her, but also a little thrilled that precious Aunt Bailey might be diminished now, in Lily's estimation.

Of more immediate concern, though, was Bailey's plan to leave the girls on their own. "Bailey," I said, "they've never been to the movies alone before. They're too young."

Charlotte corrected me. "Dad sometimes drops us off."

I didn't remember any arrangements like that. I didn't remember Ellis ever asking me whether I thought it was okay. So, if he'd dropped them off, where had he *gone* before picking them up and bringing them home? And why hadn't he told me?

"Really?" The revelation threw me. But if Ellis thought it was safe in New Jersey, it had to be okay in pokey old Charlottesville. I looked hard at Charlotte, to see if she really was okay with this, if she really didn't mind being left alone to be in charge of her little sister. If there was one iota of doubt, I would at least buy myself a ticket—Bailey be damned. She could drive to Crozet by herself.

"Jesus, Ivy, this is Charlottesville," Bailey said. "It's fine."

Charlotte nodded, a little gravely, and took Lily's hand, walking toward the concession stand.

Bailey sped out of the movie theater parking lot just like she'd backed out of the driveway—a bat out of hell, oblivious of any children who might have broken free of their parents' protective grip. And again, I grudgingly noted, she managed to escape tragedy. "Well," she said, "which is it? Pedicure or Skyline Drive?"

"What?"

We were waiting at a traffic light, behind a long line of cars. It was one of those complicated modern intersections caused by the proliferation of strip malls, with left-turn lanes and right-turn arrows, the kind of intersection suited more to New Jersey, it seemed to me, than to Virginia.

"To kill time," she said. "Do you want to get your toes done? Or just go for a drive?"

"Drive," I said. I didn't want to tell her that I'd never had a pedicure. Nor did it seem appropriate to be playing Barbie doll the day before Daddy's funeral. In fact, it seemed pretty horrifying.

"Okay," Bailey said, sliding easily into the merge that had plagued my teenage nightmares. And then we were heading west, down I-64 and onto Skyline Drive, the place where UVa boys would always take you to try to impress you.

And it was impressive, too. All the more impressive because it had been years. A wide ribbon of straw-colored fields, split-rail fences, barns, and woods twisting lazily through mountains the color of winter shadows.

"God, I miss driving here." She sighed and gestured at the scenery. "This is beautiful. Not as breathtaking as Big Sur, but pretty in its own way."

Like almost everything Bailey said, it landed like an insult. Maybe unintended, but still an insult. Was it her verdict on the relative breathtakingness of California and Virginia mountain ranges? Or did it just remind me of how my mother's friends might compare me to Bailey? *Pretty in her own way.*

"So what's up?" I said. I sensed an agenda beyond mere cabin fever. That Bailey wanted to talk to me sister-to-sister.

"Why does something have to be up?" She smiled.

"I don't know. You seemed pretty content lying around on the sofa all week watching television. And if you'd wanted a ride or a pedicure, you could have gone by yourself." It came out more sharply than I'd intended, but Bailey didn't rise to the bait. Instead she turned the radio on again, smiling to herself and, I thought, taking the mountain curves a bit briskly. I got a little nervous, thinking about Daddy, worried if Bailey could really stop in time should a deer leap in front of us.

"So, Ellis," she said finally. "He's a good-looking man."

"Thank you?"

"A *very* good-looking man."

"What's your point?"

She looked over at my baggy jeans.

"What?"

"It's just," she said, "you don't seem to be trying very hard."

"Trying very hard to *what?*"

"Trying very hard to hold on to your man."

"What are you saying, Bailey? That I have to dress up to please my husband?"

"And maybe lose a little weight."

I felt stunned. Insulted and at the same time shocked by Bailey's nerve. And timing! This was just too much. First Bailey lazed around the house, doing absolutely nothing. She stole the affections of my younger daughter, took over my car, changed the radio station, decided my kids could be left alone at the movies—and now she was doling out marital advice?

"Bailey, I'm not sure what exactly you're getting at here. *I* don't live in California, where everybody thinks they have to look eighteen until they're eighty-one."

"I'm not saying you have to look eighteen. I'm just pointing out that Ellis has eyes."

"What do you mean, 'Ellis has eyes'?" I was feeling angry in a way I hadn't since Nixon was president. Who did this little bitch think she was?

As the trees flew by, I had a sudden realization. Like it or not, this week would stick with me forever. This whole week—even this drive—would be the thing that divided my life into two distinct pieces: the first half, when Jack Honeycutt still walked the earth and I was happy and whole; and the second half. It was like the front door being blown open by a sudden November gust. I would never again hear my father's voice on the phone, smell his Old Spice, see him dress up as Santa. It was more than mere sadness. I had taken all these things for granted my whole life. Losing them was like losing something integral and necessary to life, like air, or the color blue.

And another worry presented itself: With Daddy gone and, someday, eventually Mommy, what would happen to the frail bonds that tied me to Bailey? I knew friends who were close to their sisters, who called them every day. Bailey and I weren't like that. We had a certain shared history, but not much in the way of shared affection. We'd barely seen each other in the past ten years. A lot of it was geography. There'd always been, on my side, jealousy and resentment. Now I was beginning to actively dislike her.

"Hey, big sis, I hate to break it to you, but he's been looking at me all week."

"Of course he's been looking at you all week. You've been sprawled out on that couch like some damn bimbo!"

"There are bimbos everywhere," she said softly.

I folded my arms and looked out the window. Not for the view but to avoid looking at her. She was raising questions about things she had no knowledge of. Assuming. Judging.

But, and this was what really got me, maybe there was some truth to what Bailey was saying. Maybe Ellis had been looking at her. Hadn't I been irked when he tossed her the keys? God, I detested her. What a bitch. A skinny, arrogant, husband-stealing little cunt.

"'You're so vain,'" I sang. "'You probably think this song is about you.'"

"Just looking out for you, sis. Listen, I know a little bit about this. Frank puts new tits on women five days a week. Why do you think I look like I do?"

Why *did* she? I'd never thought about it. She'd always made it look so effortless. But, really, now that I did think about it, there always was effort, even in high school. I thought of all the things she used to clutter the bathroom with: hair dyes, depilatories, tweezers, eyelash curlers. Was it possible that, intrinsically, Bailey was no prettier than me?

"How's the sex?"

My mouth fell open. Who *was* this woman? Had we really shared parents, a house, a childhood?

"None of your fucking business," I said through clenched teeth.

She made a *tsk, tsk, tsk* sound. "I hope you're at least giving him blow jobs." She didn't wait for a response, but turned the radio back on. I felt like a hummingbird was trapped inside my rib cage. My cheeks burned, my ears burned, my face burned, and I felt a slight little tingle down there, between my thighs, where I hadn't felt anything in a long, long time.

As a matter of fact, I'd never given Ellis a blow job. I thought it was disgusting. Was that a crime?

It was ridiculous and it was perfect. My father would have loved it. His sales manager, Ed Johnson, had organized a Buick parade to follow Daddy's hearse to the Riverview Cemetery. He'd asked the Rotary and the Kiwanis and the Elks to drive the fleet from the dealership on Pantops down High and Meade and left onto Chesapeake and then up that final little hill that would take him to his eternal view of the Rivanna. The cavalcade of Buicks added twenty minutes to the wait for those unfortunates caught in the funeral traffic. But it was a thing to see—all those gleaming new cars, inventory sheets taped to the windows, black balloons festooned to their antennas, and Honeycutt Motors license-plate frames bearing mute but emphatic tribute to Dad. The weather was cruelly glorious, and the red, white, and blue metallic streamers of the car lot danced in the breeze in a way that reminded me of whirligigs and UVa football games. I turned around to see if there was any reaction from the girls, what they thought of the parade, but they just stared forward, their hair clean and brushed and pinned into place, looking grim. Then it occurred to me: What would they know? This was their first funeral.

The girls' eyes had popped when they saw the nine-passenger limo that rolled up to Mom's house to collect us for the funeral. A Buick, of course; my mom had asked Ed Johnson to make sure the funeral hearse and limos were both Buicks. I could see Charlotte working hard to remain stoic when she saw it, but Lily was unable to stifle a little shriek. And then there was the game of musical chairs in deciding who would sit where. I was so busy attending to my mother, who, after a week of being the perfect hostess, was now—finally—surrendering to grief, that I didn't notice at first that somehow Bailey and Ellis had wound up on a bench together. I felt like a high school girl who'd just seen her boyfriend with her best friend. Stupid reaction, maybe even shameful, given the circumstances. But after my ride with Bailey, it still felt like a threat.

I thought quickly, looking for a plausible reason to shift things around. "Bailey," I said, "I think Mom should have both of her daughters next to her. Charlotte, move back with Daddy and Lily."

Ellis looked baffled, but as Bailey took the seat on the other side of Mom and crossed her shapely legs, she reminded me of a gold digger on her way to bury a wealthy husband. Was that a smirk on her face? Was she feeling satisfaction that her words the day before had gotten under my skin?

Suddenly I had an almost irresistible urge to pinch her.

The rest of the funeral, the urge continued, like an unscratchable itch. While the limo idled in front of Honeycutt Motors, I wanted to pinch her. As the cars snaked up to the gravesite, I wanted to pinch her. As Ellis and my uncles lined up as pallbearers, even as they lowered Daddy into the ground, I felt this overpowering hatred of my little sister.

At the very end, after the coffin had been lowered and everybody tossed a handful of dirt into the grave, Bailey threw her arms around Mom and started bawling. I stood there, wordlessly wondering where this sudden display of emotion had come from. This was the same sister who just the day before had thought about getting a pedicure, who'd lectured me about blow jobs? I stared—everybody stared—as Bailey planted muffled shrieks into my mother's shoulder.

When I saw my mother patting Bailey's back, I was livid. There was a matter of rank when it came to mourning, and my mother was the top mourner, the one who would go home to an empty house, the one who could be forgiven for an overheated emotional display. But Bailey had upset the natural order and was asking for comfort from the most bereaved. Suddenly my desire to pinch her gave way to an even stronger compulsion, and it took all my strength to resist. I wanted to place a nice swift kick on her perfect ass.

But when, out of the corner of my eye, I noticed the graveyard men glide in the direction of the open hole, I felt the anger suddenly fall away. It dropped like an elevator plummeting a hundred stories, and in its place was the sickening loss I'd felt a week earlier, on the floor of my house, after hanging up with Bailey. *Daddy!* I wanted to cry. *Oh, Daddy, make Bailey stop!* But Daddy was in a box, about to be covered up with dirt.

* * *

Back at Mom's house, the crowds poured in. It was almost like Christmas—the same familiar dishes stacked on the buffet, the same familiar gray heads that had been showing up at Canterbury Road for years—but without the Perry Como and the tree, and the possibility of Daddy coming down the stairs with a *Ho, ho, ho!* Here came the Nelsons and the McGoverns, the Hitchcocks and the Bagwells. There was comfort in this, in seeing them all. If the roads on the outskirts of Charlottesville were almost unrecognizable, with all the new shopping centers and chain stores, at least I had my landmarks in people like Bob Nelson, with his towering frame and his craggy smile.

Suddenly it was a party, and with those two great imperatives—food and coffee—my mother was back in her element, making people comfortable. It stunned me to see the perfect Southern hostess return, not half an hour after saying her final good-bye to Daddy and witnessing Bailey's ludicrous graveside display. Mom's posture was perfect, her living room rug so recently vacuumed, you could see the pattern of the track marks, and the light on her forty-cup percolator was already lit and ready to dispense its vital social elixir. And bless her heart, she'd even applied a fresh layer of the Dusty Rose lipstick that had been her trademark ever since I could remember. Mom's friends, I noticed, took to her kitchen as if they lived there. They knew where all the serving pieces were kept. I couldn't help noticing that they all shared her impeccable grooming as well. Their hands were manicured, their hair helmetlike in its perfection, their outfits conservative and ladylike. They wore stockings. These were women whose entire job in life was being women. Their training had begun as young ladies, and even if I'd bristled at that attempted training myself, I could see now that, in times like these, it served a higher purpose. They simply knew what to do. I wondered if my friends, perhaps more interesting, certainly better educated, more cultured, and funnier, would be of such use if Ellis died.

Bailey, I noticed, had changed into jeans. I saw her across the room, tossing her hair, amazingly recovered, and realized that she was a fixture in the familial tableau, too. The adorable younger sister. Only now she'd shed the baby fat of the cheerleader years and turned into something harder, glossier, maybe even dangerous. I avoided her, yet knew every minute exactly where she was. If she caught my eye and started crossing the room toward me, I'd find a sudden errand in the kitchen. I let Lily hang on to her, but was prepared to intervene if I saw her cozying up to Ellis.

Ted McGovern, who owned a local hardware store and had served with my father for years on various committees to beautify downtown, came up and wrapped me in a great bear hug. Then he stood back, his hands still on my shoulders, and said, "Look at you. All grown up!" His eyes glistened, ready to spill over with tears. "And two little girls! Just like you and Bailey." As if on cue, Bailey burst out laughing across the room. Ted looked over toward the laugh. "She's one looker, isn't she?" I was always put in that position, accepting praise on my sister's behalf. I took her discards, the compliments that didn't quite get to her. Always had. Always would. The gulf before my plain looks and her spectacular ones only widening with time.

But admiration for Bailey wasn't universal. About half an hour after my talk with Mr. McGovern, I walked into the kitchen to refill the half-and-half and came upon three of Mom's closest friends—Ina McGovern, Lacey Hitchcock, and Anita Bagwell— in a tight huddle. Their whispering stopped as soon as they heard me walk in, but I'd already caught the words *Bailey* and *ridiculous*. I blushed as I poured the cream, then walked over and gave each of them a quick kiss before leaving them to their gossip. As I set the pitcher down in the dining room, I knew I ought to feel some shame on my family's behalf, but I felt, instead, the smug satisfaction of the teacher's pet. Maybe I hadn't grown up to be a real Southern lady, maybe I *had* grown schlumpy, but at least I hadn't made a spectacle of myself.

Once I set down the cream, I noticed Hope Wheeler standing at the far end of the table, talking to her mortal enemy, Janet Clements. If it hadn't been for my long week of intimacy with Mom, I'd never have known how momentous this was. I poured myself a cup of coffee and watched discreetly. I could see their lips moving, but was too far away to hear. *Poor, dear Jack,* I imagined Hope saying. *I always thought he'd be the last to go.* But then they might have been trading recipes or complimenting each other's outfits, or staying with any one of a dozen safe subjects.

I could only tell that Janet had lost her advantage over the years, that she was no longer the breathless young woman with high heels and freckled cleavage. Now in her early sixties, she was dressed primly and wore a simple strand of pearls. If anything, it was Hope whose looks had improved, whose ruddy expression, a by-product of years of avid gardening, conveyed robust health.

I scanned the table, piled high with ham biscuits, beans, salads, casseroles, and sweets. Some homemade brownies caught my eye. I started to reach for one, but hesitated. How would *I* look in twenty years? It was true what Bailey had said the other day in the car. I *had* let myself go. But I was part of a whole tribe that looked like me, almost all the other mothers on the playground. Everybody wore baggy, comfortable jeans and pulled back their hair in careless ponytails. It had never occurred to me that I was supposed to look any different.

The brownies beckoned again. I shouldn't. It was time to put myself together, to think about the future. And yet . . . it was a time for comfort, wasn't it? I'd just buried my dad. Who could expect me now, this minute, to forgo the little bit of solace that was offered?

Ellis had been patient, amazingly so, but by the night of the funeral, he started to remind me of a penned-up dog.

"Tomorrow," I said as we undressed to get in bed.

"Tomorrow?"

"We'll go back home."

We'd planned on leaving two days later, but I was ready. I felt bad deserting my mom, but I had other people to consider. Ellis had work to get back to, comedians to prop up, a boss to appease. The girls simply had to get out of a house of death. And then there was the fact that I didn't want to spend one more full day under the same roof as Bailey.

"Are you sure?" he said. I knew he wanted to go, couldn't wait to get back, but he offered this to me—this chance to change my mind—like a friend freely sharing half of the last cookie.

I nodded my head. "It's time."

We got in bed, Ellis on his back, me on my side, facing away from him, grabbing an extra pillow to put between my legs to ease the strain on my back, the way I had since being pregnant with Charlotte. I'd just rested my head on the pillow when Bailey's words jumped out like a hidden snake. *I hope you're at least giving him blow jobs.*

A blow job. My heart hammered at the thought of sliding down the bed, pulling Ellis's penis out of his boxers and putting it in my mouth. It was so . . . bizarre, so out of my experience with Ellis. With anyone. Blow job. After *Jersey Turnpike,* the two scariest words in the English language.

Blow jobs made me think of Leo Disario, rest his soul; they had composed half his stand-up routine. Blow jobs were what sluts did. It was demeaning to even think about. Yet here I was, in my parents' house—*my mom's house,* I corrected myself—on the night of my father's funeral, wondering if it was time to start.

I turned around, facing Ellis, who looked almost asleep. I watched his chest rise and fall, listened to his breathing. Safely asleep, I thought, my heart starting to slow down. I could think about this tomorrow, next week, some other time.

And then his eyes popped open. He looked at me tenderly, as if scanning my face for sorrow. He clearly had no idea what I was thinking.

I leaned over and kissed him. Tentatively, I inserted my tongue in his mouth. He seemed almost startled. When had all our kisses become brief pecks?

And then I reached down and put my hand on his crotch.

His eyes widened, and I could feel his penis harden, a sudden involuntary rush of blood. He looked at me for direction, or explanation. Did I really want sex? Was that really where this was going?

I felt as scared now as a high school girl, experimenting in the backseat of a car. Was I really doing what I thought I was doing? Had I actually initiated sex? On the night we'd put my father in the ground? Was I doing it for Ellis? Or to prove something to Bailey?

My heart fluttered crazily, and I tried to convince myself that it was passion. Daddy would approve, I thought. This would be good for me, good for Ellis, good for the marriage.

But as soon as I thought the words *good for me,* I thought of spinach, broccoli, vitamins, savings plans. And I knew that I'd been fooling myself. I didn't feel anything stirring between my legs. All I felt was fear. Fear that I wouldn't come, that sex would be awkward, that I was a terrible lay, that Bailey was right after all.

Ellis leaned in closer to me, gently testing my resolve. My dread must have been obvious. He took my hand, removed it from his penis, and held it to his chest.

"It's okay, Ivy."

"Really?" I felt released from an unpleasant chore.

"Really."

He put my hand up to his mouth and kissed it. Five minutes later, I heard him snoring.

* * *

Mom kneeled down on the front stoop to kiss the girls good-bye, putting her arms around both of them at the same time. I saw grief etched in the crow's-feet around her eyes, wrinkles that had been initially earned as smile lines. They looked deeper now, or maybe it was just the contrast of the girls' downy faces, and I felt guilty leaving her so soon, so freshly widowed. Ellis was busy packing the car, lugging suitcases and arranging them in the back. I envied him, busy with the matter-of-factness of things.

"Promise to be good," Mom said with mock sternness to Lily. Under Bailey's tutelage, Lily's spoiled streak had deepened. "And you"—Mom looked at Charlotte—"don't forget to play once in a while." She worried that Charlotte was too serious, that all her time with books was keeping her from sunshine, friends, human interaction. The same worries she'd had about me.

Then Mom stood up and hugged me. She held me so tight, I could feel her heart beating, and I thought suddenly about the nine months I'd spent inside her, being rocked to sleep to the very same heartbeat. We'd been one, once. Just as my girls had each been part of me. It was heartbreaking if you thought about it. "Thank you," she said. "For everything."

Ellis, finished with packing, came up to say his good-byes, too. But his hugs were quicker, manlier—they served to separate rather than to unite. Then, just as we were turning to leave, the front door opened and Bailey made her first appearance of the day. Between her minuscule nightie and her mussed-up hair, she looked like a Victoria's Secret model. She stretched her right arm high in a catlike yawn. "Bye y'all. Be careful on the road."

"Bye, Bailey," I said. I waved good-bye, then hoisted my L.L. Bean tote bag, filled with magazines, hand wipes, maps, and the leftover ham biscuits, into the car. "Charlotte, Lily. Come on."

And then we were on the road, the girls safely clicked in, our little family hurtling back from my childhood life to my adult one. It would be a long ride, six hours at least, and though I'd been eager to leave death and Bailey, I was exhausted by our journey even before it started. After Washington, the kudzu-cloaked Virginia scenery would dissolve into the endless gray monotony of interstate. It was, it suddenly struck me, like the reverse of Dorothy's journey in *The Wizard of Oz*. I was leaving the Technicolor for the oppressive black-and-white of the Northeast.

"Did you have fun?"

The words sprang from my mouth before I had time to think.

Ellis raised his eyebrows. That's when I realized: This was just what I said to the girls after every trip, whenever we got in the car to go home. I'd slipped. Of course nobody had fun, except maybe Lily. We'd just spent a week in a house of mourning.

Mercifully, Charlotte broke the silence. "Mom, remember you promised you'd take me to that bookstore?"

"Bookstore?"

"Williams Corner," Ellis said. "You promised when she started *Gone with the Wind*." He sounded a little irked. It was *my* promise. Why didn't I remember it?

"And you're finished already?" It was hard to believe Charlotte had already finished *Gone with the Wind*. She was, after all, only nine. But more to the point: I couldn't believe that we were going to have to make a stop before we'd even started.

"Last night," she said.

Ellis made the decision, changing lanes abruptly and heading downtown. I was surprised he knew where it was, but within ten minutes, we were parked in the Water Street lot and walking down Third Street into the honeyed warmth of Williams Corner.

It wasn't until we got there that I realized how deeply I missed it. Despite yearly trips to Charlottesville, it somehow never fit into our visits. If Canterbury Road represented my childhood, it was Williams Corner, where I'd worked part-time my last three years in Virginia, that stood for my young adulthood. And a cozy home it was, with polished plank floors, long towering walls of books, cozy nooks with rocking chairs. Something about the narrowness of the bookstore cosseted you. I'd fallen for many bookstores since being up North, but none came close to this one.

Lily ran off to find the children's section, Charlotte hesitated, not knowing whether to follow her sister or look through the long fiction wall that covered the left side of the store. Ellis ambled over to biographies.

I just stood by the front window and drank it in.

It had waited for me, all this time. At any moment, the twenty-two-year-old version of me might walk in, a dozen years younger, twenty-five pounds thinner. That Ivy, it pained me to realize, would walk right past the current me: an overweight middle-aged mother of two. I would be invisible to her, nobody worth taking the time to get to know.

Who was that Ivy Honeycutt? And, more important, what had become of her?

The old Ivy—I mean the young Ivy—wasn't just a more youthful and prettier version of my current self. She was more tender, like new growth in springtime. She didn't have the automatic authority that came with motherhood. And she was, I remembered, jealous of being on the perimeter of the writers who did readings here. But she still had dreams, that Ivy, ambitions, full-blown fantasies of getting on these very bookshelves. She—I—used to write. On a typewriter, for heaven's sake. A old Royal manual, in a country kitchen, in the Virginia mountains. How beautifully, impossibly romantic, like a scene from a movie.

It suddenly felt like a phantom limb, that long-ago desire to be a serious writer, a yearning that had been absent so long, I'd almost forgotten it. What had happened? I'd gone to New York, fallen in love, settled for a job writing about restaurants, and then given even that up when we'd moved to the suburbs. I'd toyed with catering, made a mess of that. Until finally, Ambition—in the capital-A sense that I'd had it back in my Williams Corner days—had fallen away altogether, replaced by small, almost meaningless ambitions, like getting the girls to put away their toys, remembering doctor's appointments, throwing a reasonably successful dinner party.

I walked over to the local authors shelf and fingered the spines. There they all were, the local eminences—Rita Mae Brown, Ann Beattie, and Peter Taylor—joined by dozens of rising stars, a whole twinkling firmament of literary talent. I pulled out a few volumes, looked at the author pictures, smiled at the incestuous way they all blurbed each other, and felt that familiar blend of contempt and jealousy. I remembered the glorious literary battles that were recounted raucously at Williams Corner: an accomplished poet whose flirtations led to fistfights between her many lovers; a professor of fiction writing who fell for a first-year graduate student and whose wife, in revenge, scattered his clothes, photos, and books—including a signed Carl Sandburg—on the front lawn, where everything got drenched in a springtime storm.

Lily ran up with a whole pile of little chapter books. "Mommy, Mommy, I want these," she said. Her piggishness annoyed me, reminding me of Bailey. "Pick one," I snapped. Charlotte was moving slowly down the long wall of fiction. She looked to be lost in the Gs.

I was walking to the back of the store when I suddenly recognized Julia Eckleberry, an up-and-comer in the writing scene when I was waiting tables and ringing up the cash register at Williams Corner. She was just leaving Mike Williams's office.

Though I hadn't thought of her for years, I knew her instantly. Her looks were extremely memorable; I always thought they'd opened up bedroom doors and helped to propel a fairly meager talent. In her twenties, Julia had been skinny to the point of anorexia. Her tiny face framed enormous brown eyes. I recognized her now even though the long chestnut hair that had been her trademark was chopped off and streaked with blond. Her eyes remained huge, her body even skinnier than I remembered. She was even more stunning as a woman than she'd been as a girl.

"Julia!" I said.

She looked up. I watched as she searched my face and found nothing.

"Ivy," I said. "Ivy Honeycutt."

Still nothing.

"Nick's girlfriend." She'd been a regular at the restaurant, sitting late many nights, smoking and laughing and drinking red wine. She'd known me. She'd probably slept with Nick. We'd taken a fiction class together. "And I worked here," I added.

None of it was registering. I realized that Nick was probably long gone, too, and that a bookstore clerk was the world's most replaceable commodity.

"Honeycutt," she said finally. "Like in Honeycutt Motors?"

"Yes."

"Do you live in Charlottesville?"

"No, not anymore."

"Sorry, I don't remember you." Her voice didn't sound sorry, though. She didn't even try to place me. She did, though, hand me a postcard before hurrying off. "I have a reading tonight if you're still around," she said.

We paid for the girls' books and finally left Charlottesville. As we waited at one of the traffic lights just north of town, I thought about that day I'd left on the train so many years before. I remembered my parents standing on that platform, growing smaller as I rushed toward my new adventure. There was only one of them now. It had never occurred to me that they wouldn't always be there, both of them, whenever I chose to return.

I spent the first leg of the drive trying to fill my heart up, like it was a suitcase, with all the memories of my childhood, all the *Virginianess* I had so willingly relinquished when I boarded that Amtrak. I looked out the window, trying to memorize the farms and the antiques stores, even the gas stations, along Route 29. But as soon as we hit Washington, the big interstates and their monstrous trucks smashed my delicate memories like bullies.

Just before Baltimore, I pulled Julia Eckleberry's postcard out of my purse. It was very plain, just a black-and-white portrait with the title of her new novel in white block letters. Her eyes stared out haughtily, as if to say, *Look at my perfect cheekbones; see what I've made of myself.* And the corollary, *What the hell have you been doing?*

Ellis stepped on the accelerator. That was another thing I'd noticed. The restraint he'd shown driving down to Virginia the week before, in deference to my mourning? That was gone. I looked over and saw the speedometer hovering near eighty.

# Six

## 1995—ELLIS

1995 AUDI CABRIOLET CONVERTIBLE,
AUTOMATIC, V-6, RED (RENTAL)

Like Randy Newman, I love L.A. Every goddamned little thing about it. Driving a convertible, staying at the Beverly Hills Hotel on the company's dime, the weather, all that sunshine, year-round summer, all those perfect eighty-degree days. I love the tropical backdrop, the palmettos, beautiful girls in bikinis. Everything is vivid in L.A., as long as you stay away from South Central. No wonder Technicolor was invented here. The whole place is Technicolor, full of life. I don't even mind the assholes in muscle cars blasting music with their windows down. In their low-class way, they add to the atmosphere.

HWG started sending me to L.A. in the early '90s. My business required me to stay weekends, to see the big acts in the comedy clubs. Night work. That gave me all day on Saturdays and Sundays to play. I loved tooling around without a care, driving as fast as I wanted, no East Coast boss to report to, no white-knuckled wife digging her fingernails in the armrest. I loved starting out a Saturday morning driving to Santa Monica or Venice Beach, watching the surfers, picking up some cheap knickknacks or T-shirts to take back to the girls. I'd get a little sun, jog a little, maybe even go in the water. Then when I'd had enough beach, I'd get on the Pacific Coast Highway and just drive. I'd sail through Malibu, maybe hug the coast all the way up to Santa Barbara. Sometimes, I'd skip the morning at the beach and just head for the highway immediately, see how far I could get toward Big Sur before I had to turn around. It was four hours to get to San Simeon, where I could see Hearst Castle, and if I started early enough—like seven or eight in the morning—I could turn around after lunch. I only did that once. Got snagged in Santa Barbara traffic, spent ten hours on the road, but made it back just in time to see Ricky Santori grab the mic. Loved every minute of that trip. Well, maybe not the two-hour bumper-to-bumper on the 101, but every minute of the *other* eight hours, sailing along the very edge of the earth, that sheared-off rim that separates California, at skyscraper height, from the Pacific Ocean. Top down, sun on my arms, wind through my hair, Sade on the CD player. Nobody watching the speedometer, no kids fighting in the back. Sheer bliss.

California always made me feel young. Here I was, on the far side of forty, a man with a mortgage and a briefcase and a closet full of expensive suits. But when I went to L.A. on business, I could wear what I wanted, sleep late, eat at restaurants—never have to rinse a dish. It was my job to hang out in comedy clubs. Not bad work if you could get it.

Of course, being from the right coast, I always felt a little square. Out in L.A., they were always five years ahead on the pop culture curve. CEOs did yoga. Men went for plastic surgery. I felt a little like a straight arrow: a young Dick Van Dyke. Somebody would start talking about the Melrose Roll, and I'd ask, "Who plays there?" and everybody would laugh. The Melrose Roll was a sushi roll with softshell crab and mango. When I came home, it was the opposite: I was the cool one. For a week after every trip to California, even if I took the red-eye home, people would say I looked tanned and well rested.

Ivy hated it, me going to L.A. She hated me coming back tanned and relaxed. I'd walk into the living room after a long overnight flight, and there'd be crap everywhere: cereal bowls, coffee cups, decapitated Barbies, broken crayons, Charlotte's books, half-folded baskets of laundry. The house fell apart when I was gone, and half the time Ivy fell apart, too. I'd take a long breath before walking in the house, not sure whether I'd get a hug or a lecture. If I was lucky, she'd have taken the girls to school and gone back to bed to sleep off the previous night's insomnia. She never could sleep when I was out of town. Never. And that, of course, was my fault. Like just about everything else.

It was the year of the O. J. Simpson joke. Actually the second year of the O. J. Simpson joke. From the moment the white Bronco made its way down the 405, it was like a twenty-four-hour, all-you-can-eat smorgasbord for comedians. A year later, with the trial going on, not only had every last comic heard of Johnnie Cochran and Mark Fuhrman, but they could all do Judge Ito impressions, too. Nothing was off-limits, nothing in such bad taste that it couldn't get a laugh. Bond traders spent more time circulating O.J. jokes than they did trading bonds. For comedians, it was like shooting fish in a barrel. But the real prize was to get on Leno. Leno was the undisputed master of ceremonies of the official

O.J. circus. There wasn't a comic alive who didn't think he could out-Leno Leno, and it was my job to get our most promising young comic, Rick Santori, a spot on the show.

That was the year my bosses decided I had to subscribe to cable. I'd wanted it, for HBO, ever since I'd seen a tape of *The Larry Sanders Show.* But it always seemed like an indulgence, a monthly expense we just couldn't afford. Because of O.J., my bosses decided I needed round-the-clock access to CNN. Now I got *Larry Sanders,* but that was just a one-hour diversion every week from the daily black comedy that was *California v. O. J. Simpson.*

Ivy despised it, the whole O.J. circus. She didn't see the fun in it, thought it coarsened public discourse, cheapened everything. She hated if I talked or joked about it in front of the girls. Maybe she was right. Maybe our whole national obsession with O.J. was sick. After all, two human beings had been murdered. And who needed Charlotte and Lily to think about the essential truth of the case, that somebody's daddy had murdered their mommy? Especially Charlotte, my sensitive one, who'd been an inveterate worrier since preschool.

But Ivy being right didn't make me want to watch it any less.

When I was out in L.A., I could not only watch the O.J. saga as much as I wanted, but I was supposed to. It was everywhere. In every office, coffee shop, elevator. You could monitor it poolside. A reference to the O.J. trial passed as a greeting. Like *shalom* in Israel, it could start a conversation or end one. If there were children out in L.A. who might be traumatized by the Simpson coverage, they didn't travel in my circles. Maybe there were house-holds in the Valley where husbands had to watch it privately, in the den. I don't know.

My longtime client, Ricky Santori, looked like he might be the first in HWG's talent stable to make it into the O.J. end zone. And it was late in the game, September. It looked like the trial might be wrapping up. "Get him on Leno," said Murray Geltzman, one of HWG's senior partners, who'd personally called to assign me the trip. His voice sounded like ground marbles; he'd started in the business when everybody smoked during two-martini lunches at 21. "I don't care how long it takes or who you have to blow. Just do it." I'd never gotten a call directly from Geltzman before. His secretary, yes. But the big man? Never. I wasn't even sure he knew who I was. When I happened to ride the same car in the elevator, he never showed any sign of recognition.

"Okay, Mr. Geltzman," I'd said, and immediately regretted the *Mr.* I felt like a fourteen-year-old getting offered a lawn-mowing job.

But it was obvious why he'd called me. I was the perfect person to prime Ricky Santori for an appearance on Leno. I'd practically raised Ricky Santori from a pup. I'd discovered him as a twenty-two-year-old kid in a two-bit nightclub in West Orange, so green his folks were still coming to his shows. He was doing bringer shows: Bring five paying guests and you get five minutes at the microphone. Bringer shows are the purgatory of stand-up. Amateurs can stay there for years, forcing the same routine on all their friends and relatives until they finally run out of willing victims.

But Santori was ready to break out, I thought. I liked his routine. He wasn't angry and he didn't need to talk dirty to get a laugh. He was—I don't know—just *likable*. He talked about his Italian upbringing—basic, basic, basic, you saw it five times a night—but when he told it, it was different. All the other Italian comics talked about their overbearing Italian mothers, tiny castrating gnomes who cooked nonstop. Ricky Santori's mother was the only Italian mother in the neighborhood who *couldn't* cook. She thought she was a WASP, spent the afternoons lying in a chaise longue, drinking gin and tonics. Must have been some kind of mix-up at the hospital when she was a baby. On Mother's Day, they took her to the Olive Garden.

I started getting him into clubs in New York. He watched better comics, learned, grew more sophisticated, dropped the Italian-mom jokes, developed an edge—but still remained likable. Then he got some small part in a TV sitcom that got canceled five weeks after he got to L.A. But he liked it out there, stayed, started doing those clubs. I always took him for a nice expense-account dinner when I went out. He stayed a client. And now Geltzman had heard through the grapevine that Santori was cracking them up at the Comedy Store and the Laugh Factory, had great material on O.J.

Ivy leaned against her dresser, her arms crossed tightly, frowning as I packed. I could see the effort she was making not to cry, not to rage, not to complain. And yet, even if she bit her lip, her disapproval was palpable. I acknowledged none of it, concentrating instead on what I needed to bring. Tape recorder, notebooks, khakis, jeans, swim trunks, suntan lotion. A tie and a jacket, just in case.

"How long did you say?" she said finally.

"Impossible to know. Until I get Santori on Leno. Or the trial ends. Whichever comes first."

"And what if he doesn't get on Leno and the trial goes through December? We see you at Christmas?"

"Ivy," I started. But I didn't know what to say. *Ivy, don't be ridiculous? Ivy, this is my job? Ivy, I have to do it?* I'd said all these things a thousand times before. It never made a difference.

"You know how busy I am. The school year's just starting. There are ten million forms to fill out, back-to-school night, sign-ups for soccer, ballet." She was getting ready to hyperventilate. "Then *my* classes. Shit, I can't believe this. Sometimes I think you *want* me to fail."

It was getting hard to be sympathetic. It's true, there was more on Ivy's plate this year. Last spring she'd applied to graduate school for creative writing and had been accepted. Her first semester had just begun. But when she started to accuse me of sabotaging her, it just pissed me off. I'd practically *begged* her to go back to school when she first floated the idea, told her she was wasting her talent, not to worry, we'd find the money to pay for it. Truth is, she'd been floundering for years—the restaurant writing, the catering, the full-time-mom stuff—flitting from interest to interest without any real commitment.

I walked into the bathroom to start packing toiletries. Ivy followed.

"And now I'll have to do your stuff, too. The trash. The recycling. Changing lightbulbs. Making the girls' lunches. Nobody to help clean up. And of course, you know I can't sleep when you're away. God, I'm exhausted just thinking about it."

I packed the little bag with my toothpaste, toothbrush, and deodorant, went back to the bedroom to put it in the suitcase, and zipped it up. I didn't want to listen to her worries yet again. I wanted her to buck up, become a grown-up. But what I wanted was different from what was necessary. "Come here," I said. I put my arms around her, stroked her hair, read from my usual script, assuring her that she would indeed survive my absence.

I got to L.A. on a Friday afternoon. Ricky was playing Saturday night. I don't know why, but I didn't spend my Saturday the way I usually did, driving out to the beach towns, zipping up the coast on the PCH. I felt like I should be working. I picked up every newspaper I could find and sat by the pool at the Beverly Hills Hotel, soaking in the sun and every O.J. detail I could find. Some Jews study the Talmud on Saturdays. I studied O.J.

In the afternoon, I went back to my room, took a nap. It felt decadent, sleeping in the middle of the day, in a king-sized bed, no less. I felt a little guilty, thinking of Ivy schlepping the girls to their different Saturday activities. Then I rationalized. Long hours, working weekends, jet lag. I deserved a nap.

On impulse, I went to Pink's and got myself a nice juicy Polish pastrami dog for dinner. Why I wanted a hot dog, when I could eat in any restaurant in L.A. on the expense account, I couldn't say. Just slumming it, I guess. Or maybe I just woke up from my nap

with the realization that I'd been suffering from hot dog depriva-
tion all these years. Ivy never bought hot dogs, didn't allow them at
our barbecues. When the girls were small, she worried about
them choking. Then she worried about the sulfates, or sulfites—
whatever it was they poisoned you with.

I got to the club early, in time to see the 6 P.M. open mic. Just
like going to Pink's, another form of slumming. Ricky Santori always reminded me you could find new talent in a dung heap. And
what a dung heap it was, the open mic crowd, a sideshow of freaks
in every possible variation. *Ladies and gentlemen, step right up, see
people who wet their beds as kids! We've got nerds, geeks, three-hundred-
pound women, forty-year-old men who live with their mothers!* God
save us. You had to laugh at their pathetic streams-of-consciousness,
out of mere politeness, but when you did, it was like sacrificing a
small piece of your soul.

"Who are you here for?" the girl at the window asked when I
handed her my five bucks.

"Nobody."

She raised an eyebrow suspiciously. Nobody came to these
shows for sheer entertainment value. Everybody was part of some
poor schmuck's quota. I winked knowingly. It would have come
off better if I'd been wearing a hat and could have tipped it, Cary
Grant–style. Oh man, those were days. Cary Grant. Nobody had
class like that anymore.

I found myself a table at the back, away from all the friends and
relatives who came as bringers. Later, when Ricky showed up,
he'd introduce me to everybody as the big shot from New York
who'd plucked him from obscurity. But for now, during amateur

hour, I didn't want anybody knowing who I was. I ordered a beer and, for lack of anything better to do, looked around the room. I'd been in big clubs and small clubs, swank places and dives. No matter how much you tried to dress them up, though, they were all pretty much the same. Uncomfortable little chairs and small tables too close together, overworked waitresses and sticky floors.

It was painful to watch. They were all there, all the stereotypes of stand-up: the black guy talking about his huge dong, the fat girl with the bad sex life, the nerd who never got a date, the brainiac talking Kierkegaard and Hegel. Oh, boy. I tried to remember my routine, back in the days when I still had the nerve to step up on a stage, back when I first met Ivy. Had I been this bad? I winced to think so. The lineup went on. A buxom redhead blaming her weight on her Irish ancestors' love affair with the potato, an Asian guy joking about being good at math, a couple of Jews, a few Italians. The black guys had the foulest mouths of the lot, and tended to be the funniest. The hot dog was giving me indigestion. I was starting to wish I'd been a good boy and had a salad.

I leaned back and stretched my legs. Just another day at the office. Sometimes my job seemed glamorous. Parties, screenings, free concerts. Other times, it was just the stench of desperation and old men's breath. The American dream: Anyone could grow up to be a movie star. But if you got close enough, nothing was beautiful. Not even the beautiful people were beautiful. All of Hollywood was just a 6 P.M. open mic night. Sick, raw, desperate. Porn with clothes.

"You're not falling asleep in the middle of Gonzo Boy?"

I heard someone plop into the chair next to mine, and opened my eyes to see the Irish chick. She pointed to the stage, where a geeky comic in a superhero mask was making odd guttural noises.

"Oh," I said. "Thanks for the heads-up." Like a freshman called out for nodding off in Econ 101, I made a show of sitting up straight and pretending to pay attention.

"You weren't missing anything." She sipped something amber-colored. Jack Daniel's, probably. She looked relaxed, like we'd known each other for years. I wondered if I *did* know her, or was supposed to.

"I'm sorry," I said. "Have we met?"

She laughed. "Well, you *do* know about most of my neuroses and my trouble with men. Unless you slept through that, too." She reached over to shake my hand. "Daphne Eagan." Her handshake was strong, a girl who'd grown up with a houseful of brothers.

"Ellis Halpern." Then I remembered my manners. She'd been onstage. "Nice set." I struggled to remember a specific joke I could praise, something besides the potatoes, but drew a blank.

"Thanks."

She leaned in closer and crossed her legs, which I noticed were paler than the typical California girl's. Either new to town or so hopelessly Irish, she'd never get a tan. She was wearing a short smocked dress, which showcased a chest full of freckles, and shoes with big cork wedges. She was sort of sloppily, effortlessly sexy. Not your regular California goddess, that was for sure. She was close enough that I could smell the bourbon on her breath.

"Never seen you here before," she said.

"I'm from out of town."

"Oh."

The emcee had walked onstage and was asking everybody to give it up for Gonzo Boy. We both watched as he introduced the next comic.

A few minutes later, the girl—Daphne—turned to me again. "Where?"

"Where what?"

"Where are you from?"

"New York."

I wondered immediately why I didn't say New Jersey. New York was always the answer if I was being a suit. But when I wasn't on business, if Ivy and I were traveling together, it was always Jersey. I wasn't being a suit now—not until Ricky Santori came on, anyway. So why was I showing off? I started fidgeting with my wedding ring.

"Yeah, I thought about New York," Daphne said. "There's a lot of stand-up there, too, of course."

I was starting to feel uncomfortable. Was she coming on to me? Or was she just a big goofy Irish setter who couldn't help making friends with anybody she found in the park? If we kept talking, I'd wind up telling her what I did for a living and why I was at the show. She'd start to hope I could do something for her career. I didn't want that, didn't think her act merited a miracle.

I cleared my throat. "Listen, Daphne. I'm married." I was still fingering my wedding band. From out of town, married. If she was coming on, that should be enough to drive her away, right?

"Yeah, I know," she said, reaching over to touch my ring. "I love married men. They're so incredibly grateful when you fuck them."

Most of the night went by in a blur. The pressure in my cock was so intense, for so long, my whole world felt like it had been reduced to a few inches of panicky desire. What Daphne had offered was unmistakable: no-strings-attached sex, something I hadn't experienced in, well, forever. I'd never cheated on Ivy. The last time I'd seen a naked woman not my wife was the night of my bachelor party. I'd had desires, yes. I'd masturbated, fantasized, sneaked a porno now and then. Even seeing my sister-in-law made me horny. But never, ever had I acted on any of these impulses with another human being.

Daphne must have known she had me. What blood that hadn't rushed immediately to my penis rushed to face. My ears turned bright red. I should have said, *Then I'm afraid you're going to be disappointed,* stood up, left the club, gone back to the hotel, whacked off, and come back an hour later for the headliners. I could have relieved the pressure and returned, safe in my fidelity, to a businesslike evening of stand-up comedy. But I didn't. Maybe I was just dumbstruck by her audacity. Or flattered. Or maybe I couldn't stand up because I didn't want her to see my hard-on. All I know is that I sat there, her captive, wavering on a moral teeter-totter, my heart clattering so loud, I felt sure it must be disturbing the performers up on stage.

I started babbling. Verbal diarrhea. Talking at least had the merit of not breaking any commandments. At least it wasn't fucking. I told her my job, the purpose of my business trip, all about discovering Ricky Santori, O.J., Leno. Except for widened eyes when I mentioned Ricky, she took it all in without a flutter. She was smart, Daphne. Didn't say, *Oh my God, can you help me?* She knew that her prospects went up exponentially once she got me into bed. A cool customer.

But fun. Lively. A congenially dirty mouth. She told me about herself, growing up in Minnesota, an alcoholic mother, six brothers (I was right!), tomboy, class clown, a regular in the high school principal's office. There were, of course, no comedy clubs where she grew up—just biker bars. What she knew about comedy she learned on television.

College, apparently, hadn't even been a consideration. She'd worked in a bar after high school, first as a waitress, then as a bartender. Better money. Harder job than people thought, Daphne said. Part bouncer, not taking crap from anybody. Part mixology, memorizing all the silly drinks people kept making up and expected her to know.

"What do you think is in a Godfather?" she said.

"Blood?"

"Scotch and amaretto. Brass Monkey?"

I shook my head, smiled.

"Rum, vodka, orange juice. Dreamsicle?"

"I don't know. Something with orange juice?"

"Yep, with Baileys. Blow Job?"

*"What?"*

"The drink. A Blow Job."

The tips of my ears reddened.

"Kahlúa, Baileys, and a squirt of whipped cream. Fuck Me Silly?"

I started laughing. "Girl, you should really put this in your act."

"Fuck Me Silly: amaretto, peach schnapps, sloe gin, Southern Comfort. And, of course, as always . . ."

"Baileys?"

"No. Orange juice. The guys used to love it, coming in and asking for Anal Sex or Tie Me to the Bedpost. At first it made me blush. Then I got used to it. Bought a book. Kept it behind the bar. Trust me, standing up here in front of a microphone is nothing compared to being a bartender."

"School of hard knocks," I said.

"You wouldn't believe the big lugs who would come in and order a peach schnapps. Losers! I prefer Jack." She swished her drink around in its plastic cup. "I suppose I *should* put it in my act."

"You really should."

The show ended; the waitress collected money. It was at least an hour until the main show. By now, Daphne had grown sloppy, like that Irish setter again, friendly, paws everywhere. I'd paced her Jack Daniel's with beer, and was starting, slightly, to relax. Maybe she didn't really want to fuck me. Maybe that was a joke. She was just trying to shock me. She was a fun girl—that was all. Just somebody else in the business. Who knew? Maybe she did have some talent.

"Wanna go for a walk?" I said. "Get something to eat?"

"Sure. Let me go back and get my bag." She disappeared to the area where the comics dropped their stuff, and for a second I thought: *I could just leave. Right now. Leave Daphne backstage getting her purse and never see her again.* She'd be miffed, maybe even a little hurt, when she came out and couldn't find me. Maybe she'd ask somebody if they'd seen me. Maybe she'd wait by the men's room door for a few minutes. But she was a tough cookie. She'd been through worse, knew the score. She'd get over it. And I'd be safe.

But that would have been like walking right past a free sushi bar and not taking any. And besides, she knew I'd be back to see Ricky. She'd just come back and give me the evil eye. I gulped, wondered what I was doing. Daphne came out, cheerful, smiling, carrying a canvas messenger bag.

"Did you have any bringers you have to say good-bye to?" I asked.

"They left a while ago." Then, changing the subject: "There's a little Cuban place right down the street." She kept it light, casual. Inexpensive.

"Sure," I said.

We drank more, switching to rum and Cokes. She talked more about her life in L.A.—"La La Land," she called it. When she wasn't doing stand-up, she was working as a bartender. Decent tips. Of course, she'd do even better if she did stripping. That was, she said, obviously, an option. La La Land was expensive. She was so nonchalant, she might have been talking about changing majors in college. As for the comedy, she didn't know. Was thinking about trying improv, too. There was a lot of that in L.A. She might even take some classes at Groundlings. But that cost money, too. Another reason to go for bigger tips.

"And what about you?" she said. "Tell me about your family."

I felt a small little stab where my heart was. Call it conscience. Inwardly, I shivered at the idea of discussing Ivy, Charlotte, and Lily with someone who pity-fucked husbands—or even joked about it. But Daphne made it sound innocent, like one of the assistants at HWG who came into my office and smiled at the pictures on my desk.

I took a deep breath, exhaled. "Well, Charlotte's eleven, very serious, studious, straight-A student. Read *Gone with the Wind* in one week, when she was just nine. Wants to be perfect, comes close. Cried when she couldn't get Roman numerals."

Daphne looked slightly bored.

"And Lily, she's like this blond-haired angel—or devil, actually. Looks like an angel, acts like a devil. Used to getting her way."

"And your wife?" She was eager to get to the juicy part.

I looked behind Daphne at the large framed VISIT CUBA poster on the wall. One of those old travel posters that had been resurrected and now showed up in frames everywhere: giant palmetto, biplane slicing a stylized yellow sky, PAN AMERICAN AIRLINES in deco lettering. Not the air travel of today, with dreary airports, long security lines, pallid passengers sandwiched in like sardines. Travel like a Carmen Miranda movie.

Ivy. What was I going to say about Ivy?

"Smart," I answered finally. "Going back to school to get her MFA."

"What's an MFA?"

I admired Daphne's frankness. Most people would pretend they knew what you were talking about rather than admit ignorance.

"Master of Fine Arts. In creative writing. She's from the South. A good cook. Pretty funny. Worries a lot. Bites her nails. Afraid to drive on highways."

"She wouldn't last long around here." Daphne laughed.

"No, I suppose she wouldn't."

"Pretty?"

Even on the precipice of betrayal, I felt a tug of loyalty to poor Ivy, who after all wasn't around to defend herself. What was Daphne implying? That my wife wasn't pretty? It wasn't a fair contest, this redheaded girl, robust with good health and high spirits and *youth,* just starting her first adventure in life, versus a grown woman who had borne children—*my* children—and who'd been worn down over the years by responsibilities, chores, neuroses. But then, why did I think of it as a contest? Maybe Daphne wasn't implying anything. Maybe she was just curious. No, on second thought, it *was* a contest. Everything between women was a contest. I'd seen *All About Eve.*

"Of course she's pretty."

"How did you meet?"

"Comedy club, open mic night. I was doing stand-up. She was in the audience."

Daphne threw her head back and laughed, showing off a young, unlined neck. "I guess you have a thing about girls in comedy clubs."

"I believe *you* picked *me* up," I said.

She set her drink on the table and smiled a wide salacious grin. "In the end," she said, "it won't make much difference."

I wobbled back to the club. My knees were weak, my bloodstream a turbulent confluence of beer and Cuban rum. I felt as scared and excited as a boy in high school going out with the town nymphomaniac: both amazed and terrified at my own luck.

But once we got to the club, I started to get my bearings. I picked up my comp, paid Daphne's cover, let the hostess lead us to a good table, ordered more beer. Though my brain had been muddy on the walk back from the restaurant, I snapped to attention once the house lights went down. Call it professionalism; call it just plain habit. Or maybe it was just the voltage of a headliner show in L.A. on a Saturday night. Having been there for the open mic, it was almost like seeing a neighborhood gentrifying in super-speeded-up motion. An hour ago, I'd left behind a motley crew of wannabes, half of whom didn't know how to work a mic. I'd returned to a room full of professionals and people paying a twenty-dollar cover. I leaned back and let the transformation wash over me. I was going to be fine. I was going to do what I'd been sent for: to gauge Ricky's performance, fine-tune it, pitch the *L.A. Times, Billboard, Variety,* and pull whatever strings I could at Leno. I felt competent, back in my groove.

Ricky was up third. The crowd clapped like mad when he was introduced, and while I waited for him to bound onto the stage, I sneaked a glance at Daphne to see if she was impressed. After all, I didn't just know him; I'd *discovered* him. But tonight,

Ricky wasn't doing any bounding. He lumbered up to the stool, looking as eager to be there as someone going to the dentist. He sat down and stared dolefully at the audience. We waited. There was an uncomfortable silence, a few nervous laughs. This was something new, this Mexican standoff, and whether he pulled it off tonight or not, I knew it wouldn't play on Leno. I prayed silently. *Come on, Ricky. Don't overdo this.* It was always dangerous to toy with an audience. They could turn on you in an instant. A few more seconds, and this one would.

Then, like a high-wire performer only pretending to hesitate in order to heighten the tension, Ricky began.

"Sorry," he said. "I'm just a little depressed. O.J. filed for trademark protection for his name this week. My lawyer tells me that not only can't I mention him in my act, but I have to pay him a dollar every time I have a glass of orange juice."

Huge laugh. Bigger, I thought, than the joke really deserved— more a testament to how badly an audience really wants the talent in front of it to succeed. *We'll give you a big laugh. Just don't leave us hanging here again.* But the important thing was, he got the laugh. He made it across the high wire. And make-believe legal advice to the contrary, he wasn't just having a little fun at O.J.'s expense, he was dining on the poor homicidal schmuck. Murray Geltzman's intelligence was apparently correct. With the exception of the sack-and-ashes opening, Ricky Santori's act was Leno-worthy.

Daphne turned to me when Ricky left the stage. "You were nervous at the beginning, weren't you?"

"No. I knew he'd . . . Well, yes, actually."

"Yeah, I thought he overdid it myself."

When the show was over, Ricky came up and squeezed into the banquette. He thunked a wet glass down on the table and turned to Daphne. "And who is this pretty lady?"

"This is my niece. Daphne."

Daphne, sipping rum, started to make sounds like she was choking.

I patted her, hard, on the back. "You okay, honey?"

She stopped sputtering. "Okeydokey."

"Niece?" said Ricky. "I didn't know you had a niece in L.A."

Daphne improvised. "New to town." Under the table, she placed her hand on my thigh, right below my crotch. A tease? A warning?

We sat for a few minutes and made small talk, Daphne complimenting Ricky lavishly on his act, Ricky asking how I liked the opening, me demurring, saying we'd discuss that later. Under the table, Daphne's hand had moved upward. Oh God, if there was anything hotter than being with a hot chick, it was being with a hot chick who could carry on a conversation with a straight face even as she stroked your manhood through a layer of denim.

"So, kids," Ricky said. "Time to go paint the town? Go for a drink? See another show? Grab a bite?" He was back to his old frisky puppy self, the kind of comic who bounded energetically onto a stage, ready to help show my niece a good time.

"You know, I promised her parents an early night," I said. Even as I said it, I knew it was ridiculous. It wasn't even a school night. "Tomorrow, come by the hotel. We'll have brunch."

"Sure," he said. "Sunday brunch at the Beverly Hills Hotel." He stood up, put his hands on our shoulders. "Good night, kids." He looked slightly hurt, or maybe he was just looking forward to an evening on the HWG expense account. Then he yelled to another comic.

"Niece," Daphne said, smiling. "I'm from such a small town, nobody could use that trick. Everybody knew *exactly* who I was related to."

"Welcome to the big city. Can I give you a ride?"

Daphne actually did need a ride. She'd caught a lift to the show with one of the paying guests she'd had to supply as her price for doing five minutes of stand-up. But I didn't take her home. Daphne, it turned out, shared a Silver Lake rental with an aspiring actress, an aspiring screenwriter, and an aspiring animator. And although nothing had been explicitly promised, she'd teased the living daylights out of me all evening. If we were going to fuck—if I was going to be one of those oh-so-grateful married men she'd mentioned earlier—it wasn't going to be at a crowded flat filled with twentysomethings.

And Daphne *was* interested in a close-up look at the legendary Beverly Hills Hotel, a place she'd seen only in movies. "Will we see Bruce Willis?" she asked eagerly. "Or Tatum O'Neal?"

"Um, they live here. In L.A., I mean. It's a hotel, remember?"

"Can we go skinny-dipping?"

"Yes, right after the animal balloons and the cocaine party." I patted her knee. It was actually touching to see such childlike enthusiasm.

I was glad the hotel was just a few miles down the Strip—that I didn't have to get on a freeway or follow any complicated directions. I'd lost count of the number of drinks I had. All I knew was that I'd consumed, in one evening, my typical alcohol ration for a year. If Ivy had been here, she wouldn't have let me near the wheel. Of course, if Ivy had been here, I wouldn't have had all those drinks in the first place. Or spent the evening entertaining a girl half my age. Or been driving said girl to my fancy-schmancy hotel. Or, for that matter, spent any more than the absolute minimum time necessary inside a comedy club. If Ivy had been here, I'd have been on a short leash.

I did my best to put Ivy out of my mind.

We pulled up to the valet and Daphne got out, slamming the door and loudly taking in her surroundings. At least it seemed loud to my delicate suburban sensibilities. "Oh my God," she said. "This is so rad." Then, switching from Valley girl to Bette Davis, she tilted her shoulders back, swung her hips in an exaggerated movie star strut, and said, "Come on, daaaahling." It wasn't an implausible impression, and it might have been perfectly fun to watch on a stage, but we weren't in a comedy club; we were in the Beverly Hills Hotel. You weren't supposed to be impressed by the wealth or the proximity of movie stars. You weren't supposed to do a clown act. You were supposed to act like you belonged.

"Come on, come see the room," I said, wanting to hurry her through the lobby. "It's really amazing."

"Oh yeah?"

"A suite," I said. "With like thousand-thread sheets. And a minibar."

I think it was the minibar that sold her. The idea of tiny little bottles of booze and fifteen-dollar candy bars.

When I unlocked the door, I saw the light on the phone next to the bed blinking. Shit, a message. Ivy? Ricky? Murray Geltzman? It pulsed like a machine in the hospital, with the steady, implacable rhythm of a heart monitor. Or no, it pulsed menacingly, like Edgar Allan Poe's tell-tale heart. A reminder of all the things I was connected to, all the people I was responsible for, the fact that even in this tawdry little episode, I couldn't escape the gravitational pull of my own life.

I took my jacket off and laid it over the phone. You could still see the little flashing light, but just barely.

"Here," Daphne said, helpfully taking off her dress and laying it over my jacket. Then she sat on the bed, in bra and panties, and pulled me toward her. She bit the top button off my fifty-nine-dollar shirt, yanked my pants down, laid me on my back, and took my penis in her mouth. And then, when I was good and hard, she pulled off her panties and expertly straddled me. She rocked like a girl on a mechanical bull, without shame, her eyes wild and glazed, seeking her own pleasure as directly as a man. And when we came, together, explosively, I felt such pure delight that I pulled her face down to me and kissed her.

That was the part that felt like a betrayal, that kiss.

Finally, Daphne fell asleep, and I took the dress and the jacket off the phone and picked up the message. It was Ivy calling me with good news. She'd gotten an A on a short story. In the background, I could hear the TV, Lily yelling at Charlotte, Ivy making popcorn, the sounds of my own family. It must have been ten o'clock or so when she'd called. Movie night—one of the weekend treats Ivy had invented to make my travel bearable. She sounded so happy. She'd been praised by Hamish McDonough, the chair of the creative writing program, who apparently never praised anyone. She was, he said, a natural.

"You don't have to call back," Ivy said. "You're probably out at Ricky's show. I just couldn't keep it in all weekend. 'A natural'!"

I replaced the phone quietly, careful not to wake Daphne. I inhaled deeply, and in that long second that hovered between inhale and exhale, tried to remember who I was. I honestly couldn't say. Was I the family man, the good husband? Or a lying, cheating bastard, driven by hungers and needs and opportunity? Or both?

And then, when the breath was completed, I put the thought out of my brain. That was the safest thing. Not to think about it. New Jersey was three thousand miles from L.A. Separate. Totally separate. And it would stay that way. It didn't matter, because it would never happen again. And Ivy would never find out.

I needed air. I needed a drive.

I sat up, put my feet on the floor, stared at the hair on my toes for a minute, then picked up my clothes and got dressed. Before leaving the room, I turned around. Daphne was still sleeping, her red hair spread like a fan across the high-quality down pillows.

When I found the valet and asked for my car, I thought I saw a question in his expression, but then, like a good member of the service class, he held the question back. I gave him twenty bucks.

I got on Sunset and headed west. The Santa Monica Pier, I thought, or maybe the Pacific Coast Highway. I would decide when I got there. The pier had the advantage of sensation. Rides and lights and the throb of the crowd. It was late, but the board-walk stayed open late on weekends. And there was also the ocean. You could walk down from the pier onto the sand.

But the PCH had the advantage of the heights. I could look down at the little houses built into the palisades.

I turned on the radio and started driving fast, faster than I should have. I don't know which of the hairpin turns on Sunset got me. All I remember is skidding across the road, narrowly missing a minivan, and winding up in somebody's lawn. The rest is a blur: the lights and the vindictive sirens and the alcohol test and the trip to the ER and, finally, Ricky Santori coming to Los Angeles County Jail to bail me out.

"Where's your niece?" he said once he'd handed over the cash that was the price of my freedom, and buckled me into the passenger seat of his RX-7.

I was dazed. I had a concussion. I didn't know what he was talking about.

He turned on the ignition, then gave me a look filled with disgust. "I thought so."

## Seven

## 1997—Ivy

1992 BUICK ROADMASTER ESTATE WAGON,
AUTOMATIC, V-8, SILVER

Ellis was in L.A. As usual. Sometimes it felt like he lived there. Starting with that trip two years ago to get Ricky Santori on Leno. Disgusting. Profiting from the murder of poor dead Nicole Simpson. Ellis just laughed when I said that, that haughty you're-so-naïve-I-can-barely-believe-it laugh. As if (the laugh said) my taking offense at O.J. Simpson jokes was going to change anything, as if I could bring back Nicole Simpson or even, by virtue of my high personal standards, restore dignity to the world. Of course, he was right. When it came to that slick, oily, endlessly fatuous world of show business, Ellis was always right. And P.S.: Santori *did* get on Leno, Ellis got a huge bonus, which paid for a new roof and all of my graduate school, and he instantly became Murray Geltzman's new best bitch. He was traveling to the coast all the time now. I'd lost track of the clients, the reasons, the talk shows. I'd grown uninterested in the green rooms. I didn't want to hear about the great weather, either. Or even the cute seals that Ellis occasionally saw on the beach during his time off.

It was late August, the dregs of summer, that time of year when the garden is dead, the neighbors are all on vacation, and the kids have no one to play with. You're taking in everybody's mail and newspapers and watering their plants, and it feels like the Rapture. Everybody must have been called to heaven. Or Maine. You've been to the pool so many times, it's about as thrilling as going to the grocery store, but the air is so thick and hot, you go anyway. Then, on the way home, you pass the garden center, where the newly arrived mums taunt you with the imminent arrival of fall. That means haircuts, doctor's appointments, trips to Kmart for socks and backpacks, school emergency contact cards to be filled out in triplicate. As long as it's dead, you'd like to get into Staples for the girls' school supplies, but you know that even if you did, there'd be some protractor or calculator you hadn't known about and you'd be back there anyway, a week later, with all the lines. There's nothing on TV except the Jerry Lewis telethon. And the whole month is set to a soundtrack of cicadas, a reminder that all things—summer, youth, life—must come to an end.

Happy thoughts.

I'd never liked it when Ellis was away, especially when the girls were babies, but now that they were thirteen and ten, it was at least manageable. For a few years now, I'd been able to run out to the store for milk if I had to, without bringing them along. Last year, Charlotte had gotten her Red Cross babysitting certificate, and I could even go to the movies or book group when Ellis was out of town. And since Ellis really was a company star, with a salary to match, I used his business trips as an excuse to take the girls out for dinner three or four nights a week. There was always more to do when he was away—all my jobs plus his—so if we wound up at Friendly's or the Tick Tock every other night, it wasn't like I didn't deserve it. And if I allowed the girls to plop in front of the TV so I could write, so be it.

Truth be told, it had started not to make that much difference having Ellis gone. Sure, when he was home, he did certain chores: taking out garbage, going down to the basement if a fuse blew. But even when he was home, it didn't feel like we saw him that much. He'd been working longer hours, spending more time on the phone, and watching television deep into the night. We'd gotten cable for the O.J. case, ostensibly, but now he hardly turned it off. He watched crap like *Men Behaving Badly* and *Married . . . with Children*. One night when I couldn't sleep, I wandered downstairs and found Ellis watching an infomercial on vacuum cleaners. When I'd complain about his television habits, he'd sweep his arm toward the TV like Vanna White and remind me: This was what paid the bills.

As he spent more time under the enchanted spell of the idiot box, I was going in the opposite direction. I'd gone back and started reading the classics: *Middlemarch, Sense and Sensibility, Sons and Lovers, Crime and Punishment*. I'd finished my course work for my master's but was still working on my thesis—a half-finished novel about the descendants of Thomas Jefferson and Sally Hemings—and I was going to work part-time helping Hamish McDonough, my graduate school adviser and head of the creative writing program, taking over some small undergraduate sections and grading papers.

Hamish McDonough. Sigh.

I fell in love with him that very first day, when I'd sat down in his classroom with my spiral notebook, trying to imagine myself as the new Flannery O'Connor or Eudora Welty, the very latest in the storied line of fine Southern women writers. I sat straight-backed and attentive, but not—I hoped—overeager. And then Hamish, a lanky form slouching lazily in his chair, suddenly crossed his legs, leaned forward, and began to speak. That's when I lost all consciousness of myself.

It wasn't just his Scottish accent, almost impenetrable the first time you heard him, which only made you listen harder. Or his sad green eyes, usually hidden under a misbehaving thatch of sandy hair, or the depths of a loss that we couldn't ask about directly, but could only guess at from clues woven into his writing. A dead baby, a wife who'd left? Sudden infant death syndrome? That seemed the most likely. But there were rumors, too, of grand-parents babysitting and the child accidentally falling headfirst out of a high chair. There were no hints in his attic office, no photo-graphs that gave it away. Just a shadow of tragedy like an airplane's shadow passing softly over patchwork fields. And then there were those who said there was no tragedy at all, no dead child, no abandonment; that Hamish wore his mantle of doom as an affectation.

It wasn't just these things—the accent, the mystery—but also the gold that he spun so effortlessly, the stories he told, the way he could parse a fairy tale into protagonist, antagonist, stakes, and crisis. You felt, as he talked, that he was unpeeling rolls of cotton from your eyes, so that you could suddenly see—as plain as a chil-dren's drawing of the grass and sky—what made a story a *story,* and the almost sacred role the writer had in explaining the human condition.

Love? Maybe not love. More like a schoolgirl crush. I allowed myself to fantasize, once in a while, that Ellis would die, freeing me up to become Hamish's lover. I could see it like a movie: soft focus, violins. Two tragic characters bound by an unspeakable grief. I never speculated how Ellis would die—heart attack? plane crash?—and felt terrible for even imagining it. Beyond that, nothing. No secret kisses, certainly no sordid affair. Just the hidden sparks my heart gave off whenever Hamish entered the room.

The sparks were fed by Hamish's praise, all the more precious for its rareness, like an unexpected box from Tiffany's.

Like Charlotte, I'd always been a teacher's pet. The one who raised my hand, turned in the best paper, was asked to read my essay for the class. It may have been Bailey who sat in the passenger seat of the convertible at the Charlottesville Dogwood Festival, her honey-blond hair whipping in the wind, but it was my stolid intelligence that impressed the teachers and gave me special privileges, like the right to bang the chalk out of Mrs. Herald's erasers every Friday afternoon in fifth grade.

And now I was Hamish's favorite. So much better than pounding Mrs. Herald's erasers.

The knowledge of this crept up slowly. First in the As my stories received, then in comments written in the margins of papers handed back, then in small and offhand invitations. A faculty tea. A meeting of prospective graduate students. And finally the offer to be his fall TA.

And so I found myself in Hamish's stuffy office one afternoon the last week of August, a day so hot, you could imagine you smelled the electric wires slowly charring the rafters. We were

discussing the upcoming school year, and I was complaining—
okay, flirting—that Ellis was awash in the glamour of Hollywood, while I stayed home and took out the trash.

"And subsisting," I added, "on Oriental chicken salads at
Friendly's. Our special treat when Daddy's away."

"Oh, that's awful," Hamish said. "Completely unacceptable.
That stuff will kill you, you know."

"And what do you suggest?"

"Come to my house for dinner. At least once. I can cook, you
know. I'm really quite good. Come on. I live out near Culvers
Lake. It's beautiful this time of year at sunset. I'll take you for a
ride in my canoe, then dinner. How about Saturday?"

Culvers Lake? Where the hell was that? Far, I knew that. It
was nowhere I'd ever heard of. I'd die if I had to confess to Hamish
my abnormal fear of driving.

"But what about—?"

"The girls? They'll be fine. Your eldest is thirteen, didn't you
say?"

"And Ellis?"

"What about Ellis?"

"What do I tell him?"

"Why do you have to tell him anything?" He leaned back in
his chair and smiled. "You're a big girl."

I frowned, thinking.

"Tell him your new boss invited you out to discuss your job for
next year."

But I didn't tell Ellis. I marked it on my calendar—"Dinner

w/H"—surprising myself with my secrecy. Like anyone gave a rat's ass about my calendar.

I was sitting on the porch the next morning reading the *New Yorker,* grabbing the last little bit of shade and breeze and quiet I'd get all day. It was midmorning, and the girls were still asleep. Charlotte was already a teenager and Lily—ten going on seventeen—had acquired a teenager's sleeping habits, too. It was folly letting them sleep until noon, when the next week we'd all have to go back to school-time hours. All the experts said the only way to yank whacked-out circadian rhythms back into alignment was by forcing yourself to get up early. A little deal with the devil, letting the girls sleep in, but I'd sell their souls all over again for another hour of peace and quiet.

Soon enough, Charlotte would be banging on the piano and Lily would be blaring the television, each of them ratcheting up the volume on their instruments, leading to the inevitable crescendo of screams. All this because of the recreation habits of *Homo suburbanis,* a lemminglike species that deserts its natural habitat en masse every August. I tried to see our forced togetherness as a sort of modern *Little Women*: Father away at the war, the girls and I huddled together, making do. A stretch. Maybe if there'd been snow . . .

I should have been writing. But I was wallowing in self-pity and had talked myself into the idea that I deserved a break. And I wasn't even reading the *New Yorker.* I was actually skimming the cartoons and daydreaming about Hamish, wondering whether my trip there on Saturday should be classified as a "date," and if it was, did that constitute infidelity?

I heard the sound of whistling on the front walk. Alas, civilization! We weren't alone after all! Here came Bob the Mailman, bringing word from the outside world. Mostly bills, to be sure. Still. I set the magazine down, knowing that I was in for a good five or ten minutes of chitchat. Bob was a relic of a more loquacious age, when people passed the day conversing with their greengrocers, knife sharpeners, butchers, wenches selling flowers, cops walking their beats.

Nobody had time for this kind of interaction anymore—the greengrocers had been replaced by the produce aisle, the butchers by the meat aisle, the wenches by FTD—but Bob hadn't caught on. Even I was busy, sitting on the front porch, busy daydreaming during the short window of morning that I had to myself. Yet here Bob was, ready to talk, and probably about the Berkshires again. He was planning to retire within a few years, and when he'd learned that my mother-in-law lived in Pittsfield, he starting pumping me endlessly for information about the real estate market. I couldn't quite picture him with a blanket and a bottle of Beaujolais nouveau at Tanglewood. I had him pegged for the Poconos. Still, whenever he asked, I'd dutifully report whatever I'd heard last about prices, or taxes, or the fixing of roads.

In exchange, he offered up lots of juicy information about my neighbors. Just today, he told me the McKenzies' house had been broken into, the Lipmans were getting a divorce, Jenn Paterson had been called from the waiting list last-minute and was going to Yale. I'd always wondered how it was he learned so much—he should have been a journalist or a spy—until the day last year everybody got the postcards with their property tax bills. I was out in the front yard that day, planting iris bulbs. Bob put my mail down on the grass next to where I was working.

"Guess what the Davises are paying in property taxes?" he'd asked, referring to the family that lived around the corner in a Victorian mansion.

I shrugged.

"Twenty-eight thousand!"

Yes, Bob was a vector of information, the vast store of his knowledge coming from return addresses and the backs of postcards.

And today, somehow, he knew that Ellis was in L.A. How, I wondered? Had he run into Ellis some Saturday morning? Or was there some telltale clue in our mail? Bob talked about summer ending, the outlook for the weather. Finally, he handed over the mail.

"Sorry to give you this," he said, indicating the envelope on top. "It's gonna be a whopper."

"A what?" I looked at the envelope, one of those official government ones with plain black type, the kind that almost always contain bad news. Unpaid parking tickets, if you're lucky, a court summons if you're not. This one said STATE OF NEW JERSEY ASSIGNED RISK POOL, and I had no idea what it meant. Assigned risk? For what? My heart sped up. It was like that old story "The Lady, or the Tiger?" Every day, the mail arrived, its sealed envelopes containing the power to delight or destroy. But this envelope, I was certain, contained no delight. This envelope contained the tiger. And how did I know? Because Bob said. Suddenly my fear gave way to a rising fury as I realized I'd be an anecdote at Bob's next stop.

I wanted to tear it open immediately, but couldn't give Bob the satisfaction. I was so determined to appear nonchalant that I asked Bob about his plans for Labor Day. He obliged me with a long, boring story about going to visit an aunt and uncle down in Keyport and a deck he was helping them build. I smiled stiffly until he left and didn't tear open the envelope until he was safely next door at the Rileys. We'd been assigned to the New Jersey Assigned Risk Pool, the letter explained, because we'd exceeded our seven insurance points and our regular car insurance had been suspended. And here was the amount of our new insurance bill: $6,389.

Three times what we'd been paying. Twice what we presently had in the bank account.

It had to be a mistake. Surely, it had been misdelivered. I'd accidentally opened someone else's mail; it would be embarrassing to have to return it. But no, Bob wouldn't have made a point of specifically commenting on it unless he was sure of the name. I put my glasses on and checked. No mistake. Our names, our motor vehicles, our address, our $6,389. Still . . . seven motor vehicle points?

I didn't have any points. I was sure of that. I'd been stopped by a policeman exactly once in my life, in Virginia, for exceeding the speed limit by four miles per hour. The only person in the history of the automobile to get a ticket for going twenty-nine miles per hour. And that was more than sixteen years ago.

And then it came to me. All the times I'd sat in the passenger seat and looked over to see the speedometer creep past seventy, sometimes past eighty. The times I'd seen Ellis accelerate suddenly and jump into the left lane, setting off a symphony of angry horns. The way he drove in New York City, aggressive as a cabdriver, squeezing through impossible openings, ignoring all road markings. It was our recurrent fight. He was going too fast; he would get a ticket; he was scaring me. Which always got the same answer, often with the drama of him screeching to the shoulder and turning off the car. *Then why don't you drive?*

It was Ellis, all right. But when had he gotten the points? Where were the tickets? How come I didn't know anything about this?

I turned the letter over and over, as if it were some kind of Rubik's Cube whose pieces would fall into place if I simply looked at it the right way. Still, there was no answer. I picked up the phone and called the hotel in California, but of course, Ellis wasn't in his room. He never was. Odd, though. It wasn't even seven, local time. I left a message in my sternest voice, telling him to call home immediately.

Charlotte was practicing piano in the next room, still stuck in an endless succession of scales and arpeggios. That was the girl's nature, a doggedness I'd always admired. Unless we were away on vacation somewhere without a piano, Charlotte never missed a day. She never even skipped the boring parts. She hammered out each scale until she'd mastered it, and then moved on to her actual pieces, which she had to play perfectly, too. Sometimes practice, which was only supposed to take half an hour, turned into two hours.

I'd been busying myself with household chores while I waited for the phone to ring. The kitchen shone, the Tupperware was organized, I was folding the last load of laundry. I was too preoccupied to try anything creative, too agitated to do anything relaxing. The piano was giving me a headache.

For the past hour, I'd tried my best to block out the incessant do-re-mi-fa-so-la-ti-do of Charlotte's scales, ungraceful and heavy-handed. It was obvious all the practice in the world was never going to amount to anything approaching talent. I was matching up socks. Each note landed on my brain like a hammer.

"Charlotte!" I shouted.

She stopped midscale and turned around. "What?"

"Please stop."

"Why?" She looked like a puppy that had just been whacked with a newspaper. She was just doing what she was supposed to do, practicing diligently.

"Please. I have a headache."

If it had been Lily, instead of Charlotte, she'd have said, *Who told you to listen? Why don't you go upstairs?* But it was Charlotte, the good one, the easy one, the one who never even *thought* about giving lip.

She pulled the lid down on the keyboard—not quite a slam, but harder than usual—then pushed the piano bench and marched up to her bedroom.

It wasn't fair, I knew. I was mad at Ellis but had yelled at Charlotte.

I went back to the socks, but the silence of the piano just made the questions in my head louder. Why was this coming as a surprise? When did he get these tickets? Why hadn't he told me? And, if he could hide this from me, what else could he hide?

"What's wrong?"

Ellis called the next morning at 10 A.M., twenty-four hours after my first call to him, ten hours since I'd ransacked his drawers and his closet, twelve since I'd called Sheba, frustrated and desperate, twenty since I'd yelled at Charlotte. He apologized for not getting back sooner, explaining that he'd been in meetings *all day* yesterday and stuck at a dinner until eleven and hadn't heard my messages until it was well past 2 A.M., my time. I left so many messages, he'd thought about calling, but just couldn't bring himself to, because of the hour. He said he had a hard time falling asleep, wondering what it was that had me so upset.

"*You* had trouble sleeping?" I sneered. Ellis could fall sleep riding a bicycle. I was the family's designated insomniac, the one who knew our house at every hour of day and night. I knew every bump of the heat vents, every trickle in the girls' bathroom. I was the family worrier. Ellis never worried about anything. It was me who'd been up all night, waiting for his call, wondering what else he hadn't told me.

"Yes," he said. "Yes, I did."

"Poor you."

"Ivy, what's wrong?"

"Car insurance is what's wrong! State assigned risk pool is

what's wrong! Seven points! Over six thousand dollars for car insurance!"

"What?"

"Don't 'what' me! Tell me, when did you get seven points on your license?"

There was silence. I could hear Ellis sigh all the way across the country. And then, I could have sworn, it sounded like a shower going on behind him.

"What's that?" I said.

"What's what?"

"The shower?"

"You're hearing things."

"Then tell me about the points."

He sighed again, and finally confessed to a car accident in L.A. in 1995. And a drunk-driving rap. "But I was only point-one over the legal limit. And it was fixed by the best lawyers money could buy."

"So how come you're over the points limit?"

"A couple more speeding tickets in California."

"And how come I never heard about them? Shouldn't something have come to the house?"

"When I rent the car, I do it through my company, so the ticket goes there."

"And you didn't tell me?"

"I knew you'd be mad."

"And you thought I'd never find out?" I shouted. "You thought it would just go away? That there would be no consequences?" *Consequences.* A parenting word. We didn't dole out punishments to our kids anymore. There were *consequences* for inappropriate behavior.

"I'm sorry."

"I bet you are."

Silence.

"You're such a little boy." I slammed down the phone. But the satisfaction of hanging up on him lasted only a second.

At least I'd had a second's worth of satisfaction. In fact, for the whole conversation, I'd held the high ground. It had been quite the opposite when I called Sheba the night before.

I didn't know exactly what I'd expected when I called her. It was more like a lashing out, the way you'd call the mother of the bully who tormented your kid on the bus. I wanted Sheba to condemn Ellis for his driving record, to be shocked at his lack of honesty with me, to offer to pay for the increase in car insurance, which was going up through no fault of mine. And, in complete contradiction to my murderous rage, I also wanted her to assure me that Ellis wasn't dead, even though I'd been calling him, unsuccessfully, for hours. I sobbed it all out, half-shouting, half-crying, wiping the snot from my nose with my fist. When I'd finished, I sniffled, waiting for some words of comfort.

I was met by a silence that was so cold, I almost thought I'd lost the telephone connection.

Finally she spoke. "I don't know why you're calling me with this."

My face suddenly felt incredibly flushed, hot, red, as if she'd reached through the telephone receiver and slapped me. I didn't know what words I could add to those I'd already tried. Was she saying I had no right to be mad at her son, or just that it didn't concern her?

"He's your son," I sputtered.

"He's your husband." Her voice was controlled, steady, and I suddenly understood the legendary family story about how, when her boys were little and came to her in tears, Sheba would offer a tissue instead of a hug. No doubt if I was sitting in her study now, she'd hand me the tissue box. Her proxy for human warmth.

I wanted to engage her, to fight with her, to convince her that my problems were her problems, but knew instinctively that if I did, I would lose. She was a queen, sitting on her throne, high above the world, passing judgment. I had come before her, a sniveling supplicant, crawling on my belly. In fact, I realized, I'd already lost. I'd lost the minute I picked up the phone.

"Do you think he's okay?" I said. Even if she wouldn't get angry on my behalf, maybe she'd share my concern about the fact that I hadn't been able to reach Ellis for twelve hours.

"No news is good news," she said simply.

I wondered how Ellis had survived a childhood with this woman. And though my pity dissipated over the hours I waited for him to call me back, a part of me understood how he might have learned to hide unpleasant facts from the women in his life.

Later that day, when I came home from grocery shopping, there was a box of flowers—two dozen long-stemmed red roses, it turned out—on the front porch. The card said, LOVE FROM LOS ANGELES.

At first I reacted automatically. I smiled. I walked over to the china cabinet, took out my tallest vase, and walked back to the kitchen to fill it. I even got out a pair of sturdy scissors to cut the stems. Then I put down the scissors. What did the roses symbolize? I asked myself. What was Ellis trying to do here? Obviously, they symbolized contrition. But he couldn't even bring himself to use the words *I'm sorry*. What kind of apology was that? A cowardly one, I decided. An expensive one. And perhaps worst of all, a trite one. Red roses? Could he have found a more predictable flower? How long had it taken him to think of it? Two seconds? Had he even ordered them himself, or had he gotten a secretary to do it? That would explain the impersonal LOVE FROM LOS ANGELES.

I emptied the water, dried the vase, returned it to the cabinet, then took the whole box out to the side of the house and stashed it next to the garbage cans.

The next morning, I had to take out some trash and I smelled the sickly sweet smell of roses decomposing. I took glum satisfaction in picturing them turning to a blood-colored mush inside the box, in knowing that I hadn't allowed Ellis to buy me off.

I considered calling my mother, knowing I'd certainly get a more sympathetic reaction from her than I had from Sheba. But every time I started to dial, I stopped. She'd be too sympathetic. She'd take my side in a heartbeat, then condemn Ellis so vigorously, I'd wonder why I married him in the first place. It was so unlike Dad, she'd never understand it. Getting fired by your insurance company? Paying more than six thousand dollars in insurance?

In the end, it would wind up being an indictment of every choice I'd ever made in my adult life: moving up North, living in New Jersey, picking a life partner who wasn't Daddy. They'd had a good marriage, as far as I knew, but after his death, he'd become Saint Jack. Ellis couldn't measure up under the best of circumstances. This would be a slaughter.

It was Daddy, I realized, who would have been the one to comfort me. He'd have been thoughtful and steady, understanding my distress but sympathetic to Ellis as well. He wouldn't approve of Ellis's driving record, but he'd find the silver lining. At least his recklessness wasn't being punished by something worse. Like a crash. *If this is the worst thing that happens, you're one lucky girl,* he'd have said. *Some people never learn until it's too late.*

I cried, thinking how unfair it was that my father, Mr. Safety, had been the one to die in a car accident.

The girls, sensitive to my mood, inhabited the house more quietly. They'd heard me yell and slam the phone. They'd seen me crying. When they asked what was going on, I just said, "Grown-up stuff, nothing that concerns you." They kept to their rooms, edging carefully around me, the way you'd avoid a strange and unpredictable dog.

It was the last Thursday in the month, and if it hadn't been for the fact that everybody in the universe was away in Maine, it would have been the night for book group. The only other person around was Rita.

We'd been best friends ever since my first playgroup, when Rita's son Cody and Lily were just toddlers. Over the years, I'd lost track of the other moms. Once we'd exhausted the subjects of nursery schools and pediatricians, there wasn't much left to talk about. But Rita was different. Even after Cody and Lily wanted nothing to do with each other, we remained friends. Rita had an outsized personality. Her laugh was so loud, it caused people to turn around in restaurants. She broke all the rules of suburban etiquette, said exactly what was on her mind, and might have been shunned by just about every woman in town except for two things. She had a hot tub in her backyard, and she loved to invite people over in the middle of the winter to enjoy the hot fudge sundae effect of experiencing extreme heat and extreme cold at the same time. And she was an Avon distributor with a corner on the local market for Skin So Soft.

Rita called Thursday morning to suggest a girl's night out, just the two of us, since there was no book club.

"I don't know," I said. I was wilted by the August heat, and sulking about Ellis. I still hadn't told her about the insurance letter, or the phone call to Sheba, or the flowers. Anything.

"The Office has two-for-one margaritas," she said.

"Too fattening."

"There's the hot tub."

"In this weather?"

"I'll give you a whole makeover."

There were advantages to being best friends with the only Avon dealer in town. It might be adolescent, but there were times when all you wanted was to have someone try out new shades of lipstick on you. Besides, maybe I'd get some beauty tips to prepare for my Saturday adventure with Hamish. Something to chop, oh, ten or fifteen years off my age. I hadn't mentioned that to Rita, either. In fact, I was so angry all week, I'd barely had time to think about it.

"Okay," I said. It would be good for me to get out of the house and talk to someone over the age of thirteen.

"I'll pick up Thai food," she said. "And I'll tell you about my new job."

"New job?"

"Tonight."

I'd left the girls a well-balanced meal of chicken, peas, and mashed potatoes and instructions to clean up the kitchen and go to bed at a "decent" hour. There wasn't much point in enforcing a strict bedtime—there was nothing they had to wake up for the next day—but I was still worried about the transition to school hours the next week. A perfect example of my ineffectual parenting. The experts said "set firm limits." I gave instructions that tax lawyers could debate for hours.

But once I walked into Rita's refreshingly frigid house—it was like walking into the freezer aisle of ShopRite—I perked up. Parenting? Children? What children? My nose sucked in a fragrant mixture of lemongrass and cilantro. Rita was reheating some soup in the microwave. Thai food was still pretty new to me. Ellis and I had been to a Thai restaurant once, but we'd never just picked it up to bring home. I wouldn't have even known what to order.

Rita opened the freezer and took out two frosted mugs. Then she opened two bottles of beer. "Sit," she ordered.

"I'm not a beer drinker," I reminded her.

She pulled a lime from the fridge, cut it into wedges, squeezed one into my mug, handing it to me like medicine. "It's Thai beer. I had to go to three different stores to find it."

"Okay." I let the mug sit there. I would have preferred Diet Coke.

I stabbed my fork into a pile of crispy noodles garnished with shrimp. As soon as I tasted it, my eyes opened wide. It was sweet, almost cloyingly so, but also savory. Fish sauce and sugar, something spicy, something tomatoey. Not like Chinese sweet-and-sour, infinitely more nuanced. I took another bite, then a third, not wanting to stop, but conscious that the pile of noodles was fairly small.

"What?" I said simply, pointing at the dish. I'd been reduced to monosyllables.

Rita smiled. She'd pulled me out of my sour mood in a record five minutes. "Mee krob."

"Oh my God. I think it's the best thing I've ever tasted." Having entered the kingdom of heaven, I sat back and took a swig of beer. "So, what's the new job?"

"Funeral home," she said.

Beer sprayed from my mouth and I started coughing.

"You really *aren't* a beer person."

Maybe I hadn't heard her right. "Funeral home?"

"Doing makeup, of course."

I stared at her.

"It's great hours. I can work at night. And the pay is fantastic."

"Have you heard of Elizabeth Arden? Clinique? The Short Hills Mall? You couldn't put makeup on *live* people?"

"I could," she said. "And I do. But the dead deserve to look good, too."

I suddenly understood. She was goofing on me. Cheering me up. She knew how tired and cranky I got when Ellis was gone on a long trip. I smiled knowingly. "I get it," I said. "You're joking, right?"

"Nope."

She walked over to a Lucite cookbook holder crammed with menus, recipes, L.L. Bean catalogs and school lists, and pulled out a Polaroid photo. She slid it across the table.

I looked. There was a woman, sixty, maybe sixty-five years old, eyes closed, hands folded over her chest. But for the fact that she was wearing glasses, she could have been sleeping. Well, that and the coffin. Suddenly I recognized Mrs. Herr, a reference librarian who'd yelled at me a few months ago for reshelving *Writer's Digest* in the wrong place.

I flicked the Polaroid away like a gigantic bug. "Ew, Rita!"

It was creepy, to say the least. Death, pulled so casually from among the Chinese food menus. Mrs. Herr without the animating force of life. Morbid. Freakish. It disturbed me to think about the nomenclature, how someone could turn so suddenly from a "person" into a "body," or worse yet, "remains." I pictured myself driving out to Culvers Lake on Saturday, down I-78, plodding along in the right lane, and a gigantic fuel truck merging onto the highway. A misunderstanding. He expects me to slow down or move to the center lane. I speed up. A huge explosion, like a bomb, with smoke rising so high, it can be seen for miles. And then me on a slab, at a funeral home, my face charred beyond even Rita's handiwork.

I thought about Rita, in the basement of a funeral home at night, applying makeup to Mrs. Herr while listening to the radio. What would she have on? Classical music? Rock? The radio shrink? How could she be so nonchalant?

I thought about my dad for the second time that day. But this time, rather than thinking about his ability to comfort, it was the physical reality of his death. I thought of his body, or what was left of it. *The worms go in; the worms go out; the worms play pinochle on your snout.*

I put down my fork. "I think I've lost my appetite."

"Come on. It's just a dead person."

"It's *Mrs. Herr.* Look at my face. It's green, right?"

"Makeover?"

"I *definitely* don't want the makeover." I suddenly shivered. "That makeup, your brushes, the lipstick. Do they touch . . . ?"

"Of course not," she said. "I have a whole separate kit."

"Still. I can't get the image out of my head."

"Hot tub?"

But it didn't matter what she pulled out of her bag of tricks. For Rita, life was a Fourth of July barbecue. Hot dogs! Fudge! Brass bands! She saw every day as an opportunity to gather treats and share them with her friends. On today's menu: mee krob, Thai beer, makeup, hot tub. Inadvertently, she'd served up death. For her, that didn't spoil the barbecue. For me, it did.

"I think I need to lie down."

She unjollied herself, in deference to me, then led me into the family room. After settling me on the sofa and fussing with the pillows, she stared at me like a painting that needed straightening, trying to figure out what I needed next.

"Can I get you some tea?"

I thought of Peter Rabbit drinking chamomile tea after being chased from Mr. McGregor's garden and nodded.

She came back a little while later with a tray, a pot of hot water, a teacup, milk, sugar, and a choice of herbal teas. I had to admit: She didn't do anything halfway. The only thing missing was a floral tablecloth. I found some chamomile and dunked it in the hot water. "Please," I pleaded, "don't tell me any more about the job. Or show me any more pictures."

"Okay, then. What's new with you?"

It poured out: the insurance letter, Ellis's points, the dead roses still in the box by the side of the house.

"That little shit," she said loyally.

"Yeah." Deep sigh. "I keep wishing he had some of his *own* money to pay this insurance out of. Instead of *our* money. It doesn't seem fair."

"I know."

"I even called his mother."

"Why?"

"I don't know. I guess I was sort of tattletaling."

"How did it go?"

"Terrible. She made me feel like an idiot."

She shook her head. "It's funny, though. It just doesn't seem like Ellis. Hiding something like that."

It was true. It didn't seem like Ellis. It was strange. You were married for years and you thought you knew everything about a person. You shared a mortgage, a bank account, a bedroom, a phone number, *children*. You knew his social security number, his favorite flavor of ice cream, what kind of pillow he preferred. And yet, out of the blue, something hidden. Something the state of California knew, the state of New Jersey knew, the insurance companies knew. Everybody but you.

I'd been obsessed with the insurance letter all week. But it was Rita saying *It just doesn't seem like Ellis* that upset me most. She was right. It didn't seem like Ellis.

Finally, I mentioned my dinner with Hamish on Saturday. I tried to make it sound casual. I didn't mention that Hamish lived out in the country. That it was an hour drive. *On a highway.* (She was my best friend. She knew the lengths I'd go to avoid driving on highways.) I omitted the fact that whenever I thought about Hamish, I felt something go all squishy in my chest. That I felt like I was thirteen again.

"He's the hunky one, right?"

I swallowed. "We're just going to discuss the school year coming up."

Rita smiled a knowing smile, which reminded me of the wolf in "Little Red Riding Hood." "It looks like Ellis isn't the only one in the Halpern family with a secret," she said.

I got home around ten-thirty and expected to find the girls sound asleep, but I heard a noise coming from the kitchen. The refrigerator door opening, closing again. That sweet, satisfying thwack of rubber locking into more rubber. Well, someone was up. Probably hungry.

I walked in and saw Charlotte standing in front of the fridge, a plastic container in her hand, looking like a thief caught midheist.

"Hungry, honey?"

She shook her head. Her shoulders began to tremble and she stared at her feet. I recognized it as her confessional mode; the quivering was an attempt to stave off tears. She'd done something wrong, at least something she considered wrong or bad. Whatever it was, though, I knew it was nothing. It's so sad when the good feel guilty.

Finally she confessed. She'd forgotten to put the chicken away after dinner. Even though I'd reminded her. She'd practiced piano, watched TV, and hadn't remembered until she'd walked into the kitchen around nine-thirty to get some water for next to her bed.

"So you put it away then?" I asked.

Her face got all rubbery. "Yes, but"—the waterworks began—"you're always telling us about food poisoning. *E. coli* and salmonella and stuff. And it had been *sitting* there."

I took the plastic container out of her hands, opened it, and gave it a sniff. "It smells okay."

"But germs are *invisible*," she cried. "And they don't always smell bad!"

"Okay, then, we'll throw it out." I put the container on the counter and pulled Charlotte's head toward my chest. I breathed her in, the clean smell of whatever shampoo she was using these days. I felt her sink into me, relax. It was nice to have the power to comfort somebody. But, oh boy. I'd raised another worrier, another Ivy.

Charlotte pulled her head away suddenly and looked up. "Oh yeah, and Daddy called."

"He did?" I wasn't sure how I felt about that. If it had been anybody but Charlotte, I might have said, *Oh yeah, what did the jerk want?* I was still furious. I thought I might always be furious. At the same time, part of me was grateful. He wasn't usually so solicitous when he was in L.A. for business, calling for no special reason on a Thursday night. Usually I had to call him.

"He asked how we liked the flowers."

I had to stifle a smile. "And what did you say?"

"I said, 'What flowers?'"

I pictured Ellis sputtering then, wondering if his secretary had sent the flowers after all, or if the flower company had fucked up.

"He sounded confused."

"I bet he did," I said. "I bet he did."


Friday morning, I got a New Jersey map out of the car, brought it to my room, closed the door, and studied it. Hamish had given me highway directions to his "cottage," as he called it, but I wasn't going to take the highway. I began to map out an elaborate route of back roads. By the time I was through, my route had twenty-eight turns. I thought I could manage getting there, but what about the trip back? It would be dark. Maybe I'd have had some wine. I pictured myself driving through the night, the directions pressed against the steering wheel, a miniature flashlight clamped between my lips. It felt dangerous. Exceedingly dangerous. Well, that was the one great advantage of being a coward. Everything was a thrill. Who needed roller coasters?

Maybe I should cancel. I'd already left the girls home alone once this week, and look what a state Charlotte had been in when I got back. And now—with us in the high-risk motorists pool— what if I got in an accident? Funny, what bothered me now, even more than the idea of death, was the thought of getting another letter and learning that our insurance had gone up yet again. Maybe that was progress, having my fear response go all bureaucratic on me. Maybe just a sign of middle age, to be more worried about money than about death.

But I wasn't going to cancel. I couldn't see myself going up to Hamish and telling him I'd chickened out. I wanted his admiration. Hell, I wanted to be a grown-up, the kind of person who could accept an invitation to a cool little farmhouse in the country without turning it into a huge production. Besides, Hamish was a great writer. A genius. This could be a once-in-a-lifetime deal. I didn't want to read years later that Hamish McDonough had won the Nobel Prize in Literature and have to say to my grandchildren, *I knew him once. He invited me over to his house for dinner, but I didn't go. . . .*

I wrote the directions out in neat block lettering. I drew the route in yellow highlighter the way AAA did. I practiced folding up the map and unfolding it. I did everything an honor student would do faced with a challenging assignment. I overstudied.

Regression. For the third time in two days, I thought of my father. I remembered how he coached me to ride a bike, running alongside and assuring me everything would be okay. I imagined him running alongside my car, shouting the same assurances.

I wasn't the kind of gal who could jump in her car and drive out to the country without a second thought. I also wasn't the kind of gal who could just slip on a pair of jeans and high heels, or even flip-flops, and exude an effortless sexiness.

I knew who was: Bailey.

That was the problem, wasn't it? It wasn't just today, this minute, now, this week, worries about Ellis, an invitation from a future Nobel Prize winner, the number on the scale. It was me. Imprisoned in a tower of pitiless self-examination and fear. Why was it that Bailey looked up and saw a blue sky? The sun was always smiling down on her. For me, it just cast shadows.

I would get in an accident, I would die, our insurance would go up, and to top it all off, I would look fat. Rita, at the undertaker's, would look at my body and shake her head. *She should have taken better care of herself.*

Half my wardrobe was spread over the bed. My yellow sundress (a stain over the right breast), my white shorts (too tight, too short), my French blue pedal pushers (too eager), my comfortable jeans (too sloppy), my tight jeans (uncomfortable). Should I bring a bathing suit for the canoe? A second outfit in case I got wet? It was hard enough to find a first outfit.

There was a light knock on the door and Charlotte came in.

She pushed aside a pile of clothes and jumped up on the bed. "Okay," she said. "I'm ready for my instructions!" I looked over to see a pencil and a notebook on her lap.

I swapped an orange T-shirt for a red button-down. "Instructions?"

"For tonight. Babysitting?"

Charlotte opened up to a printed form in her notebook, which I now recognized from her Red Cross babysitting course. She pointed the business end of her pencil toward me. "First," she said, "what's the number you can be reached at while I'm babysitting?"

"Oh, darling, I have it somewhere. I'll write it down before you leave."

"Next," she said, "how much does Lily weigh?"

"How much does Lily *weigh*?"

"Yeah, just in case. I don't know. In case she swallows something poisonous and I have to call the poison control hotline or something like that."

"Oh my God, Charlotte. This is your own sister. I really don't think we have to get so formal, do we?"

She ignored my question. " 'What are the household rules? How do you want me to handle misbehavior?' "

"Charlotte, honey," I said. "This is your own house. You know the household rules."

She put the eraser in her mouth. Her eyebrows were knit with worry. "I'd prefer if they were spelled out."

"Okay." I sighed. "No food in the living room. No fighting. Bedtime by ten."

"Why ten? It's Saturday night."

"Right," I said. "Midnight, then. But I'm sure I'll be home long before that."

She looked down at the notebook and read aloud. " 'Does your family have a fire escape plan? If not, can you have one in place before I begin?' "

"Charlotte." I was starting to get exasperated. "Here's our fire escape plan: If there's a fire, escape."

"Mom, I'm serious."

"Charlotte, why are you doing this?" Accidental poisoning? A house fire? Clearly, Charlotte—or at least the Red Cross—had foreseen dangers that hadn't even occurred to me. But why now? Why when I was struggling to find an outfit? Ellis and I had left Charlotte in charge dozens of times in the past year. We'd gone to dinner, movies. Even New Year's Eve. She'd never pulled out the Red Cross babysitting guidebook before. I'd have understood if she was going, for the first time, to babysit an *infant*. But this was her own sister, her own house. All she had to do was watch television and not answer the door until I got home.

She closed the notebook and stared at the clothes scattered everywhere. I knew how bad it looked. Like a single mom getting ready to go on a date.

"I don't want to make another mistake," she said finally.

"Another mistake? Like what? What was the first mistake?"

"Not putting away the chicken."

"Oh, honey," I said. "We'll order pizza, okay? I'll order it now. It'll be here before I leave. You won't even have to pay the pizza guy."

From outside the door, we heard a small shout—"Pizza!

Yay!"—and Lily rushed in. She jumped on the bed, stood up, and started using it as a trampoline.

"Lily, what in the world are you doing?" I said.

"Pizza dance!"

I put my hand in front of my mouth to hide my smile, because I didn't want to encourage her. Yet the notion of a pizza dance was so joyous—so *Lily*—I couldn't help myself. When she'd exhausted herself and finally folded into a panting heap on the bed, she took in the whole scene, all the clothes dumped everywhere, and pointed at a brown gauze dress that was hanging on the back of my closet door. "Wear that," she said decisively.

She was, of course, absolutely right. The brown dress was flattering, showed off my tan, hid my stomach and my thighs. Bailey Jr.

Poor Charlotte was still sitting there with her Red Cross notebook, a natural relief worker, ready to take responsibility for all the world's calamities. I wanted to comfort her, to tell her that forgetting to put away the chicken was nothing, that she didn't have to be so hyper-responsible. Life wasn't a jungle she had to hack through with a machete. It was—as Lily had so elegantly demonstrated—a pizza dance. But I didn't have time. I had to order the pizza, pick shoes, put on makeup. Besides, Charlotte wouldn't have believed me anyway.

By the time I'd dressed, done my makeup, ordered pizza, reassured Charlotte, located my keys, gathered my directions, and found a bottle of wine, I was already an hour behind schedule. Each delay made me more agitated. My neck was getting tight. I could feel a backache starting. At this point, just three hours before sunset, a one-hour jaunt out to the country felt more like a suicide mission than a social call. I was like Lestat from Anne Rice's *Interview with the Vampire,* who had to rush back to his coffin before the sun came up—only in reverse. I had to race back home before the sun set. Even though I knew it was futile, I was hoping to get my dinner with Hamish over and done with early so I wouldn't have to drive home in the dark. I looked again at my watch. It was impossible. To leave before dusk, I'd have to turn around as soon as I got there.

In the back of my mind, I could hear Ellis making fun of me. "You know, there's a fancy new invention. It's called headlights."

My heartbeat quickening, I started to think of plausible reasons to cancel. I could say one of the kids was sick, or that the car had a dead battery. I could pretend I had a fever. Yet I knew Hamish would see through every one of my bogus excuses, the same way he shot down implausible plot developments. My only out was confessing the truth. Admitting that I was a complete and total wimp.

I couldn't. I just couldn't.

I looked at my elaborate directions again. I'd scrawled *R*s and *L*s up and down a long sheet of legal paper. State road this ran into state road that, which turned around the bend into state road something else altogether. It seemed increasingly probable that in attempting to circumvent the U.S. highway system, I'd done nothing but construct an elaborate corn maze. Just one missing road sign, and I'd be out in the middle of nowhere, utterly lost, the dark gathering, passing nothing but cornfields until I ran out of gas.

I'd be forced to lock the car and sleep in it until morning. Hamish would wonder why I hadn't showed up. Charlotte would be certain I was dead.

I was cornered, caught between fear and pride. There was only one thing to do: get up my courage and take to the highway.

I took a deep breath, just the same way I did when I confronted any unpleasantness, like going to the dentist. Then I adjusted my mirrors and took off for the Garden State Parkway, following the directions Hamish had given me in the first place.

The Garden State Parkway is, luckily, like training wheels for the highway phobe. Trucks aren't allowed. So even if I did crash when I merged into the flow of traffic, I wasn't going to crash into an oil tanker. I feared the Garden State Parkway, it was true, and over the years had found elaborate ways to circumvent it. But I didn't fear it nearly as much as the Turnpike. I even had to admit that it was pretty in places, especially as it curled through the verdant landscape on the way to the beach.

And I was in luck. When I got through the tollbooth, I looked to my left and found a nice big hole in the stream of traffic. After all my ruminations about merging, it was surprisingly easy. Nobody slammed their brakes. Nobody flipped me the bird. "Yes," I said aloud, to nobody, making a little power fist. "Yes!" You might have thought I'd scaled a skyscraper.

Then I took the next daring step: taking my eyes off the road for a split second in order to find the FM button on the radio. I turned the dial until I came upon music, something by Bruce Springsteen, found myself tapping the steering wheel along with the beat. As if I were the kind of person who drove on highways with the radio blaring! What was next? Buying a convertible? Wearing high heels? I glanced in the mirror, and there she was, a stranger—myself!—wearing sunglasses, driving a car, and smiling. It was nothing short of amazing.

Suddenly it came to me: I was channeling Bailey.

*Okay,* I thought, *I'll channel Bailey.* It might do me some good to channel Bailey. Just like it would do Charlotte some good to channel Lily, to jump on the bed and do a pizza dance. I was doing my version of a pizza dance: driving off to the country on the last weekend of summer.

And maybe, while I was at it, I could channel some other things about Bailey. Her sexiness, for example. Maybe I could swing my hips a little, or copy her sultry little pout. I pictured Bailey throwing back a glass of wine and then stretching a languid arm across the table to get a refill, positioning her cleavage for maximum effect. I tried to imagine myself doing that. Or just sashaying a little as I walked from my car to Hamish's little cottage. My luck, I'd trip and fall on the gravel. Oh God, how ridiculous. He'd see through me in a second. He'd see through me and laugh. I didn't think I could bear the idea of Hamish laughing at me.

Then an even scarier idea came to me: What if he didn't laugh? What if he took me seriously? What if he enveloped me in an embrace, kissed my lips, touched my thighs under my dress? What if there was undressing and condoms?

I felt, suddenly, a flush between my legs—oh my God, sexual desire, where had *that* come from?—and then, right after it, guilt. Ah, my old friend guilt. Even as a kid, I had a highly developed sense of right and wrong, particularly wrong. I was the kid who, when the teacher turned to the class with a stern face and wanted to know who was responsible for throwing that piece of chalk at her back and if someone didn't confess, we'd *all* miss recess for a week, raised my hand out of the pure agony of *knowing*. I didn't have to be the one who threw the chalk to experience the full, sickening burden of self-reproach. Nor did I have to actually betray my wedding vows. No, just thinking about it activated my guilty conscience.

And then, suddenly, the easy part of the journey was over. I took the off-ramp, slowed down for the tollbooth, and gulped as I looked down to the highway I was approaching, I-78. This was not the Parkway. Massive tractor-trailers rampaged down the highway like mighty elephants, ready to mow down the slower, dumber animals in their path. I almost squeezed my eyes shut, the way I did when Ellis got too close to another car, before I remembered that I was the one behind the steering wheel. I hung back in the merge lane, letting two monster trucks barrel past, just feet away, so large and so close, I could feel metal rattling. Then, timidly, like a shy student raising her hand for the first time in class, I poked out into the flow of traffic.

There's an almost postapocalyptic ugliness to 78 where it meets the Parkway. It's an unremitting span of concrete, with no shade or scenery to offer any solace. The only vegetation you notice are the weeds spiking out of the highway dividers. It's bad enough in winter, this highway, but in August, the bleak, shadeless landscape makes you feel like you're in a desert. Adding to the horror are the black rubber slivers of truck tires that show up on the shoulder.

Blowouts, you remember. A whole new category of highway disaster to think about.

And yet, after a while, it all begins to be quite normal. You look at the speedometer and you see that you are going fifty-five. Thrillingly, you allow the needle to edge up just a little higher: now fifty-seven, now fifty-eight, now sixty-one. You're driving so fast, at least in coward's terms, that there is no margin of error. One tiny mistake, and you'll be thrown onto the asphalt, squashed dead like a bug. And yet the cars next to you whiz by even faster. The cars behind pass you one by one. Everybody is impatient. Even when you are going the speed limit, even when you're *exceeding* the speed limit, the whole world is rolling its eyes.

I glanced at Hamish's map, kept an eye on the exit numbers, listened to music. With relief, but not so much relief as I would have expected, I exited the highway and followed the country roads that led, finally, to the little gravel road he'd described. There were no house numbers, but I knew immediately it was Hamish's house—he called it a cottage—because of his description. A yellow saltbox with yellow roses climbing a trellis to the right of the door. Lovely. Subtle, the yellow on yellow. Much more original than the embalmed red roses Ellis had sent. The roses told a whole story, I thought. They epitomized the difference between these two men. Hamish was authentic. His roses grew from the earth; they had thorns; they could draw blood. Ellis had, over the years, become just like his company Amex card. Ellis and his roses were just the same: plastic.

Hamish's truck was out front. Against all cultural norms, he drove a pickup. He seemed to like to think of himself as some kind of cowboy, to enjoy the stares of fellow faculty members when he clunked up to one of their cocktail parties in his mud-splattered Laredo. I'd never seen him in cowboy boots. That would have been taking it too far. Still, he might have gotten away with it.

Two loud barking Labs jumped on me as soon as I got out of the wagon. So much for sashaying sexily up to Hamish's door. I put my hand out, as tentatively as I'd merged onto 78, trying to pretend that big strange dogs didn't fill me with dread. One put its snout straight up to my crotch. I imagined it taking a great big bite out of my private parts, punishment for my ruminations about adultery. I held up the wine bottle in my right hand, conscious that it looked like a weapon.

Hamish opened the door and laughed at the spectacle. "Shelley! Byron! Down!" He rushed to take the bottle out of my hand and gave me a chaste kiss on the cheek. "I forgot to ask, are you afraid of dogs?"

"A little late now." I smiled. I was going for cute, sassy, Myrna Loy. Still a reach, but closer to my real personality than Bailey. "Shelley? Byron?" I raised my eyebrows.

I was relieved when we went into the house and Shelley and Byron relaxed into docile, lumbering beasts and lay down on a big round plaid pillow. I stood in the living room, adjusting my eyes to the light, looking around, collecting and classifying the clues. It all felt strangely familiar, like I'd been here before. The bamboo shades, the coffee table made out of big wooden cable reel, books piled everywhere, record albums—vinyl—stacked in plastic grocery crates. A bong. Then I had it. It was the bong that triggered the recognition. Nick's house, outside Charlottesville. And not just

Nick, but everybody from that time. All the houses of all our friends. They'd all had this flavor, slouchy and sloppy and yet slyly smart. Eventually, someone had given it a name: shabby chic. I noticed an open laptop on Hamish's coffee table. That was the main difference. Back in the day, it would have been a typewriter.

"Want a tour?" Hamish said. I nodded and he led me into a modest country kitchen with open cabinets, an old-fashioned linoleum floor, and a chrome-edged red table that looked like it had been stolen from a diner. We passed a tiny bathroom, and then he opened the door and gestured to his bedroom. The room was insanely small, like something you'd rent in the Adirondacks, with just about enough room for a double bed and a single dresser. A guitar lay on the bed. There was a thin quilt, so worn, it was shiny.

We returned to the living room and sat down. Hamish might have offered me a drink, but I heard nothing. I was too busy in my own thoughts. Time traveling, back to an era when I wore tube tops and smoked pot daily, when sex was no big deal and my parents were certain I was ruining my life. It was before the era of acquisition, before mortgages, homeowners insurance, parent–teacher conferences, window treatments, book group. Before my Macy's credit card. I still shopped Goodwill and Salvation Army in those days, and everything I possessed in life could fit in my car. I was suddenly jealous of Byron and Shelley. I wanted to fall in a lazy heap and live with Hamish, too.

Suddenly I was aware of Hamish looking at me. "I just asked if you wanted something to drink." He studied me with concern, as if I'd lost consciousness, which I guess in a way I had.

I turned back to the room. Something was missing, but I

couldn't figure it out. Then it came to me. "You don't have a television!"

"I basically prefer the nineteenth century," he said. "More time to read."

I looked over at a deep green armchair next to a floor lamp. It was the kind of lamp popular in the 1960s, with a little round table built in at arm level. The lamp table was piled with books, many so old, they had hard covers but no dust jackets. I noticed Roth, Mailer, Dreyfus, Barthelme, Styron, Woolf, and a couple of the Russians. More books sat in uneven stacks all around the chair. I'd always wondered why Hamish lived so far out in the country, about the two hours he lost commuting, but now that I could picture him reading, I could see the appeal. Here, in this little cottage, you could forget you lived in New Jersey, or even in the twentieth century. Time stretched out into something approaching infinity.

I pointed to the laptop. "What about that?"

"Oh yes, well, everybody has a weakness, I guess." He smiled. The word *winsome* popped into my head.

I was startled when I looked closer and noticed that the laptop was an Apple. I didn't know anybody who had one. I heard the only people who did lived in California.

"Let me get some lemonade," Hamish said. He returned a few minutes later with two mismatched coffee mugs and put them on the table. No need for coasters.

Then he pointed to the bong. "Want some?"

Boy, did I. It had been years. I hadn't smoked pot since . . . since I'd lived in the city. Since Bill Bennett had become the first drug czar. Since I'd had kids. Years ago it had come to me that if I was caught, they could take away Charlotte and Lily. Since then, I'd practically forgotten that marijuana existed. I remembered it, now, as something that gave me interesting thoughts, one idea leading to another like a widening circle of ripples on a lake. What had happened to all those ideas? Were they all subsumed by my growing collection of neuroses? It was like something out of *1984*. *Make her straight. Make her afraid. Take all the drugs you want, honey, as long as they're sold by Big Pharma.* Now that I was no longer subversive, I was a basket case. I'd never made that connection before.

I shook my head and smiled. "No, no, I'm going to have to drive."

"It dissipates in two hours," he said, his sentence rising at the end, full of all kinds of possibilities.

"Okay." In for a dime, in for a dollar. I'd already driven on two highways. Why the hell not?

The person who came out after I smoked the pot was different from the one who'd torn up her closet looking for just the right outfit. Different from the one who hunched over a map with a yellow highlighter, determined to avoid highways. Different even from the one who'd slid right onto the Parkway and tapped her fingers to the radio.

It was like, after smoking the pot, I didn't have enough brain cells available to create all the psychological resistance I was used to creating, to double- and triple-thinking myself. I imagined myself as one of those Russian nesting dolls. The outer layer—the biggest doll—was fear. Next was self-consciousness. Then resentment. You had to go through all those layers to get down to the bottom, the real, the essential Ivy, and that is what the pot had miraculously done. Suddenly, I wasn't channeling Bailey or even Myrna Loy. I was channeling myself.

We skipped the little canoeing trip Hamish had promised when he invited me out to the country. "I'm too fucked up," he said.

"I agree. I don't think I could even stand up, let alone get into a boat."

" 'I agree,' " he said, mocking me lightly. "You sound like you're answering a question on some game show."

"*Hollywood Squares!*"

We both erupted in giggles. It seemed hilarious that I'd said *I agree* so formally, rather than *yeah* or *me too*. A second later, I couldn't remember what we'd been laughing about.

My head felt heavy and my neck weak, like a bowling ball balanced precariously on a dainty stem. I found a nice cushion at the end of Hamish's couch, and managed to get very comfortable, kicking off my sandals and stretching out. If it hadn't been for my expansive mood, I might have gagged on the pungent odor of dog that emanated from the pillow. But I felt part canine myself. If I'd had a tail, I'd have wagged it.

"Come on, let's cook," Hamish said, grabbing my hands and trying to pull me up.

"I'm too lazy." Was this the same person who'd stood frozen, wine bottle at the ready, like some parody of a scullery maid holding a rolling pin, when Shelley and Byron had greeted me an hour earlier? "But I *am* hungry!"

Hamish laughed.

I was a pasha now, pampered and supine, ready to snap my fingers and have all my wants and needs indulged. "Do you have any chips or anything?"

"I have a cheese tray."

"Excellent."

I closed my eyes and got lost in the Jefferson Airplane record Hamish had put on, which was punctuated by occasional sounds of him bumping around his kitchen. He returned with a spread of Wheat Thins, goat cheese, Gruyère, green grapes, and black olives. He'd even made a little tapenade with sun-dried tomatoes.

I devoured it all, surprised by the power of the munchies, licking the goat cheese from my fingers unself-consciously. I don't think I'd eaten with so much abandon since my first year in college. It even crossed my mind to lick Hamish's fingers. The fact that I didn't was more a matter of timing than of discretion. He'd moved his hand before I got there.

I'd never come close to cheating on Ellis. I figured I didn't have the libido for one man, let alone two. But if Hamish's hand had lingered near the goat cheese for a second longer, who knows what might have happened.

Instead we talked. Pot had always made me cerebral. Hamish and I lolled around like a couple of lazy undergraduates. He introduced me to Irma Thomas and stuffed artichokes. I blathered on about Virginia Woolf's *To the Lighthouse*. The white sheets on the furniture after the war. I'd read the book years ago, but now, suddenly, I couldn't stop thinking about it, this abandoned beach house on the Isle of Skye. How Woolf had killed off her main character in the middle of the book. Ellis would have mocked me, said something like, *That's the joke we always say when we're trying to find a vehicle for a has-been actress. We'll cast her in* To the Lighthouse. But Hamish loved *To the Lighthouse* as much as I did.

The hours just flew, and somewhere between the cheese plate and *To the Lighthouse,* the sun managed to set without my noticing it. All I noticed at first was that Hamish's cottage had grown increasingly cozy. A little later, I realized it was the lighting. Hamish possessed the lamps of a true reader. Lamps that put out a concentrated amber warmth, which could keep you in a novel deep into the night. Nothing white or bluish or overhead or diffused. It was the circuitous way the brain worked on Mary Jane that had led me to notice the lamps before I noticed it was dark outside. Had it really been just a few hours ago that I'd wanted to cancel this visit because I might have to drive home at night?

I really wished I could spend the night—not so I could sleep with Hamish, or even to avoid driving in the dark—but just to hold on to this sense of suspended animation. Suspended worry. Suspended self-consciousness. I'd have gladly taken the couch, even the dog pillow. I didn't have any toiletries, but I'd have settled for putting some toothpaste on my finger and rubbing it on my teeth. But I was a mother, with two little girls waiting for me at home. Having an impromptu sleepover wasn't an option. I had to drive back to my previously scheduled life.

Hamish walked me outside. It was profoundly dark. Dark in a way that I'd forgotten it could be. It had been years since I'd lived in the country. I'd become used to neighbors and streetlights and porch lights and cars driving by at all hours. And to not seeing—not even looking up to see—stars. I looked up now and thought how funny it was that those celestial pinpricks had been there all along, all the years I hadn't been paying attention, how they'd been there before me and would be there after me, and how the very same sky was shared by the entire earth, even Los Angeles. When I started the car, Byron and Shelley woke up and pushed their way out the screen door, jumping up on the driver's-side door, barking and licking me through the open window. Hamish pushed them aside and bent down to give me a quick kiss. On the lips. My heart pumped frantically, not knowing how to process it. Why now? When I was in the car?

"All right, boys," he said to the dogs. Then to me: "Safe home."

He walked back to the house and watched me from the front door. I decided that the kiss meant nothing. If it had, I wouldn't still be in the car.

I turned on the headlights and inhaled deeply. I wasn't going to revert to my old neurotic self. I wasn't going to get out that folded piece of yellow legal paper with the twenty-eight turns. I was going to be a grown-up. I was pretty sure the pot had worn off, but as I turned the car around on the crunchy gravel, I carefully scrutinized my driving. Made sure I knew where all the controls were and didn't send the car lurching when I stepped on the gas. I didn't want to blow it. Not this late, this far away, by myself, with the kids home waiting and on top of our new insurance problems. For one thing, it would be pretty embarrassing to have spent the week scolding Ellis and then wind up in a ditch myself.

I was cautious and attentive—but not scared—as my headlights groped for the edges of the country road that led back to the highway. Still thinking about the evening, not sure whether to be regretful or relieved that it hadn't turned into something else. I hadn't felt so comfortable with anyone since the early days of Ellis. Well, that wasn't quite true. Of course I was still comfortable with Ellis, comfortable as an old bathrobe. What I felt with Hamish went beyond comfortable. It was more like a great swelling of the heart, the lifting of a boat. Yes, that was it. It had been a long time since I'd felt so gently lifted. I couldn't tell if Hamish felt the same way about me. The day before, I'd have said it was impossible. I was too dumpy. He was too . . . wonderful. But pot had been a great equalizer.

Suddenly my headlights caught a tiny flicker of movement—three deer, graceful as prima ballerinas, leaping across the road. My heart jumped; I slammed the brakes, braced for impact. My brakes made a horrible sound, and I whipped forward and then back, but the car stopped. I looked up and saw the tail of the last deer disappear through some birch trees off to the left. The whole thing was over in a second. I hadn't been hit. I should have been happy that my reactions were intact, but instead I felt like an idiot. What was I, some reckless fraternity boy? Then I remembered this was exactly the last thing my father had seen before he died.

I felt bile rise in my throat. Then I took my foot off the brake and started again.

I was actually relieved when I saw the sign for 78, which promised to deliver me, like a great deer-free assembly line, to my home. It was the first time in my life I was happy to get on a highway. It was lit up like a cathedral, and the headway between cars was long. I took the eastbound ramp and slid easily into the right lane. And then, safely on the assembly line, I reached down and switched on the radio. To settle my nerves.

It was still on the rock station I'd found that afternoon, but I wasn't in a rock station kind of mood anymore. I turned the dial to the left, looking for NPR. Classical music would be good company at this hour. Or talk. It hardly mattered. Just some palpable intelligence to keep me awake and drown out my own thoughts.

It didn't take half a sentence for me to tell something had happened. There's this tone that newscasters get when the news is really bad. You can hear it in the way their voices catch, falter. They reel off tragedy after tragedy, day after day, and yet *this* news story is different. *This* news story makes them quaver. The world is not as whole it was yesterday. It's as palpable as a soundtrack in a movie or the sudden ring of a telephone in the middle of the night.

And then I heard, "Princess Diana has been seriously injured in a car accident in Paris."

If the universe had been plotting to trip me up, it had executed its plan perfectly. First the deer, now this.

I listened, my hands clenched on the wheel. You think of those other moments when the world changes. Jack Kennedy. Martin Luther King. The *Challenger.* Diana was just a woman. Just a beautiful, tormented woman. She didn't run a country. She didn't hold the keys to the world's security. She wasn't even a member of the royal family anymore. Yet the entire world had become a hospital waiting room.

The newscasters were circling, like birds of prey, waiting to report her death. It wasn't enough that the world's most photographed woman had been hurt in a car crash. It wasn't epochal enough for a princess to have a broken arm and some crushed ribs. We all knew the fairy tales. The princess had to die.

What had seemed solid just seconds ago was now quicksilver. The windshield in front of me, dashboard, mirrors, taillights, headlights—everything shiny, reflective, in motion, dizzying. A truck behind me started passing on the left. I knew I would flinch and wander into its path.

I'd always known it, hadn't I? Ever since those days of driver's ed. But the world had laughed. Everybody thought it was so funny, the daughter of a Buick dealer afraid to get her driver's license. The neurotic New Jersey housewife who'd do anything to avoid a highway. But they were wrong. Look at Princess Diana! Didn't that prove it? Cars were dangerous, dangerous places and it was folly to think otherwise.

I wanted to turn the radio off, but I was already part of it, invested in the vigil myself. Half breathing, I sat listening over and over to the story. The paparazzi, the chauffeur, Dodi, dinner at the Ritz. I heard reports from London, from Paris, from the hospital, from the highway. I listened as the smashed Mercedes was pulled from the tunnel.

I was being punished, I realized, for having too good a time with Hamish. Too bad Diana had to go down with me.

I considered pulling over to the shoulder of the highway to wait it out. To let the waves of nausea and panic wash over me and eventually subside. But I knew they wouldn't stop. Because the story wouldn't stop. And I'd still have to get home. I could wait until morning and Princess Diana would still be the lead story on the radio. And if I stopped, I'd have to, eventually, accelerate into traffic from a full stop. You couldn't call AAA to come tow you because of a panic attack, could you?

Finally, miraculously, I made it to the Parkway, the home stretch. I was driving past the Holy Sepulchre cemetery when the vigil ended. Princess Diana was dead.

"Oh my God," I said softly, surprised that I didn't scream or cry or crash the car in shock. I wondered if all the other drivers on the road had just heard the same news. Well, of course they had. I wondered if Ellis knew. He must; it was just the middle of the evening in California. If I knew Ellis, he was already work-ing on an angle. Lining up clients to perform at the funeral. And then I realized Hamish probably hadn't heard. He didn't have a TV, after all, and there was no reason for him to turn on a radio. He was probably sitting in that great armchair, reading.

When I got home, the two little heads were in front of the television, their faces wet with tears. Even they knew. Of course they knew. It was a *princess* who'd died.

They both jumped up to hug me.

"I was so scared," Lily said, her face dampening my dress. "I was afraid you were dead."

Oh my God. It hadn't occurred to me. The girls were just as convinced as I was that I would die on my way home from Hamish's. Who knows what they'd been watching when the newscasters broke in. It didn't matter. Every channel would have had it. They would have heard the story over and over, with no parent reassuring them, no parent telling them to turn it off. They were waiting, like Princes Will and Harry, for news of their mother's death.

I looked down at Lily's quavering little lips, her red-rimmed eyes. I expected that from Charlotte, but not from Lily. But then I remembered how Bailey had fallen apart in the first few hours after Daddy died.

"I told her it would be okay," Charlotte said. She had been crying, too, but it was clear she considered it her duty to be strong. After all, she was the sitter. "I was scared, too, when we heard about Princess Diana's crash and you weren't home. But I figured out a way to keep you alive."

She said it so calmly, so clinically, it almost seemed plausible.

"How, honey?"

"I took all the clothes out of my hamper and put them in the washer. Then, when they were done, I took all the clothes out of Lily's hamper, and put the other wash in the dryer. I just kept doing washes and folding them and I knew you'd come home, because God wouldn't let me go to all that trouble and not let you appreciate it."

Indeed, there were three laundry baskets of neatly folded clothes lined up on the dining room table.

I laughed. Lily glanced at me and then at Charlotte, and made that little spinning motion with her index finger up to her head. *Cuckoo.*

Charlotte glared. Her dignity was wounded, and I was an ingrate. She'd gone to the trouble of *saving my life,* and here I was, laughing. Mocking her. Trading conspiratorial glances with Lily.

"I'm sorry," I said, pulling Charlotte toward me for another hug. But her body was stiff, unyielding. She was having none of it. I tried to smooth her hair and she yanked her head back.

"Charlotte," I pleaded. Suddenly it mattered more than anything else in the world that she forgive me. I felt like I was on trial for every stupid insensitive thing I'd ever said or done, for thirteen years of ineptitude as a mother.

Charlotte stood there glowering like a judge.

"I'm sorry," I said. "I'm sorry I laughed. And that I kept you waiting. And that you both had to listen to all this Princess Diana stuff without a grown-up here to help you through it."

Charlotte let out a small, almost inaudible sigh.

"And thank you for doing all that laundry. What a big help!"

Nothing. She wasn't falling for the big maternal thank-you. The tiny exhalation was all I was going to get.

I glanced at the TV and saw they were now doing the big visual retrospectives: Diana, Princess of Wales, 1961–1997. Video from the wedding, the polo matches, with AIDS victims, with Charles, with Dodi, with Andrew Morton, with Will and Harry on the teacups in Disney World. I suddenly wanted, needed, to see every last bit of it.

I looked up and Charlotte was gone. I heard a door slam. Lily came over and grabbed my hand. "Let's watch it, Mommy."

Was it terrible to let a ten-year-old wallow in all this? Or was it just like an extended Barbie doll fashion show? I didn't know. I had one child who was furious, and another who wanted to watch the real-life fairy tale about a tragic princess. I was still shaken by the news, by driving home, by the close call with the deer, by Charlotte's odd reaction to the news of Princess Diana's death. Not to mention the kiss—though that seemed like it must have happened in another lifetime. And I was tired. Dead tired. Like I was wearing one of those lead aprons they put on you in the dentist's office. Like I was swimming in one.

I plopped down on the sofa and Lily nestled up against me. Her weight against me felt absolutely luscious. I dozed off and on, but heard little snatches of Lily's running commentary. My heart felt heavy, physically heavy, as if the weight of Diana's death were borne by me and me alone. The last thing I remembered before falling asleep was Lily saying, "That's the ugliest hat I've ever seen."

I looked up. Diana was wearing a red cap, trimmed with blue-gray fur and a dotted veil in the same unlikely blue. It *was* the ugliest hat. It looked like something Santa Claus might wear in church.

# *Eight*

## 2001—ELLIS

### 2001 CHRYSLER SEBRING CONVERTIBLE,
### FOUR-SPEED AUTOMATIC, FOUR-CYLINDER, RED (RENTAL)

It all started with a simple photograph.

Ivy saw a picture I'd taken of Big Sur on my laptop screensaver and was blown away. It was, I have to admit, a very nice photograph, taken an hour before sunset, with that long, slanting afternoon sun turning the huge jagged cliffs of the California coastline an insanely luminous gold. At the top, you could see the candy ribbon curve of the road; at the bottom, waves smashing huge rocks. It was, Ivy declared, the most beautiful thing she'd seen in her life. "Is this what California really looks like?" she asked. "Like a car commercial?"

I was, to put it mildly, surprised. A winding road right on the edge of a bluff: This was the kind of thing that usually filled Ivy with dread. And of *course* she knew what California looked like. Anybody with a television knew what California looked like. But, the photo reminded her: She'd never been there in real life. "All those years that Bailey's been out there. And you, too. All those business trips. Why didn't you ever take me?" She sounded petulant, like a small child left home from the fair. One random

glance at a laptop, and Ivy had discovered the vacant center at the core of her being.

Of course, Ivy was always discovering a vacant center at the core of her being, always on the verge of discovering the one thing she absolutely needed to complete her life. I'd met her when that great new thing was New York City, which was replaced, in succession, by marriage, moving to the suburbs, motherhood, cooking, and writing. But writing was getting old. She'd been writing her heart out for years, and all she'd managed to get published was one story in a little literary journal that paid her by sending her five copies. And her unfinished novel? What were the chances she'd really finish it? It was time, past time, for something new. And the next new thing was—ta-da!—California!

So Ivy began planning a trip. And not just any trip, but a special vacation, a second honeymoon—just the two of us—a celebration of twenty years of being together. The girls were big, fourteen and seventeen, and it was about time we went away together, didn't I think? Especially after everything we'd been through with Charlotte. We needed time away; every couple needed time away. It was an investment in the marriage. She'd read it in a magazine. The girls could stay with one of the grandmothers. We'd go in August, when there was no camp, no school. They wouldn't miss anything.

In theory, I agreed. I just wasn't sure about California.

For one thing—okay, the only thing—there was Daphne. She had turned out to be a bad habit I couldn't drop, a drug I couldn't resist, a bag of potato chips I couldn't keep my hands out of. Daphne and California had become hopelessly intertwined; they

were of a piece. It was an organizing technique, a way of keeping the different parts of my life separate, like a second set of dishes in a kosher household. In New Jersey, I was the good husband, the good father. Devoted. Even doting, some would say. From the earliest days, I'd always done more than my share of housework. Diapered babies. Washed the clothes. And through the rough times of Charlotte's OCD crisis, I'd been there for every major doctor's visit, every school consultation. I wasn't just a good provider—though I prided myself on that—I was also a sensitive and caring spouse and father. I listened to Ivy's worries, read the first drafts of her stories, and scraped her up off the ground when an offhand remark by Hamish McDonough knocked the wind out of her sails.

In New Jersey, I was a family man. In California, I got to swing my dick around. In New Jersey, I memorized the train schedule and wore suits to the office. In California, I wore sandals and did half my business poolside. In New Jersey, I had Ivy—my high-strung, complicated, smart, funny, and frigid wife. In California, I had a girlfriend who never tired of sex.

I had the best of both worlds, in other words. I didn't want to fuck it up.

Of course, it was already fucked up. I knew that. I didn't like to think about what I was doing. I'd never forgiven my father for his indiscretions, or the fact that because of them my parents had split up and I'd been stuck with Sheba. I'd given up Daphne a hundred times, or tried to. Told her I couldn't see her anymore. Told her she should find a serious boyfriend, one she'd have a future with. I'd tried not telling Daphne when I was coming out to L.A., I'd changed my cell phone number, but she always managed to find me. She knew she'd find me at the clubs, or the Beverly Hills Hotel or Spago. She seemed to have an uncanny instinct for finding me when I was slumming it at Pink's. Seriously, if I'd been a nuclear bomb, the Russians could have hired her as a tracking missile. If I was in the Pacific time zone, Daphne somehow knew it, and within hours was busy sucking my dick.

I wasn't a strong enough man to resist.

But Daphne had started to become a liability. The first few years, she had been incredibly discreet. If I was in a club, talking to a comic or a manager, she'd just give me a signal from across the room. She'd take her tongue and slowly roll it across the bottom of her upper lip—a not-too-subtle suggestion that she was hot, wet, and ready—and wait until I'd disentangled myself from whatever business was at hand. But in the last few years, she'd lost all sense of discretion. I could be talking with Michael Ovitz, and she'd come up from behind and clap her hands across my eyes in an infantile game of peek-a-boo. If I was sitting in a restaurant booth across from Jay Leno's booking guy, she'd appear from nowhere and slide in next to me. She'd show up at private pool parties, straining the confines of a too-tight bikini, and plop right on my lap. It could be awkward, especially if she did it in front of a colleague who knew Ivy. It was risky for my marriage, and for my career; even in swinging L.A., people didn't like to see your dick hanging out of your shorts.

And the indiscretions didn't stop there. A couple of times, just for fun, Daphne raced me for the ringing phone in my hotel room.

She *wanted* it to be Ivy, to see how close to the edge she could take things. She'd go into an incredibly hokey foreign accent, pretending to be a maid. Once, she was Mexican. Another time, Eastern European. Then, after handing me the phone, she'd sit next to me with a self-satisfied look, looking like she might start giggling at any moment. I'd seriously wanted to kill her.

"Do you think we should fly into L.A. and drive up to Big Sur?" Ivy asked me. "Or fly into San Franscisco?"

"San Francisco," I answered quickly. Safer.

"But I want to see Bailey. And stay at the Beverly Hills Hotel."

I groaned inwardly. They all knew me at the Beverly Hills Hotel, and they all knew the bouncy redhead that hung all over me.

I had no plans to let Daphne know I would be vacationing in California. First of all, she'd want to get a whiff of Ivy. I knew Daphne. She'd find it impossible to resist her rival. And she did consider Ivy a rival. It was stupid; I'd told her a hundred times that I was never going to leave my wife. Daphne was hot; she was fun, a barrel of laughs. She wasn't even half-bad as a comic, though she was never going to rise far above the New Talent Night level. But she wasn't in Ivy's league. And she wasn't the mother of my children. She was my West Coast plaything, and one I was more than ready to retire to the bottom of the toy chest.

I started having California nightmares. And all of them, strangely, involved driving. In one, Ivy and I are driving on the 405 and there's a car stopped on the side of the road. Next to it, a woman on her knees is trying to change her own tire. Ivy yells for me to stop, and when I do, the woman turns out to be Daphne.

Next thing, she's sucking my cock. In another dream, I'm driving down Sunset Boulevard with Ivy, and a car rear-ends us. I drive a little farther and it bumps us again. I get out, furious, and it's Daphne. She starts screaming at me in a crazy Mexican accent, and Ivy suddenly knows—just from the stupid accent—that I've been fucking this woman for the past six years.

I jolt to consciousness, my heart pounding against my rib cage, and fearing the worst: that I've yelled out *Daphne.*

And yet somehow Ivy is oblivious. I wipe the sweat from my forehead while Ivy sleeps peacefully. No doubt dreaming sweet California dreams. With the help of the Internet, she is planning it all. A few days in L.A., a visit with her sister, a tour of Paramount, window-shopping on Rodeo Drive, side trips to Venice Beach, Topanga Canyon, and Malibu. And then, up the Pacific Coast Highway to the Hearst Castle and, finally, Big Sur, the place that remains at the center of all her dreams. She has no idea how much driving she's actually signing up for. She has no concept of California distances. And I know she will hate the Pacific Coast Highway, she will hate Big Sur. It's different in a photograph than in real life. Yes, she's gotten braver in recent years. But she's never been on a twisty mountain road that drops a thousand feet to the ocean.

"Have you heard of a place called Deetjen's?" she says.

I swallow. I have heard of Deetjen's. I've been there with Daphne. That's when I took the picture.

If you found some little fairy world nestled in the roots of an old oak, constructed of little twigs and pine needles, and you could sprinkle magic dust to make it grow, then you would have Deetjen's.

Deetjen's is a hotel built in Big Sur in the 1930s, a collection of rustic cottages tucked in the woods, furnished in a style that's half L.L. Bean and half Goldilocks, with antiques and fireplaces, as well as a four-star restaurant. There's nothing girly about it—not a single doily or piece of flowered wallpaper—still, it's the kind of place that makes chicks go ape-shit. I'd never heard of it, being a Jersey boy, but somehow Daphne knew, and she got me to take her there one weekend the first year I started seeing her.

As soon as we parked my rental car and walked in, I thought: *Except for the road to get here, Ivy would love this place.* Then for the next two days, I fucked like a college boy and put Ivy completely out of my mind.

I didn't want to go back. Not because they'd remember me—I was there for only two nights, and that was years ago—but because *I'd* remember. I'd remember and I'd be haunted, and I'd have to spend the whole time pretending not to be.

Ivy, I knew, would swoon over Deetjen's. It's the country inn all the rest *try* to be but never are—the gold standard of understated romantic getaways. I could try to talk her out of it, but how? *Oh, honey pie, let's not go to Deetjen's. It would remind me of a weekend I spent with my mistress.* No, that wouldn't do. I could tell Ivy that the roads of Big Sur would scare her to death, but I'd sound like a mean-hearted bastard out to spoil her fun. No, there was no getting around it.

I would just have to go and bite my tongue. Be careful what I said. Pretend to be bowled over for the first time. I'd have to ignore the ghost of Daphne, who'd be hiding behind every piece of camp-style furniture, licking her lips and taunting me. It would be hard, but I was the one who'd gotten myself into this predicament.

But there was one other thing I was worried about. Every room in Deetjen's comes with a diary, and at least in the room I stayed in, it was crammed with long, elaborate, and disarmingly confessional entries from previous guests. Daphne and I lay in bed that first night, sweaty and exhausted from sex, and read them aloud, laughing. Some were sappily sincere, others just hilarious. There was the couple who had taken peyote and spent their whole night in paradise throwing up, another couple who'd fought in the car on the trip all the way down from San Francisco and seemed on the verge of divorce, and a wife who'd fled there with a lover because her husband hadn't been able to get it up for thirty years. Nestled high up on a ledge overlooking the Pacific Ocean, Deetjen's was the site of some high-stakes romantic drama.

The question was, Had I been drunk and stupid enough to write one of these missives myself? Or had Daphne?

Los Angeles is a city of four million souls, spread over five hundred square miles. Statistically, the chance of accidentally running into one specific person during a three-day visit to the City of Angels is so small as to be infinitesimal. True, there are certain neighborhoods where you're likely to see the same people again and again—if you're trying to avoid a thrift store shopper, don't visit Melrose Avenue; dodging a celebrity wannabe, stay away from Spago—but I was careful to avoid all the neighborhoods where

Daphne and I had a history. I'd jumped at Bailey's invitation to put us up at her house (otherwise Ivy would have demanded the Beverly Hills Hotel), I avoided all comedy clubs, and insisted that Pink's wasn't worth our time—even if its hot dogs were written up in all the guides. I thought I was safe. So why was it that on the final day of our three-day visit to Los Angeles, the first leg of Ivy's ambitious California odyssey, the person behind the wheel of the little golf cart tour bus at Paramount Studios was none other than Daphne?

Oh, she played it cool. I had to hand it to her. She was so good at acting like she'd never met me that she pretended to trip on my name. "Elliott?" she asked, after Ivy, oblivious of the sexual tsunami she'd just entered, nudged me into the seat right next to Daphne and then slid in on my other side.

"No, *Ellis*," I said.

"Really, all the way from New Jersey?" She made New Jersey sound exotic, like Australia, a far-off place that never sent representatives out this way. "Is this your first time in California?"

"For me," Ivy said, glowing with the excitement of her California adventure. "But Ellis comes out all the time for business trips."

I imagined Daphne's glee at that little nugget and slunk a little lower in my seat.

From a strictly professional point of view—Daphne was, after all, a performer—I had to be impressed. She was the picture of the friendly tour guide: making small talk, prattling on about her life as a struggling comic, weaving the bus around the soundstages where they filmed *Sunset Boulevard* and *Rear Window* while rolling off snippets of Hollywood history, stopping the cart so we could take pictures of the famous New York Street Scene set. The whole spiel, casual as could be, no hint that she knew me or was holding the atom bomb that could destroy my marriage.

But I felt like my heart was just going to burst right through my chest. Over the years, I'd built an elaborate structure to keep these two women apart—the one I loved, and the one I loved to fuck—both in my mind and in real life. I'd hardened my heart so that I didn't think of Ivy when I was with Daphne, and vice versa. I'd given Daphne strict protocols about getting in touch with me, and never answered a phone without checking caller ID. And now this whole organizing principle had collapsed in on itself.

There were other people sitting in the cart behind us, a family of three from Kansas and an elderly couple from San Bernardino, and I prayed that their presence would provide some kind of protective buffer. Daphne wouldn't decide to spring her little secret on Ivy right in the middle of a tour, would she? With other people around? It would be professional suicide. These studio tour jobs were good gigs; they came with benefits and were considered a possible route to getting cast in the sitcoms that were still being filmed there.

And yet. Love hath no fury like a mistress scorned. Daphne had to know that I'd been avoiding her, not telling her about my trips to L.A., ignoring her calls when her number came up on my cell phone. The question was, Would it be more fun for her to continue the charade of being an innocent tour guide, content with the fact that she was making me squirm? Or would she be unsatisfied until she drew blood? I could just imagine some studio executives sitting inside their air-conditioned office, listening to a pitch for a big car-chase picture and suddenly, from outside, the animal howling of my wife. I could picture hair being pulled and fingernails tearing skin as the Paramount cart careened into some irreplaceable artifact of movie history and pitched the old couple from San Bernardino onto the street. The whole thing winding up in the *Hollywood Reporter.* My marriage over, my career a joke. Even Ellis Halpern couldn't spin that disaster.

I tried studying Daphne out of the corner of my eye. Did she look amused? Angry? Nervous? Maniacal? Hard to tell. Her face was as much a mask as the studio-issue polo shirt and khaki pants. I could see the corners of her mouth turned up into a tight smile. It wasn't any more telling than *Mona Lisa*'s smile, but if I had to bet, I'd guess amused.

We passed the playground and child care center that Lucille Ball had built, and Daphne seemed to think this was a good place to casually mention Desi's long history of infidelities.

I felt sick. I kept thinking about the Aesop's fable of the scorpion and the frog. To my right sat Ivy, so innocently, taking Daphne and everything she said at face value. To my left sat Daphne, her stinger and venom at the ready. And yet I had to keep a smile pasted on my face, to look like I was enjoying all this great Hollywood history.

Daphne started pumping Ivy for information on where we were going next. Of course it didn't sound like pumping. It just sounded like a Californian wanting to make sure an out-of-towner was going to see all the important sites.

"We're driving up to San Simeon, then making our way to Big Sur on the Pacific Coast Highway," Ivy said. She seemed proud to have remembered all the names.

"And where are you staying in Big Sur?"

"A place called . . . Ellis, what is it called?"

I pretended not to remember.

"Deetjen's?" Daphne offered helpfully.

"Yes! Deetjen's. It looked great on the Internet."

"Oh, you'll love it," Daphne said. "I went there once. Very romantic." She looked over and winked.

It took all my powers of self-control not to throttle the life out of her right then and there, although Ivy hadn't seemed to notice anything.

When the tour ended, Daphne offered to take pictures of everybody in front of the Paramount gate. The old couple from San Bernardino didn't have a camera, but the family from Kansas offered to take their picture and send it to them. When that transaction was completed, the Kansans handed their camera to Daphne, so she could take a picture of them. I wanted to escape, but Ivy was patiently waiting her turn. Running off would have looked unfriendly.

I watched as Ivy handed the camera over, and in that moment— Ivy's hand outstretched toward Daphne's—I thought of Michelangelo's painting, in the Sistine Chapel, of God creating Adam. I felt queasy all over again, almost as if Ivy were passing something much more valuable to Daphne than a mere camera. Ivy unwittingly passing her husband over to the other woman? Giving away her innocence? But then, as Daphne held up the camera and started calling the shots—"There. Yes, a little to the right. Now smile!"—I suddenly understood. Ivy was allowing Daphne to make monkeys out of us. We stood there, framed against the studio entrance, my arm around Ivy's shoulder, dopey little tourists. Waiting, literally, for Daphne's release.

"And I have to take a picture of you, too!" Ivy said. "You were so much fun."

Daphne handed back our camera and moved to the spot where everybody had posed.

"Ellis," Ivy said, motioning at me to stand next to Daphne. "Move into the picture."

I walked over and stood next to Daphne, careful to keep an inch or two between us. I couldn't see her expression and didn't want to. In fact, I was already thinking about how I'd have to remember to throw out the picture when we got the film back. I'd been thinking about buying a digital camera before the trip. Now I wished I had. I could have lost the picture with a single click.

Ivy looked through the camera, framing her shot, focusing. "C'mon, Ellis," she said. "Smile! You look like your dog just died."

"I don't have a dog."

The shutter clicked. At last it was over. For now, at least, my secret was safe. But for how long? Daphne knew everywhere we were going.

I'm not usually overly philosophical, but I couldn't help thinking how close two people could be and yet how utterly far apart.

The day after the Paramount tour, after our final thank-you-for-putting-us-up dinner with Bailey and Frank, Ivy and I drove up California's Central Coast in our usual formation. Me on the left in the driver's seat, Ivy on the right. We had rented a convertible, a red Sebring. I often rented a convertible when I traveled to L.A., but this was Ivy's first time. She'd bought a scarf on the boardwalk in Venice Beach just to pull back her hair when we were driving, and when I looked over at her on the highway, I saw her smiling out at the parched California mountains, looking unusually girlish and happy.

Yet, despite being separated by just a matter of inches, we were miles apart, alone in our heads, having two entirely separate vacations. Ivy was enchanted by the ruggedness of the landscape, by the sun and the breeze, by being away from the kids for the first time in years. She had been dog-earing the pages in *Frommer's* and *Lonely Planet,* making sure we didn't miss any of the must-see experiences she'd read about, like the A-plus schoolgirl she always was, for weeks before the trip. She had no idea I writhing in a private prison of guilt and fear, sure that our Lucy-and-Ricky trip to California was about to turn into *Fatal Attraction.*

But maybe I'm exaggerating. Maybe it wasn't like that all the time. It just felt like it during the long trip up the Central Coast on our way to San Simeon.

The drive did have its moments. I got to reprise my old role as Ivy's private tour guide, showing her Cali just like I'd shown her New York back in 1981. When I took her to a nice little café I knew in Los Olivos, where we could sit outdoors on a wisteria-covered patio, she was charmed. Afterwards, when I took her for a little side trip through the winding hills of wine country and stopped the car at the front gate of Michael Jackson's Neverland, she was blown away. We got out of the car and posed together in front of the big black iron gate, setting the camera on self-timer. We felt giddy and silly and young, and I looked like a genius for taking her there. Ivy would have been satisfied with the café, but Neverland was like icing on the cake. Well, as they say, *Dayenu*.

And Ivy was different. The two little worry lines that usually creased her forehead were gone, I noticed, and she seemed less angry. When was it, I wondered, that she'd started seeming angry all the time? But now that she was genuinely on an adventure, she didn't seem angry at all. *We* were on an adventure. The first in, like, forever. Family vacations didn't count. That was just parenting with wheels.

Ivy even surprised me by offering to drive after we left Neverland. I looked at her as if she'd just grown a second head.

"Really?" I asked.

"Yes," she said, reaching for my keys as if it were the most ordinary thing in the world.

I knew she wouldn't last long—a half an hour or forty-five minutes was the best I could expect—and she wouldn't let me fall asleep. She wanted me awake to supply directions and conversation. But the fact that she'd voluntarily offered to drive at all was worth striking a commemorative stamp.

When we finally arrived at the hotel in San Simeon, we found our room had a king-sized bed, a gas fireplace, and a view straight to the Pacific. I had a little involuntary shiver when I thought about what I'd be doing in that bed if it had been Daphne I'd brought to this hotel rather than Ivy. It was a terrible thought, and I shook it off as fast as I could. It didn't make me horny, just ashamed.

Still, the room was nice, much better than I'd expected. After a day of driving, all I wanted to do was flop down on the bed, but Ivy opened the sliding glass door and walked out to the balcony. She put her feet up on the railing and looked out at the ocean. It was sweet, seeing her like that: content to just sit, to take it all in. She didn't bring out a guidebook or even a novel to amuse herself. She didn't turn around and gesture me to join her. She didn't even pick up her cell phone to check with the girls. She just sat. I opened a bottle of California zinfandel we'd picked up in Los Olivos, found two glasses, and poured them. We sat there for almost an hour, looking at the ocean and watching the sunset. Saying nothing, yet perfectly content.

After dinner, we saw that the hotel had set up bonfires along the beach. It was cold. We both put on jackets and headed down. Even with the jackets, it was chilly. In the blackness, all that was left of the ocean was the sound of it pounding on the sand.

There were three bonfires, each surrounded by a cluster of people sitting in plastic Adirondack chairs. We hung back a minute, looking at all three groups, trying to figure out which might be the most congenial. Feeling a little shy, we settled on the closest.

An arrestingly beautiful young Latino couple, both wearing tight jeans, shared a single chair. Across from them sat an older couple. The man had on a fishing hat and the kind of multi-pocketed vest photographers wear. He looked like the kind of guy who would travel around South America taking pictures, maybe even a CIA operative or a mercenary; you could almost smell the testosterone. But maybe he was just a fisherman. His wife was knitting a sweater. She wore a baseball cap outfitted with a headlight, like a coal miner's hat, to illuminate her work.

The man in the vest was talking. He barely nodded when we sat down. He was holding forth, explaining how the world worked, something about John Ashcroft and an airplane. You know guys like that. You find them everywhere, in diners and train stations, on park benches and behind you at the dry cleaners. Angry men who are convinced that they're the only ones smart enough to detect all the secret patterns and hidden conspiracies the rest of us are too stupid to notice. Was it my imagination, or did the young couple look trapped, like butterflies impaled by a biologist's pin?

"At taxpayer expense," the man said. "Don't you see? Everybody else has to fly commercial, but they're sending him up in a government jet."

I wondered vaguely if he was a left-wing nut or a right-wing nut. I was starting to wish we'd chosen another bonfire. But then his wife bent down and pulled a joint out of her knitting bag. Her eyes twinkled as she held it up, like she'd just landed a nice-sized carp. When she put it to her mouth, the man leaned over to cup his hands over her face, so she could get a light. Still he didn't stop talking. Frankly, with the ocean just a few feet away, I was surprised they managed to get the thing lit. But I smelled it, the unmistakable musk of burning ganja. The woman drew in deeply, smiled, then reached out and pushed the joint in our direction.

I looked quickly at Ivy. Neither of us had smoked pot in years. Well, at least not together; sometimes it got passed around during a party in L.A, especially those parties up in the hills. I wondered if Ivy would disapprove. She'd smoked a little pot that first year in New York, but hadn't smoked at all since she got pregnant with Charlotte. Was she intrigued? Or scared? After all, if she was terrified to sit in a car going sixty-five miles an hour, how would she feel being handed an illegal substance by the wife of a raving stranger on a semi-public beach? I was interested in smoking some dope, but not if it was going to freak her out.

But to my surprise, Ivy reached out and took the joint. I cupped my hands over it for her and then took it myself, inhaling deeply. I wasn't an expert on marijuana, but I could tell this was some good shit.

"British Columbia," the man said.

*Ah,* I thought. *Now we really are on the West Coast.* The real West Coast, the one that starts in Mexico and goes all the way up to Alaska.

We introduced ourselves. The beautiful young people were newlyweds from Orange County. He worked, he said, in security. I supposed that meant night shift at a bank. She was a dental hygienist. I wondered why they were out on the beach, listening to some crazy conspiracy theorist instead of back in their room, fucking. The older couple, it turned out, came from Oregon, where he'd recently retired as a professor of engineering. I almost laughed aloud. He'd been sounding all Unabomber, and yet he turned out to be a college professor from one of the most liberal places in the country. He and his wife were heading to Santa

Barbara to see their daughter—a pediatrician—and had just spent a few days in Big Sur.

"Deetjen's?" Ivy asked. If there was anything that my star pupil wanted in life, it was confirmation that all the homework she'd done had really paid off.

"No," the woman said. "Esalen."

It was, she explained, a place for "transformational psychology," where they took yoga and meditation classes and worked on "intimacy issues" and got to bathe nude in natural hot springs overlooking the Pacific. A bunch of West Coast crap.

"Oh," Ivy said. "But you've heard of Deetjen's, right?"

"Touristy," the man proclaimed. "No point in going to Big Sur unless you're going to Esalen." He launched into a new story about meeting Tim Leary in the early days of LSD.

I reached over and grasped Ivy's hand. I could feel the joy leaking out of her. It was important to Ivy to always make the right choice, especially if it meant parting with money. She could spend weeks researching a new dishwasher. And then months later, sitting in somebody's kitchen, fret that she should have picked the Whirlpool instead of the General Electric. Our stay at Deetjen's was to be the crown jewel of our trip to California. And now this blowhard had called it touristy. I wanted to slug him.

But my anger was soon replaced by something else. Something mildly disturbing, like a vaguely remembered dream. And then, suddenly, I remembered. The word *Esalen* had finally penetrated through the pleasant marijuana fog and landed, with the force of the ocean pounding the beach, in whatever corner of the brain is responsible for storing all the painful memories of youth. Maybe it was the word *intimacy* that triggered it. All of a sudden, I felt physically ill, almost like someone had put their hand around my heart and was squeezing it. For the first time in my life, I wondered if I was having a heart attack. In the darkness of the beach, would anyone even notice my face turning blue? And even if they did, was there a hospital close enough to make a difference?

My parents had been to Esalen. A few months later, they'd split up.

My mind flooded with a million ideas at once. I was remembering my parents as young therapists, going off for weekend retreats, leaving us with five twenty-dollar bills and a list of emergency phone numbers. Some strange bronze sculpture on a bookshelf in my father's den, which my friend Billy Davis, in fifth grade, had embarrassingly identified as phallic art. Odd phone calls late at night and doors slamming and my mother secretly weeping. Sheba weeping! A black-and-white photograph, which showed my mother and father with another couple—all of them in bathing suits, arms and flesh linked—which had disappeared around the same time my father had.

And the word, which had meant nothing until now: *Esalen.*

The invisible hand that gripped my heart now reached down and squeezed my intestines. I was afraid I'd shit myself right there on the beach. Daphne, I suddenly knew, hadn't just shown up *accidentally* on the Paramount Studios lot. It was no *coincidence.* She had to have infiltrated my plans. Called my secretary, hacked into my e-mail. And she would continue to shadow me, springing out of nowhere—whenever and wherever I least expected—with her wild red curls, an Irish Medusa in a jack-in-the-box, my own personal horror movie.

Because that was, of course, what I deserved. To be exposed for the creep and fraud I was.

Just like my dad.

Right? Hadn't my dad betrayed my mom? Wasn't that the reason for their sudden divorce, my mom's half-hidden sobs, the abrupt bifurcation of my childhood? But I wasn't sure. Funny, for a family of therapists: We'd never really talked about it.

The Oregon professor was going on at great length about his first acid trip.

But, no. I was wrong, overreacting. It was just marijuana-induced paranoia. Yes, perhaps a trip to Esalen had preceded my parents' split-up. But the thing about Daphne, that *was* just a coincidence.

I heard, now, a sound like a mosquito, right by my left ear. The buzzing grew until it eclipsed all other sound. The ocean churning, the blowhard pontificating, both receded, like a distant radio station fading slowly out of range. I saw Ivy leaning toward me and tugging my sleeve. Her mouth was open, moving, her eyebrows knit together in concern. But I couldn't hear anything above the buzzing of a million mosquitoes between my ears.

"Do you hear that?" I asked. I looked around and saw all their faces, licked by the shadows of the bonfire, staring at me.

And then I was sitting on the sand, and someone was pushing my head down between my knees. "You fainted," said a voice from above me. I smelled spearmint. It was the dental hygienist with a lilting little accent, Cuban or Puerto Rican, I couldn't tell. "We're getting blood to your head."

I glanced up and noticed the old man and his wife skulking away.

"Afraid they'll get busted," the hygienist's husband explained. "If someone from the hotel comes out, smells pot, and sees you lying on the sand."

Phonies.

I felt something cold and wet on my forehead. It was Ivy, crouching in front of me, wiping my forehead with a sleeve of her jacket. She'd dunked it in the ocean.

After a minute or two, I felt better. I sat upright and swallowed a big gulp of ocean air. I was a mess—there was wet sand caking my hair and stuck to my jeans—but at least I hadn't shit my pants.

The next morning, we woke to a thick layer of fog. It felt like the tendrils of my unconscious, pulling me back down into sleep, but Ivy's schedule beckoned. We had tickets for Hearst Castle at 10:40 and sandy clothes to get to the hotel laundry service. We were checking out and, after Hearst, heading up to Big Sur. I barely had time to chug a cup of coffee.

It wasn't until we'd started up the road to the Hearst Castle parking lot that Ivy asked, "Are you okay?"

"I'm fine."

She frowned.

"Just some strong pot." But I wasn't fine. I didn't like the idea that I could just black out. Especially *now,* this week, when I was going to be driving on roads that dropped a mile straight down to the Pacific Ocean. And I didn't like this coincidence, or whatever it was, that had Daphne just happen to show up as our tour guide on the Paramount lot. I was already jumpy, half-expecting Daphne to greet us at Hearst Castle. Daphne, the omnipresent tour guide. She'd probably be at the Henry Miller museum, too. Maybe she'd pop out from under the bed in Deetjen's.

But it wasn't like I could share any of this with Ivy. It was her job to worry, my job to brush anxiety away. And besides, what was I going to say? *You know that cute little tour guide at Paramount Studios? I've been bonking her ever since the O.J. trial.* Maybe I could have talked to her about the Esalen stuff. I mean, Ivy ate psychological shit like that up, at least with her girlfriends. Here, we'd booked this trip to California, including Big Sur, and it never once occurred to me that this was the place that had broken up my parents' marriage. Or *possibly* broken up my parents' marriage. I had a strong feeling that something had happened there. Ivy would have found it fascinating. But I didn't want to stray into the dangerous subject of marital intimacy, or get within a thousand miles of the subject of cheating.

But there wasn't time for any of that anyway, because we were already at the parking lot, and then boarding the bus, riding up the twisty road and listening as a canned tour told us to look for zebras—descendants of the ones that William Randolph Hearst had imported way back during the Woodrow Wilson administration. The bus released us moments later to a summit where fog was banished, and William Randolph Hearst's shrine to publishing and himself glared in brilliant morning sun. We stood obediently behind thick velvet ropes, listened to long item-ized lists of fixtures and art objects, and tried to imagine Charlie Chaplin and Marion Davies, castle regulars, as real-life movie stars escaping the blinding flashbulbs of those big old-fashioned news cameras. Like everyone else, we laughed at the bottles of ketchup and mustard sitting next to all the silver in Hearst's formal din-ing room.

Ivy was loving it. Growing up in the shadow of Monticello, less a mansion than a blueprint of Thomas Jefferson's orderly mind, Ivy was always surprised and delighted by the gaudy ex-cess of real piles.

I leaned over and whispered in Ivy's ear, "Do you think there'll be tours of Neverland someday?"

She giggled.

I loved it when Ivy giggled. A tiny little eruption of—what?—happiness? Approval? Validation? Every time Ivy laughed at one of my jokes, I felt like I was drawing another tally on some invisible chalkboard. You can take the boy out of the comedy club, I guess, but you can't take the comedy club out of the boy.

Maybe that was it, why I fell in love with her. She was always my best audience.

It's just a few miles north of San Simeon that the Pacific Coast Highway begins to show what it's really about. Up until then, driving north from L.A., it's just a pleasant drive—some of it on the coast, some inland—with pleasant scenery. But as you begin the drive from San Simeon to Big Sur, the winding two-lane road soars to unimaginable heights, and you discover that the left coast of the United States is a sheer bluff falling straight down to the Pacific Ocean. This is the stuff of car commercials and high-flown poetry. It feels like God, working with sculpting clay, went into a manic phase—throwing rocks and mud and stone down with increasing frenzy—until finally, in one single violent gesture, he decided to just take his sculpture and shear it in half. You knew the jagged edges of Big Sur really have something to do with geology and plate tectonics, and you wished you'd paid more attention in geology class. But in the end, it doesn't matter. You just round corner after corner, from sublime to sublime, your mouth agape.

You also handle the road respectfully.

When you are driving north, there's one lane of traffic between you and the edge of the universe. God pity the Englishman who gets confused about which side of the road to drive on.

I knew Ivy had read everything there was about driving the Pacific Coast Highway. She wouldn't have been Ivy if she hadn't. But I still glanced over at her from time to time to see how she was handling it.

"Keep your eyes on the road," she said, white-lipped.

There were times during the climb when I could tell she was moved by the sheer physical beauty of the scenery. You could tell because that's when she busied herself with the camera. But then she put the camera down, and the guidebooks down, and crossed her arms tightly across her lap, as if unconsciously trying to strap herself in with a second seat belt.

"When it's safe," she said. "Let's pull over and put up the roof."

"Are you chilly?"

"No." She sucked in a deep breath, and I didn't think she was going to exhale until we got to Deetjen's. "I could just use a little more of a barrier between me and reality."

There weren't many places to pull over, but I found one.

I felt bad for Ivy. I'd warned her, the guidebooks had warned her, and yet here she was, still unprepared for what had to be the most terrifying experience of her life.

"How's the Blue Ridge compare to this?" I asked, suddenly remembering that she'd grown up just a few miles from a mountain range.

She shook her head. "That's more like Iowa."

God bless her, she was trying to be brave. She reminded me of a little girl, strapped into a seat on a big roller coaster, holding on tight and waiting for the ride to be over.

Notwithstanding the carping of the blowhard on the beach in San Simeon, Deetjen's was everything Ivy had hoped for. I don't know how the bastard could have called it touristy. In my mind, touristy was Disney World. Plastic. Fake. Overpriced. Deetjen's was anything but plastic. It was even more primitive than I'd remembered, a style I'd call 1930s American Treehouse. The main sign out front looked like it had been made by Boy Scouts.

As exposed as you might have felt on the drive there, you felt exactly the opposite in Deetjen's. Snug as a pet salamander in a jeans pocket. The room we were assigned had dark paneled walls, a low ceiling, a wood-burning stove, and a built-in cubby filled with firewood. The bed was piled high with old quilts and down pillows, and the lamps on either side of the bed glowed through coarse burlap shades. Simple white curtains covered the multipaned windows, which stared onto thick woods. Best of all, it was cozy in a way that didn't make a man feel embarrassed. A lumberjack would feel as comfortable as a librarian. No doilies.

Ivy was so tickled, she dropped backwards on the bed, her arms outstretched like she was making an angel in the snow. "I could stay in this room the whole time, couldn't you?"

If you'd been a fly on the wall, you might have thought she was suggesting nonstop sex. But really, that was laughable. Sex was not our strong suit; whole seasons could come and go between our awkward attempts at coupling. Ivy was as dry as the Grand Canyon, and if I did, miraculously, manage to stay hard enough to penetrate, I'd come almost immediately due to the shock. I'd have gone down on her—believe me, I'd tried—but the very idea embarrassed her. If I edged downward on the bed to assume the cunnilingus position, she'd look stricken.

Sex, or lack thereof, had become the elephant in the room.

I'd told myself it didn't matter—it shouldn't matter—and I knew from the occasional magazine article in the dentist's office that sexual frequency in marriage was a highly variable thing. According to the experts, there were some couples who hadn't done it for *years*. That was how I'd rationalized Daphne—at least at first. Ivy wasn't interested in sex; Daphne was. Didn't a man need to release his sexual tension? I mean, I didn't want my cock to atrophy.

But just because we had problems with sex, just because I had a little nookie on the side, didn't mean that Ivy and I didn't love each other. We did. And besides, we had children together, a home, a life, a history. And the last couple of years, ever since the trouble with Charlotte, I'd felt more tender toward Ivy than ever. Still, I didn't kid myself, when Ivy suggested we stay in the room, that she was thinking about nonstop marital intimacy.

Sure enough, Ivy slipped under the covers, jeans and all, and pulled out a book.

We read, we dozed, we snuggled together—the dourest Puritan chaperone wouldn't have raised an eyebrow—and when it was time, we got up and went to dinner in the Deetjen's restaurant. While Ivy was sleeping, I found the room's guest diary and quickly leafed through it. Although I didn't see anything incriminating, any notes from Daphne or, God forbid, myself, I took the precaution of hiding the whole book in the back of the closet. My heart fluttered wildly during this minor act of subterfuge. I'd deceived Ivy before, but never at such close range. And I felt a smidgen of guilt knowing that I was denying Ivy a really good read.

The room might have been cozy, and reading novels the next best thing to sex, but even Ivy wanted to explore by the second day. She'd studied too many travel guides to stay in the room reading the whole time, even if she was in the middle of *A Prayer for Owen Meany.*

The next morning, at breakfast, she announced that we "had to" see the Henry Miller Library, just a few miles north.

"Sure," I said. Of course, just like Deetjen's, the Miller museum was another place I'd have to pretend not to have seen before.

It still was, just as it had been the time I'd visited with Daphne, a haphazard sort of place, a little down at the heels, more a specialty bookstore than anything else, with copies of *Tropic of Cancer* and *Tropic of Capricorn,* and the rest of the Henry Miller oeuvre, along with books on censorship, California history, and some thin self-published monographs of poetry.

There was also an old Macintosh computer in the front room, with one of the few Internet connections available in Big Sur. I looked around at black-and-white photographs of the bawdy genius and stared for a while at Henry Miller's old typewriter, while Ivy checked her e-mail. When she'd finished—it was a slow connection, and she didn't really understand how to use a Mac—we switched. She looked around while I checked my e-mail. We managed to squeeze about forty-five minutes of entertainment value out of the place, and then walked back to the car. How different it had been from the time Daphne and I were there—our one break from a weekend of nonstop fucking—and we'd stood there reading *Tropic of Cancer* and getting horny.

Ivy and I took our usual seats—me on the left, Ivy on the right—and looked at each other like two prisoners with life sentences and a shared cell.

"What do you think about Esalen?" she said finally.

"What about it?"

"Do you think we should try to go there? For a visit?"

*Esalen.* Just the word made my stomach clench. "I don't think they take day visitors," I said.

Ivy nodded. She thumbed through one of her guidebooks. "What about Carmel-by-the-Sea? They say they have missions there."

I sighed. Nobody but guidebook writers called it Carmel-by-the-Sea. Everybody else just called it Carmel. I knew Ivy wouldn't like it. It was one of those upscale places where everybody was very rich and very white, and everything in the tchotchke shops cost a fortune. But what were we going to do? Go back to our room and read for the rest of the day?

"Sure," I said.

"What?" There was an edge in Ivy's voice, a testiness. I felt like a cat whose fur had just been stroked the wrong way.

"What do you mean, 'what'?"

"You don't think it's a good idea," she said. "I can hear it in your voice."

"I said 'sure,' didn't I? What am I supposed to do, cartwheels?"

Ivy turned and stared out the window. "Fine."

Why did we have so many fights like this, fights over nothing? So I wasn't jumping-on-the-bed enthusiastic. Big fucking deal.

I put the key in the ignition, lifted my eyebrows, and put on an exaggerated smile. "So? Carmel?" I was trying to sound bright, enthusiastic, accommodating. But I knew, looking at the shadow that crossed her face, that it had come out as sarcastic.

"Sure," she said. We'd come full circle.

Before getting back on the road, I reached into the glove compartment and pulled out the CDs that Ivy and I had packed for the trip. I thumbed through them, figuring that whatever I picked would set the tone for the rest of the day. Leonard Cohen? Too gloomy. Billie Holiday? Too tragic. Badly Drawn Boy? Maybe. Then I came across *The 2000 Year Old Man*. Mel Brooks and Carl Reiner. Yes! I pulled the disc out of the case and slipped it into the slot, which sucked it in with satisfying efficiency.

We drove through the world's most beautiful scenery listening to Mel Brooks riff about nectarines. It was, to say the least, a little incongruous. Reiner and Brooks were a soundtrack for cramped urban spaces filled with old Jews and pickled herring. Not for the great wide-open expanses of the West. We might as well have been listening to klezmer music on the moon. And yet somehow it was just right. Ivy was still looking out the window, but she'd uncrossed her arms. She had let out a few chuckles, almost grudgingly, as if conceding a point for the opposing team. We'd just gotten to the part about the guys running into each other to make the Jewish star as we were coming up to the Bixby Bridge.

I reached over to hold her hand. A peace gesture.

"Hands on the wheel!" she ordered. But she was smiling.

I snapped off the stereo. The Bixby Bridge was, if not one of the wonders of the world, close enough. This was the quintessential car commercial moment of our trip, this arch of reinforced concrete, spanning canyons.

"Look," I said. I gestured to the scenery. You might have thought I'd built the bridge myself.

"Amazing."

Ivy pulled the camera out of her purse and started taking pictures. It was fun to see her absorbed in this, tilting the camera this way and that. I knew her pictures would turn out good, that she'd have the best one enlarged and framed, and would hang it right next to all the rest. This was Ivy's version of plunder, the ritual gathering of images, without which a vacation might as well not have happened. A month from now, back in the Jersey suburbs, it would be hard to believe we'd ever been here.

"You know," she said, finally setting down the camera, "I got a strange e-mail."

"You did?"

"Yeah, from that tour guide. From Paramount."

I felt my heart do a flip. My hands started sweating, and my neck and chest suddenly felt hot. What the hell had Daphne said? I knew suddenly I was on a different kind of precipice. One narrower, steeper, more dangerous than the Pacific Coast High-way. But I had to act cool. Perplexed, not terrified.

*"Really?"* I said, trying not to gulp down a breath. "What did she want?"

"She just wanted to know how we were liking Deetjen's."

"That's all?"

"Yeah. But the weird thing is, how do you think she got my e-mail?"

I had my own theories on that. There were lots of imaginable ways Daphne had gotten Ivy's e-mail. From my own laptop. Or from the L.A. office. Maybe there was a new secretary. One who didn't know . . . Maybe Daphne had connived her way into this secretary's confidence by saying something about a surprise party. Anything. She was capable of just about anything. Or maybe— this seemed like the worst possibility—she'd figured out my password. She'd not only have access to everything on my computer, but she could also send things out *as me*.

"God." I shook my head. "I don't know. Didn't you give your e-mail to one of the other people on the tour? When everybody was taking pictures?"

"I don't think so."

"You must have."

I shrugged, tried to act like it was just one of those things, one of those weird stories you'd hear Ira Glass tell on *This American Life*.

But inside I felt a confusion of blood and organs, of things rising and falling simultaneously, like you sometimes feel when an elevator shoots up fifty stories in a second and a half. I could feel my heart blow up like some lunatic Macy's parade balloon, threatening to topple into buildings, knock over street signs, take out the whole fucking Empire State Building. Would my heart explode? Was that possible? Would I die right here on the spot? This, I realized, was the scientific phenomenon that made polygraphs work. This primal, fight-or-flight, running-through-the-savannah-being-chased-by-tigers feeling that came from trying to hide an ugly little truth. You could put on a mask, and hope that your acting skills were adequate. You could fool some of the people some of the time. But inside, in your veins and arteries and your pulse rate and your metabolic whatever the hell it was, the truth was as plain as writing.

I looked over at Ivy. She seemed puzzled, and a little troubled, and she was concentrating mightily, as if she were trying to solve the *New York Times* Sunday crossword. It made me feel a little bad but relieved, too. She never got very far with the Sunday puzzle, never filled in more than a few squares.

We walked around Carmel, which disappointed Ivy in exactly the ways I had expected. We glanced in stores filled with the kinds of expensive playthings favored by rich, aging preppies—Lauren and Longchamp and Limoges—all at full retail price. We walked into an art gallery filled with big swaggering minimalist canvases, and then, down the street, another one with paintings the size of postage stamps, set in elaborate gilt frames. There was an over-priced bistro where we ate undistinguished fifteen-dollar sand-wiches. When Ivy went to the bathroom, I glanced at my cell phone and noticed that it again had reception. I thought about calling Daphne and asking what the hell she was doing. To cut the crap. But I didn't dare. That would be like sticking my hand in the lion's cage. I decided instead to mute the ringer. The last thing I wanted was to pick it up unprepared.

The missions Ivy had read about in her guidebooks didn't materialize. Anyway, they seemed beside the point. Carmel was the California equivalent of the Upper East Side. Two hours there felt like a lifetime. And so, feeling even more depressed than after we'd left the Henry Miller Library, we headed back.

Only now, heading south, the Pacific Ocean was on our right.

It made a difference. I could see it, immediately, in Ivy's face. This time the steep drops to the Pacific Ocean were just inches away. There wasn't the psychological buffer of a lane of traffic in between our car and the cliff. Sometimes, the curves banked up, and there'd be a little hill between us and the great views of the

Pacific. But most of the time, there was nothing but a few inches of asphalt and a dinky metal barrier between the car and a *Thelma & Louise* fall to oblivion.

And yes, it was beautiful, too. Full of awe, just like the first time you ever flew in an airplane and looked down, and saw the highways and the houses and little swimming pools in backyards as tiny little rectangles of aqua, and suddenly realized that the metal tube you were sitting in was now above the clouds.

The weather was crisp, sunny—almost, given the cooler temperatures that came with the altitude, like early fall. It was perfect driving weather. Not a molecule of moisture, not a hint of fog.

I'd driven south on Big Sur before. With Daphne. A point that didn't escape me. That time, I hadn't felt the fear at all. I remember it being like one of those driving games you play in the arcade. A fun little test of my driving prowess. And Daphne, she was giddy after spending a weekend fucking somebody else's husband. She'd leaned the seat back, put her feet up, and enjoyed the wind blowing through her hair, occasionally lifting her shirt just to tease a passing truck driver.

Ivy, on the other hand, was frozen like a block of ice. If she'd been nervous during the ride north on the Pacific Coast Highway, she was petrified heading south.

It was lucky I'd had a couple of hours in Carmel to get my blood pressure back down after Ivy's revelation about Daphne's e-mail. I'd had time to cool off, to compartmentalize my mind again, to put fear and regret back in the dark little corners where they belonged and seal them up tight.

I eased myself into a comfortable rhythm, concentrating on

the scenery, leaning into the curves. We weren't more than a few miles south of Carmel when Ivy started asking me to slow down.

"Look," I said. "I'm going with the flow of traffic. If I go any slower, I could *cause* an accident."

She bit her lip until it turned white.

Suddenly, I remembered the mother in *Portnoy's Complaint,* who made poor lusty, neurotic Alexander Portnoy promise when he went off to college that he'd never ride in a convertible. I laughed. What a strange thing the human mind is, storing away such a small detail, and then dredging it back up twenty or thirty years later.

"What?" Ivy asked suspiciously.

"Nothing."

"No, really. What were you laughing about?"

I shook my head. It wasn't worth it. It was just too hard to explain. Ivy wasn't in the mood. Besides, she'd take offense.

"You're laughing because I asked you to slow down?" Ivy said. Her voice was getting tighter, whinier. It was starting to grate on me.

"Trust me," I said. "It was nothing."

Portnoy reminded me of Mel Brooks and Carl Reiner, and the fact that *The 2000 Year Old Man* was still waiting in the car stereo. I turned it on. It had helped ease the tension earlier, taking our minds off things.

But Ivy reached over and snapped it off. "No," she said. She sounded like she did when she was telling Lily to go to bed.

So she wanted to bask in her terror, really luxuriate in it. She would brook no distraction, allow no sunshine to penetrate her private rain cloud. Ivy wasn't doing the driving, but she wanted her full concentration to pay attention to *my* driving. And God forbid she actually sit back and enjoy the scenery. No, it was all about control. It always had been. Okay, if she wanted to play it that way. I pressed my foot just the slightest bit harder on the accelerator.

Ivy reacted as if she'd been punched. "Please, Ellis."

"Please, Ellis, *what?*"

"Please slow down."

I knew I was in control of the car. I wasn't going fast. I'd been glancing from time to time in the rearview mirror, and had seen a line of cars lengthening behind me. They weren't exactly on my tail, but I could feel their drivers' impatience. I was embarrassed. Like they could all tell that I was driving a rental and were thinking *goddamn East Coast schmuck*.

"Look," I said, gesturing at the rearview mirror. "There's a long line of cars behind us." Some steel had gotten into my voice. I kept both hands on the wheel and looked straight ahead.

Minutes later, I heard her whimpering quietly. She was looking out the window again, but not rigid, as before. It was as if she sensed that a direct appeal to me would only make me go faster. Mascara ran down her left cheek.

"Please," she whispered.

I said nothing. I was driving. I had the responsibility of getting us safely back. I wasn't going to be hijacked by her emotionality. Again, I checked my rearview mirror.

Ivy looked accusingly at the mirror. "You care more about them than you do about me."

"That's not true."

"You don't love me."

"I do." But I was thinking now of our trip up to see my mother that first Thanksgiving, and the emotional blackmail of Ivy opening the door while I was driving. The snow flying in. She wouldn't do that now, would she? She wasn't that stupid. She was a mother, after all. I mean, that *would* be dangerous, if I had to fight her over the door handle.

I was getting mad now, almost as if she had done it. Again, I pressed down slightly on the gas.

"Ellis!" she screamed, grabbing on to my right arm.

"Get your fucking hand off my fucking arm!" I spat through clenched teeth. "Don't you ever grab my fucking arm while I'm driving."

Now her crying was in dead earnest.

"If you don't love *me,* think about Charlotte and Lily."

"Think what?"

"That they should have parents."

"Do you think *I* want to die?" I said. I glared at her, just a split second longer than I should have, and found myself just a hair off on a curve. I pulled the steering wheel hard left, overcorrecting, and found myself an inch over the center line. Lucky there wasn't anything coming our way.

I heard a horn behind us.

Now I was boiling mad. Ivy's fear was beginning to infect me. I could drive safely, or I could react to her theatrics, but I couldn't do both.

And then I saw one of those little turnoffs, the small sandy parking spaces by the side of the road, where you could stop and take pictures. I slowed the car down and glided in. I could almost feel the relief of the drivers who had been following us. I watched them pass, then opened the door.

"What are you doing?" Ivy asked.

"Letting you drive."

I got out of the car and gestured extravagantly toward the driver's seat. Ivy looked up like a small frightened animal. I thought of Isaac, at the summit of Mount Moriah, suddenly realizing that the sacrifice his father was preparing for slaughter was actually himself.

And yet, I felt no pity for Ivy. No love.

I felt like one of those deranged kids you read about after they've shot up a whole school, the ones who started out in third grade by drowning their pet hamster. I felt an overpowering urge to cruelty. I was tired of Ivy's weakness, her worry, her constant fear of life. I wanted to punish her.

But that wasn't actually true, either. I didn't want to hurt her, exactly. Certainly not physically. It was more like this: Her fear had become a black hole, both empty and unbearably dense, which I had grown weary of trying to fill. She was like the damsel always getting tied to the railroad track, looking up in abject terror and waiting for her Dudley Do-Right—me—to come racing to the rescue. I wanted to watch her stricken face when I refused to come running.

But then, after a minute, I couldn't bear watching anymore. I guess my appetite for cruelty wasn't quite as large as I'd thought. I walked over to a boulder a few yards away, climbed up on it, and sat down. I knew I would get back into the car after a little while, in the driver's seat, as I always did. I just didn't want to do it right away.

I looked down at the improbably named Pacific Ocean, not pacific at all, but ferocious and, I knew, bitterly cold, even in August. I took in the whole panoramic view: the steep cliffs, the eerie stillness of the coves in between, the rocks that jutted up out of the water. I saw that the sky was endless in a way that you never could comprehend back East—or even in Los Angeles. I saw an eagle spiral downward into that vastness, and tried to imagine how it would feel to be able to dive into such immense nothingness as easily as walking down the street, knowing that your wings would bear you up whenever you wanted. I wondered if eagles mated for life. I hoped they didn't.

Then I closed my eyes and concentrated on the sounds. The cars whirring by behind me. The ocean down below.

That's when I heard the door slam, and knew Ivy was getting out.

I kept my eyes closed, refusing to watch her approach the rock. She wasn't screaming—not that it mattered, up here, in the middle of nowhere, whether she made a scene. She wasn't ordering me around like I was Charlotte or Lily, telling me to get down off that damn rock immediately. Well, that was good. She was going to be tearful and apologetic, which would make what

I had to do easier. I would rescue her—again—but at least she would have to pay the price.

But when I turned around and faced her, Ivy was reaching up to me with my cell phone. Her face was drained of color.

"It's her," she whispered.

I looked down and saw Daphne's cell phone number.

# *Nine*

## 2001—IVY

2001 CHRYSLER SEBRING CONVERTIBLE,

FOUR-SPEED AUTOMATIC, FOUR-CYLINDER, RED (RENTAL)

Ellis's phone didn't ring but it did vibrate, rattling against the molded vinyl like a crazed beetle. I jumped. We hadn't gotten many calls on the trip, and there hadn't even been a signal at Deetjen's. I grabbed the phone, my heart pumping furiously, the way any mother's would who was three thousand miles from home and her children. I was expecting to hear my mother, or perhaps the grave even voice of an emergency room administrator ready to break bad news.

Instead came a female voice that was vaguely familiar, but not official in any way. If anything, she sounded faintly amused. "Oh, I was expecting your husband," she said. Then she laughed. "And, by the way, I've been fucking him for the past six years."

There are moments when the earth swallows you whole, and you think: *Oh, right, I'm going to be buried alive. I always knew that.* Even before you can gather your bearings, before your mind can process anything, you know your life has been cleaved in half.

"What?" I wasn't sure I remembered how to breathe. "Who is this?"

⌄

CARS FROM A MARRIAGE

"Does it really matter?" she said, and laughed again. "Does it really matter who the fuck he betrayed you with?"

She sounded angry, drunk. Why was she angry at me? What had *I* done? And then all of a sudden it occurred to me that this was all a mistake. There was a crazy bitch on the phone, all right, but it had to be a wrong number. It wasn't Ellis she was talking about, but somebody else's husband. It was all a misunderstanding. She'd meant to ruin somebody else's life.

I sat up straight and willed myself to talk, but it came out like a squeak. "You must be mistaken."

"Really?" she said, laughing again. "And by the way, how's Big Sur? How's Deetjen's?"

I glanced down at the caller ID and saw the name D EAGAN and a 213 area code. The number looked familiar, but I wasn't sure. Ellis was always getting phone calls from 213 numbers.

"Did you like the Henry Miller museum? He must have taken you there. It's so close. He took *me* there. We spent the whole time reading racy passages from *Tropic of Cancer,* then went back and fucked our brains out."

It was the third time she'd used the word *fuck*. She was dropping them like bombs.

The reference to the Henry Miller museum freaked me out. I was starting to feel like I was being watched. Could she see me now, sitting in the car by the side of the road, with Ellis up there on the rock? Had she heard our fight? I suddenly felt like I was in a thriller. I half expected a rock or a bullet to shatter the windshield.

Part of me wanted to just press the END button and open up

the car door to vomit. But I knew the rules of the thriller: You kept them on the line. You drew them out. You found out more.

"Six years, you say?" I asked it as matter-of-factly as I could, like we were trying to establish whether our children had been in the same class in third grade.

"O. J. Simpson trial."

And then it came to me. I recognized the voice. After all, I'd listened to it for more than an hour, just a few days earlier. It was that tour guide, the one at Paramount, the one who'd sent that strangely inappropriate e-mail.

"Daphne?" I asked.

"Can I talk to Ellis now?"

When I handed Ellis the phone, I saw him glance at the caller ID and then my face. I knew in that awful instant that everything Daphne said was essentially true. Ellis picked up the phone and held it to his ear. He listened to her but studied me, his face growing grayer by the instant, as if he were turning into a photograph from the Depression.

I stood and watched, both in and outside the moment, rubbernecking my own life, watching my marriage fall apart.

*Why?* I thought. And then I remembered. *Oh, sex.*

I flashed on that ride I'd taken with Bailey in Blue Ridge, that week we'd been down for my father's funeral. What had Bailey said? Something about bimbos. Something about blow jobs. *There are bimbos everywhere.* That was it. I'd wanted to strangle her at the time, for her knowingness, her presumptuousness, for being the resident expert on men and sex. But it turned out she was right, wasn't she? She'd tried to warn me.

An even worse thought crossed my mind: Had Ellis ever done it with Bailey?

The thing that took me out of my own head was Ellis's phone bouncing down the hill. It broke the third time it smashed into the cliff, and was now cascading toward the ocean in splinters. At first I thought Ellis had thrown it. But when I looked up, I saw him half-slumped, his face contorted by pain, his right arm holding his left. His breathing was labored.

"I think I'm having a heart attack," he croaked.

*You bastard,* I thought. *Don't you dare die and leave me here alone.*

And then, *How convenient. The minute you're caught with your pants down, you find a way to get out of it.*

And finally, *Oh my God. What about Charlotte and Lily? They can't have their father die when they're still kids.*

I got closer, looking him in the eye. "Is it true?"

"The heart attack? I don't know."

"No," I said. "Daphne."

He squeezed his eyes shut. I couldn't tell whether it was the pain or that he couldn't bear to look at me. He shook his head, almost imperceptibly, from left to right. I was flooded with relief. So it wasn't true. Yes, this woman knew a lot about him—about us—but there was no proof. She could just be some crazy client, someone he'd passed over for an important gig. Maybe she'd had a crush on him. Maybe he'd refused to have an affair with her. There were lots of reasons why someone could want to hurt somebody.

But if that was true, if Ellis was innocent, then why had he been shocked into having a heart attack, or a panic attack, whatever the hell it was? He'd shaken his head no. But his eyes had been closed. If eyes are the windows to the soul, he was keeping his locked tight.

Over the years, I'd had secret, guilty fantasies about Ellis dying, of the alternative life that might spring up for me in his absence. A TV-free, cynicism-free life. Ellis had changed, over the years, from that callow comic who'd done a whole set without profanities, then rescued me from the mean waitress, into a person I often didn't recognize. Or particularly like. Of course, everybody changes. I had changed. But with Ellis, it was like the transmutation of wood into steel. Where he'd been soft, he was now hard. Warm, now cold. It had started, I realized suddenly, when he'd begun traveling regularly to L.A. Maybe even the trip he'd made for the O. J. Simpson trial.

It had never occurred to me to ask for a divorce, yet the image of myself puttering outside Hamish's little bungalow, cutting the yellow roses, persisted like something shimmering just outside my field of vision. I glimpsed it sometimes when I closed my eyes, the way you saw the reverse image of a swimming pool in bright red-orange if you'd stared at it too long in the blazing sun.

Of course, it was a fantasy—I didn't really think that Hamish wanted me—but now it was, oddly, within my reach. I could just let Ellis die. And he would deserve it. The bastard. I knew he'd changed since the O. J. Simpson trial. I knew it! What I hadn't known was why.

But I wasn't sure. *Maybe* he would deserve it. Maybe he'd had the affair and maybe he hadn't. Maybe he would die. Or maybe he'd turn into an invalid I'd have to take care of for forty years. He'd survive his heart attack, if that's what it was, and live to hate me forever for not lifting a finger.

I reached out, knowing that if I pushed him—no harder than you'd shove a heavy planter on the patio to move it a few inches— he'd lose his balance. He would follow his phone, tumbling down the hill, his head splitting like a pumpkin. I turned around, almost involuntarily, and glanced at the road. There were cars passing by, but we were on a curve. People could see us, if they looked our way at all, for only a split second. No one would ever see. . . .

I tasted some undigested food, mixed with stomach acid, as it leaped into my mouth. What was I doing? In the space of a minute, I'd become a potential murderer. I'd been *checking for witnesses*. That's what I'd been doing when I turned around. It was shocking.

Was that all unpremeditated murder was? A sudden opening, reality parting like curtains, and a person—an ordinary person, a decent person—rushing for that opening like a commuter running for the train? If I was capable of murder, then anybody was. And if I was capable of murder, or even standing by while the father of my children struggled for breath, then what was I? A worse monster than he was. Even if . . . Even if what Daphne said was true.

But that's not what stopped me. I realized that if I let Ellis die, I would never know. Not for sure. His secrets would die, too. I would never hear his side of the story. I would never really know.

A decision had to be made, and it had to be made now.

I reached for Ellis's hand and pulled him away from the ledge, back toward the car and the road. I let him lean on me. I walked him to the car, opened the passenger door, and helped him in.

"You're going to drive?" he said. He tried to make it sound funny, but he could barely manage a wan smile.

I clicked his seat belt and gave him a perfunctory peck on the cheek. "Like I have any choice?"

I got in the car and pulled the seat forward. I went to adjust the rearview mirror and saw a grim middle-aged woman stare back at me. She could have been a coal miner's wife, or the mother of a shooting victim. It was the same ashen, unremarkable face you'd see in the fluorescent glare of a hospital waiting room. The face of a woman whose entire life had narrowed to a single purpose: begging the gods for mercy. I quickly pulled back, looking at the road behind me, removing my face from view. I was about to turn the key when Ellis suddenly announced, "You're going to have to pull a U-turn."

"What?"

"The closest hospital is in Monterey, and that's north."

"How do you know?"

"I just do."

"A U-turn?"

"Left. Back where we came from."

We were parked in a sandy little turnoff, facing south. I would have been scared enough just getting into the right-hand lane, going with the flow of traffic. Getting onto the Pacific Coast Highway, just north of Big Sur. But Ellis was saying that I had to cross that lane, pull a tight little turn and head north. The cars behind me were coming around a curve. I couldn't see them until they were practically on top of me. And I had a man—my husband, the father of my children, quite possibly a cheater, quite possibly in cardiac arrest—in the seat next to me, totally dependent on my driving.

Except in parking lots, I never made U-turns. I was too cautious, too respectful of the law. I didn't want to test the wheel-span of the station wagon, or anger the traffic gods. I knew if I tried one, a cop would materialize with a fat ticket book. Ellis, of course, was the king of the U-turn. The more improbable, the greater the danger, the closer the proximity of law enforcement, the better. He'd even managed one on Forty-second Street.

How ironic that he was now depending on me to whisk him off to the region's only hospital.

I kept my eyes steady on the rearview mirror, watching as cars whipped around the corner behind me, one after another. It felt like there would never be an opening. A succession of sports cars with California plates sped recklessly, propelled by a blind faith I couldn't fathom. And finally, when there did seem to be an opening, and I was just about to make a break for it, I glanced at the oncoming traffic to see a long line of cars going so slowly, it could have been a funeral procession. At the front was an ancient Volvo burning oil, trailed by a giant cloud of black smoke and at least fifteen cars.

"Fuck!" I said, pounding the steering wheel. "I can't do it."

Ellis reached over and put a hand on my leg. "Yes, you can," he said. "Just relax."

I felt my guts knot up. It wasn't just the impossibility of the

U-turn. The slow parade of cars had pinched something in my heart. I didn't know why at first. It was one of those cases where feeling precedes thought. But when logic caught up, when I realized that the cars slowly climbing the hill had reminded me of the Buick motorcade that had followed my father's casket into Riverview Cemetery, it felt like a big wave had come out of nowhere and knocked me to the ocean floor. Death was winking at me, taunting me, challenging me, daring me to do this impossible thing my husband had asked. And that was only half of it. The other half was the aching realization that I'd loved my father more than I loved Ellis.

"Relax?" I put the gearshift back in Park while waiting for the long line of cars to inch up the hill. I glared at Ellis. "Relax?"

I'd never been less relaxed in my entire life. Less than half an hour ago—though it felt like a lifetime—I'd been pleading, like a prisoner, for Ellis to slow down. He'd responded, not with tenderness or pity, but with anger and cruelty. Then a strange woman had called, brandishing the F-word like a weapon, and claiming she'd been sleeping with my husband for six years. And now? Now Ellis was crumpled in the seat next to me like a used rag, his face carved with pain. Maybe he was having a heart attack. I was thousands of miles from home and, quite literally, on the very edge of the earth. And fate, that incorrigible jokester, had put me behind the wheel.

"Right," I said. "I think I'll just put on some mood music." I turned on the radio and spun the dial until I finally landed on some stupid oldies station playing some stupid surfer song. I pretended to tap the steering wheel in time with the music. "Yep, that's all I needed," I said. "To relax. Oh, wait. I could use a drink with a little umbrella."

Ellis winced. "Ivy, please," he said. Look who was doing the begging now.

As the last car in the procession finally passed, I noticed that something in me had shifted. I felt my fear give way to fury: righteous blood-pounding moral indignation. I jerked the gearshift into Drive, slipped my foot off the brake, glided onto the asphalt, and wrenched the steering wheel hard left while smashing the gas pedal to the floor. It was swift and decisive, unleashing the laws of physics, turning my guidebooks and Ellis's sunglasses into projectiles. But I'd done it. I'd turned the car 180 degrees and was speeding up the hill.

I heard the squeal of air brakes first. Then I saw the truck. The laws of physics weren't finished with me. I must have turned the wheel too hard, or given it too much gas, or slid on some gravel . . . I didn't know what. All I knew was, my car was sticking out into the oncoming lane, and a truck carrying Porta Pottis was barreling straight at me. So this was how I was going to die: in a clash of metal and glass and an exploding fountain of human excrement.

I yanked the wheel to the right.

The truck driver blasted his horn. I flinched, but took it as my due, punishment for gross incompetence. I glanced back in the rearview mirror, fearing that I'd see the truck, with its Porta Pottis, fly off the mountain. But its tires held fast.

"Well done," Ellis said.

"But—"

"No harm, no foul."

I couldn't believe it. I'd fucked up royally, and Ellis was congratulating me. If the roles were reversed, if Ellis had been the one who'd almost got us killed, I'd have been beside myself. It had happened before, too many times to recount, close calls that had me flipping out in the passenger seat. But Ellis sat there like a trusting child. Once I'd calmed down, he leaned his head back against the seat and closed his eyes. I saw his eyelids flutter a few times, and then his head slumped down over his chest like a rag doll.

It occurred to me that he might be dead.

I snapped off the radio, surprised that it was still on—I hadn't been listening—and held my breath, willing my ears to work harder, just as I had all those years ago when I would walk into the nursery to check on Charlotte. It was impossible, I'd discovered, to hear a newborn's breath. Too delicate—like trying to hear a flower. At first, to reassure myself she hadn't died, I would place my hand on Charlotte's onesie and feel her speeding little heart. But I'd trained myself to detect that light rising and falling of her tiny chest, and eventually began to believe in the continuity of her existence, even when she was out of sight.

All these years later, I was straining my ears again. I heard the tires on road, the car engine, the whipping of the wind, but I wasn't tuning in anything from Ellis. Finally, I detected a faint wheezing. Air squeezed into Ellis's lungs, whistled out through his nose again. It wasn't exactly the sound of health, but it was— indisputably—breathing. It became regular. The sound of Ellis sleeping.

I exhaled, releasing some of the noxious air that had been building in me ever since Ellis stopped the car and walked over to the rock. I didn't have much to be happy about, but at least I was heading north, with a lane of traffic between me and the cliffs. And I had this to be grateful for, too: Even if nothing had turned out the way I'd wanted—not my marriage, not my career, not even this lousy vacation—at least I didn't have a corpse in the passenger seat.

I held the wheel tightly at ten and two, and kept the speedometer needle, like the bubble in a level, exactly between fifty-five and sixty. The whole time, Ellis slept. I felt surprisingly steady. I was amazed at how easy it was, once I'd gotten past the initial U-turn debacle, to keep the car on the road. It was like coloring inside the lines. True, if you thought of all the terrible things that could happen—about driving off bridges or over cliffs, or smashing into oil tankers when you merged onto a highway—you could jump out of your own skin. But the actual act of holding on to a wheel and pointing a car in the direction you wanted to go: There was nothing to it. Why, I wondered, had it taken me until now to figure this out?

If I could do this, why couldn't I drive on the New Jersey Turnpike? Or into the city? If I could do this, what was there I couldn't do?

I saw now that I'd lived my whole life inside a prison of my own making. Ellis had rescued me from a mean waitress in a comedy club once many, many years ago, and I'd been asking him to rescue me, over and over, ever since. But I didn't need to be rescued then—I could have paid for my own four-dollar Diet Cokes—and I didn't need to be rescued now. Ellis was actually right to pull over and tell me to drive if I didn't like his driving.

I followed the signs for Monterey. Then I followed the blue signs with the white *H*s. It wasn't until I pulled into the emergency room loading zone that I allowed myself to fall apart.

I ran into the emergency room and cut into the triage line, shrieking that my husband was having a heart attack. A team of orderlies ran out with a gurney, but when I tried to follow them through the big swinging doors into the treatment room, a uniformed guard physically restrained me. I wailed and pounded him with my fists; he threatened to have me sedated. I ignored everyone's suggestions to sit down, to get coffee, to go look at the beautiful water sculpture outside. What did I need with a water sculpture? I pulled my cell phone out of my purse and thought about whom to call. Sheba? My mother? Charlotte and Lily? No, I couldn't put any of them through this. Wherever they were, whatever they were doing, they were blissfully unaware of the drama that was unfolding, and for that I envied them. If everything turned out okay, then this would eventually become a knee-slapper. *Remember the time Ivy had to drive up Big Sur?*

I thought briefly of calling Bailey—she lived in California, after all—but realized she was at least five hours away. I doubted she'd be any comfort anyway. Even if she could miraculously show up by private jet and sweep into the waiting room, it would all be the Bailey Show. It always was. Bailey with her glamorous blond hair, Bailey with her perky breasts, Bailey with her tight-fitting Lucky Brand jeans. It was true that Frank was a surgeon. He could make a call to the hospital and talk to Ellis's doctors. But really, was he anything more than a playboy? What was he going to do, recommend an eyelid tuck along with an angioplasty? So

I paced the waiting room, not caring that people were staring at me the way we stare at homeless people who talk to themselves in Port Authority.

Doctors came out of the ER from time to time, looking around, trying to identify the families that were attached to the bodies they'd been busy mending. I would see them whisper to the main nurse, and then nod when they saw the blue jacket or red hair that had been provided as an identifier. I'm sure that in my case, all the nurse had to say was, *There. The crazy one.*

I inspected the doctor for clues as he walked toward me. He was young—in his thirties, I guessed—with overgrown surfer boy good looks, a tanned face, hair that glinted gold under the fluorescents and hung down past his ears. But when he got a few feet away, I could see that his good looks were compromised by dark circles under his eyes. Even with the tan, I doubted that he got to hit the waves very often. He kept a poker face up to the last minute, but when he got up to me, he pumped my hand like a politician and put his left hand on my shoulder. I knew then that Ellis wasn't dead.

"I'm Dr. Schweig," he said. "Your husband is okay. We ran an EKG, an echocardiogram, a nuclear scan. We drew blood. All normal. But, to be on the safe side, we're going to keep him here overnight."

He paused, giving me time, I guess, to emote. It seemed like something maybe he'd learned in doctor school, Bedside Manner 101. I felt pressured to perform, like a potential Miss America in the final question-answer section. I could almost hear Bert Parks, or whoever was doing it now, read from the card. *You've just learned your husband was cheating on you. Then he seems to have a heart attack. You drive him up the Pacific Coast Highway, a road you're deathly afraid of, and take him to the ER—only to discover it wasn't a heart attack after all. What do you say?*

*World peace?* I smiled stiffly, buying time.

"It looks like indigestion," the doctor added. "Or a panic attack. Did something happen to upset him?"

"Yes," I said finally. "He did have a little shock."

"Well, he's going to be fine. He's resting comfortably. Would you like to see him?"

I thought about going out and finally looking at the water sculpture. But I played the good wife, following Dr. Schweig back into the hallowed sanctuary of the ER treatment rooms. I glanced a little triumphantly at the triage nurse as if to say, *See, I got past you after all.*

The doctor led me to Ellis's bed, then drew the curtains and walked away. Despite his prognosis, Ellis was still connected to an IV and a heart monitor. He looked up at me with a piteous expression, more pitiful even than he'd looked on the rock when his cell phone tumbled down the hill. I knew immediately that he wished it had been a real heart attack.

"I'm sorry," he said.

I nodded.

"It was just sex. It meant nothing."

I thought about Bailey again, her warning, and felt a spasm of shame.

"I love you, Ivy. I've always loved you," he said. Then he smiled. "Great driving, by the way."

That's when I understood. I no longer *needed* Ellis. I didn't know yet whether I wanted him.

I felt a confusion of emotions. Humiliation, a desire to punish, mixed with the staggering number of details that would be required to split up our household: The real estate transactions, the emptying of the attic; dividing up the books, dividing up the friends. The legal fees. The faces of Charlotte and Lily as we sat down at the kitchen table and delivered the news.

Changing my own lightbulbs, even the one on the front porch. Dating again, getting naked with a stranger.

I didn't know. It was too much to decide.

I couldn't stand to look at Ellis with his pleading eyes. Instead I stared at the heart monitor and watched the green line spike up and down, accompanied by the sound of his heartbeat, *thump-thump thumpthump,* over and over again, all as steady and even as windshield wipers.